A WILD KISS

Even as he told himself he should step away, should not give in to the growing attraction he felt for her, he reached out with his free hand and stroked her cheek. Her skin was soft and warm, a delight to touch, and he ached to touch more of it. Her eyes darkened to a rich blue, and he knew she felt the same craving he did. Pushing aside all thought of the consequences and ignoring his own resolutions of but moments before, he lowered his mouth to hers. He had to have another taste.

She tasted sweet, hot, and willing, he thought as he slid an arm around her slim waist and pulled her closer. Just as he feared, she still tasted like more—more than kisses and a few gentle caresses. The way she fit against him made him wild with need, and he struggled against the fierce urge to tumble her down on the carpet. Alethea was a widow, but all his instincts, honed through years of playing love's games, told him that she was far from an experienced one. The way she again seemed so startled when he slipped his tongue into her mouth simply confirmed that opinion. That taste of innocence only made his hunger for her more intense. He wanted to be the one to show her all the pleasure a man and woman could share . . .

Books by Hannah Howell

Published by Kensington Publishing Corporation

HANNAH HOWELL

IF HE'S WILD

ZEBRA BOOKS
KENSINGTON PUBLISHING CORP.
http://www.kensingtonbooks.com

ZEBRA BOOKS are published by

Kensington Publishing Corp.
119 West 40th Street
New York, NY 10018

All Kensington titles, imprints, and distributed lines are available at special quantity discounts for bulk purchases for sales
promotion, premiums, fund-raising, educational, or institu-
tional use.

Special book excerpts or customized printings can also be
created to fit specific needs. For details, write or phone the
office of the Kensington Special Sales Manager: Attn.: Special
Sales Department. Kensington Publishing Corp., 119 West
40th Street, New York, NY 10018. Phone: 1-800-221-2647.

Zebra books and the Z logo Reg. U.S. Pat. & TM Off.

ISBN-13: 978-1-4201-0462-2
ISBN-10: 1-4201-0462-4

First Printing: June 2010
10 9 8 7 6 5 4 3 2 1

Printed in the United States of America

Chapter 1

Alethea Vaughn Channing looked up from the book she was trying to read to stare into the colorful flames in the massive fireplace and immediately tensed. That man was there again, taking shape within the dancing flames and curling smoke. She tried to tear her gaze away, to ignore him and return her attention to her book, but the vision drew her, ignoring her wants and stealing her choices.

He was almost family, for there was no denying that they had grown up together. She had been seeing glimpses of the man since she was but five years old, although he had been still a boy then. Fifteen long years of catching the occasional peek into his life had made her somewhat proprietary about the man, even though she had no idea who he was. She had seen him as a gangly, somewhat clumsy youth, and as a man. She had seen him in dreams, in visions, and had even sensed him at her side. An unwilling witness, she had seen him in pain, watched him weep, known his grief and his joy and so much more. She had even seen him on her wedding night, which had been oddly comforting since her late husband had been noticeably absent. At times, the strange connection was painfully intense; at others it was only the whisper of emotion. She did not like invading his privacy, yet nothing she had ever done had been able to banish him.

This was a strong vision, she thought as the images before her grew so clear it was as if the people were right in the room with her. Alethea set her book down and moved to kneel before the fire as a tickle of unease grew stronger within her. Suddenly she knew this was not just another fleeting intrusion into the man's life, but a warning. Perhaps, she mused as she concentrated, this was what it had all been leading to. She knew, without even a hint of doubt, that what she was seeing now was not what *was* or what *had been,* but what was to come.

He was standing on the steps of a very fine house idly adjusting his clothes. She smelled roses and then grimaced with disgust. The rogue had obviously just come from the arms of some woman. If she judged his expression right, he wore that smirk her maid, Kate, claimed men wore after they had just fed their manly hungers. Alethea had the suspicion her vision man fed those hungers a lot.

A large black carriage pulled up. She almost stuck her hand in the fire as a sudden fierce urge to pull him back when he stepped into it swept over her. Then, abruptly and without warning, her vision became a dizzying array of brief, terrifying images, one after another slamming into her mind. She cried out as she suffered his pain along with him—horrible, continuous pain. They wanted his secrets, but he would not release them. A scream tore from her throat and she collapsed, clutching her throat as a sharp, excruciating pain ripped across it. Her vision man died from that pain. It did not matter that she had not actually seen his death, that the fireplace held only flame and wispy smoke again. She had suffered it, suffered the cold inside his body as his blood flowed out of him. For one terrifying moment, she had suffered a deep, utter desolation over that loss.

The sound of her servants hurrying into the room broke through Alethea's shock as she crawled toward the table where she kept her sketchbooks and drawing materials. "Help me to my seat, Kate," she ordered her buxom young maid as the woman reached for her.

"Oh, m'lady, you have had yourself a powerful seeing this time, I be thinking," said Kate as she steadied Alethea in her seat. "You should have a cup of hot, sweet tea, you should, and some rest. Alfred, get some tea," she ordered the tall, too-thin butler who no longer even attempted to explain the hierarchy of servants to Kate.

"Not yet. I must get this all down ere I forget."

Alethea was still very weak by the time she had sketched out all she had seen and written down all she could recall. She sipped at the tea a worried Alfred served her and studied what she had done. Although she dreaded what she had to do now, she knew she had no choice.

"We leave for London in three days," she announced, and almost smiled at the look of shock on her servants' faces.

"But why?" asked Kate.

"I must."

"Where will we stay? Your uncle is at the townhouse."

"It is quite big enough to house us while I do what this vision is compelling me to do."

"And what does it compel you to do, milady?" asked Alfred.

"To stop a murder."

"You *cannot* meet with Hartley Greville. He is the Marquis of Redgrave you know."

Alethea frowned at her uncle, who was only seven years older than she was. She had been too weary to speak much with him when she had arrived in London yesterday after three days on the road. Then she had slept too late to breakfast with him. It had pleased her to share a noon meal with him, and she had quickly told him about her vision. He had been intrigued and eager to help until she had shown him the sketch she had made of the man she sought. Her uncle's handsome face had immediately darkened with a scowl.

"Why not?" she asked as she cut a piece of ham and popped it in her mouth.

"He is a rake. If he was not so wealthy, titled, and of such an impressive lineage, I doubt he would be included on many lists of invitations. If the man notches his bedpost for each of his conquests, he is probably on his third bed by now."

"Oh, my. Is he married?"

"Ah, no. Considered to be a prime marriage candidate, however. All that money and good blood, you see. Daughters would not complain, as he is also young and handsome."

"Then he cannot be quite so bad, can he? I mean,

if mothers view him as a possible match for their daughters . . ."

Iago Vaughn shook his head, his thick black hair tumbling onto his forehead. "He is still a seasoned rake. Hard, cold, dangerous, and the subject of a cartload of dark rumor. He has just not crossed that fine line which would make him completely unacceptable." He frowned. "Although I sometimes wonder if that line is a little, well, fluid as concerns men like him. I would certainly hesitate to nudge my daughter in his direction if I had one. And I certainly do not wish to bring his attention your way. Introduce a pretty young widow to Greville? People would think I was utterly mad."

"Uncle, if you will not introduce me, I *will* find someone else who will."

"Allie—"

"Do you think he has done anything that warrants his murder?"

"I suspect there are many husbands who think so," muttered Iago as he turned his attention back to his meal, frowning even more when he realized he had already finished it.

Alethea smiled her thanks to the footman who took her plate away and set several bowls of fruit between her and Iago. The moment Iago silently waved the footman out of the room, she relaxed, resting her arms on the table and picking out some blackberries to put into her small bowl. As she covered the fruit with clotted cream, she thought carefully over what she should say next. She had to do whatever she could to stop her vision from becoming a true prophecy, but she did not wish to anger her uncle in doing so.

"If wives are breaking their marriage vows, I believe

it is for more reason than a pretty face," she said. "A man should not trespass so, yet I doubt he is solely to blame for the sin." She glanced at her uncle and smiled faintly. "Can you say that you have not committed such a trespass?"

Iago scowled at her as he pushed aside his plate, grabbed an apple, and began to neatly slice and core it. "That is not the point here, and well you know it. The point here is whether or not I will introduce my niece to a known seducer, especially when she is a widow and thus considered fair game. A rogue like him would chew you up and spit you out before you even knew what had happened to you. They say he can seduce a rock."

"That would be an intriguing coupling," she murmured and savored a spoonful of her dessert.

"Brat." He grinned briefly, and then quickly grew serious again. "You have never dealt with a man like him."

"I have never dealt with any man, really, save for Edward, and considering how little he had to do with me, I suppose dealing with my late husband for a year does not really count for much."

"Ah, no, not truly. Poor sod."

"Me or him?" She smiled when he chuckled. "I understand your concerns, Uncle, but they do not matter. No," she hastily said when he started to protest. "None of them matter. We are speaking of life and death. As you say, I am a young widow. If he seduces me, then so be it. That is my business and my problem. Once this difficulty is swept aside, I can return to Coulthurst. In truth, if the man has anywhere near the number of conquests rumor claims, I will just disappear into the horde with barely any notice taken of my passing."

"Why are you being so persistent? You may have misinterpreted this vision."

Alethea shook her head. "No. 'Tis difficult to describe, but I *felt* his pain, felt his struggle not to weaken and tell them what they wanted to know, and felt his death. There is something you need to know. This is not the first time I have had visions of this man. The first was when I was just five years old. This man has been visiting me for fifteen years."

"Good God. Constantly?"

"No, but at least once a year in some form, occasionally more than that. Little peeks at his life—fleeting visions, mostly, some clearer than others. There were several rather unsettling ones, when he was in danger, but I was seeing what was or what had been. Occasional dreams, too. Even, well, feelings, as if we had suddenly touched in some way."

"How can you be so sure that this vision was not also what was happening or had already happened?"

"Because amongst the nauseating barrage of images was one of a newspaper dated a month from that day. And, of course, the fact that the man is still alive." Alethea could tell by the look upon her uncle's face that he would help her, but that he dearly wished he could think of another way than by introducing her to the man. "I even saw him on my wedding night," she added softly.

Iago's eyes widened. "Dare I ask what he was doing?"

"Staring into a fireplace, just as I was, although at least he had a drink in his hand. For a brief moment, I felt as if we were sharing a moment of contemplation, of loneliness, of disappointment, even a sadness. Not an inspiring vision, yet, odd as it was, I did feel somewhat comforted by it." She shrugged away the thought.

"I truly believe all that has gone before was leading up to this moment."

"Fifteen years of preparation seems a bit excessive," Iago drawled.

Alethea laughed, but her humor was fleeting, and she soon sighed. "It was all I could think of to explain why I have had such a long connection to this man, to a man I have never met. I just wish I knew why someone would want to hold him captive and torture him before killing him. Why do these people want his secrets?"

"We . . . ell, there have been a few rumors that he might be working for the Home Office, or the military, against the French."

"Of course! That makes much more sense than it being a fit of revenge by some cuckolded husband or jealous lover."

"It also means that a great deal more than your virtue could be in danger."

"True, but it also makes it far more important to rescue him."

"Damn. I suppose it does."

"So, will you help me?"

Iago nodded. "You do realize it will be difficult to explain things to him. People do not understand ones like us, do not believe in our gifts or are frightened by them. Imagine the reaction if, next time I was playing cards with some of my friends, I told one of them that his aunt, who had been dead for ten years, was peering over his shoulder?" He smiled when Alethea giggled.

Although his example was amusing, the hard, cold fact it illustrated was not. People did fear the gifts so many of her family had. She knew her dreams and visions would cause some people to think she had gone mad. It was one reason she shunned society. Sometimes, merely touching something could bring on a vision. Iago saw all too clearly those who had died and not yet traveled to their final destination. He could often tell when, or why, a person had died simply by touching something or being in the place where it had happened. The only thing she found unsettling about Iago's gift was that, on occasion, he could tell when someone was soon to die. She suspected that, in many ways, he was as alone, as lonely, as she was.

"It does make life more difficult," she murmured. "I sometimes comfort myself with the thought that it could be worse."

"How?"

"We could have Cousin Modred's gift." She nodded when Iago winced. "He has become a hermit, afraid to touch anyone, to even draw close to people for fear of what he will feel, hear, or see. To see so clearly into everyone's mind and heart? I think that would soon drive me mad."

"I often wonder if poor Modred is, at least just a little."

"Have you seen him recently?"

"About a month ago. He has found a few more servants, ones he cannot read, with Aunt Dob's help." Iago frowned. "He thinks he might be gaining those shields he needs, but has yet to gather the courage to test himself. But, then, how are we any better off than he? You hide at Coulthurst and I hide here."

"True." Alethea looked around the elegant dining room as she sipped her wine. "I am still surprised Aunt Leona left this place to me and not to you. She had to know you would be comfortable here."

"She was angry that I would not marry her husband's niece."

"Oh dear."

"Quite. I fear she changed her will when she was still angry and then died before the breach between us could be mended."

"You should let me give it to you."

"No. It suits me to rent it from you. I keep a watch out for another place, and, if this arrangement ever becomes inconvenient, we can discuss the matter then. Now, let us plan how we can meet up with Redgrave and make him understand the danger he is in without getting the both of us carted off to Bedlam."

Two nights later, as she and Iago entered a crowded ballroom, Alethea still lacked a sound plan, and her uncle had none to offer, either. Alethea clung to his arm as they strolled around the edges of the large room. Glancing around at all the elegant people, she felt a little like a small blackbird stuck in the midst of a flock of peacocks. There was such a vast array of beautiful, elegant women, she had to wonder why her uncle would ever think she had to worry about her virtue. A hardened rake like the Marquis of Redgrave would never even consider her worth his time and effort when there was such a bounty to choose from.

"Are you nervous?" asked Iago.

"Terrified," she replied. "Is it always like this?"

"Most of the time. Lady Bartleby's affairs are always well attended."

"And you think Lord Redgrave will be one of the crowd?"

Iago nodded. "She is his cousin, one of the few family members left to him. We must keep a sharp watch for him, however. He will come, but he will not stay long. Too many of the young women here are hunting a husband."

"I am surprised that you would venture forth if it is that dangerous."

"Ah, but I am only a lowly baron. Redgrave is a marquis."

Alethea shook her head. "You make it all sound like some sordid marketplace."

"In many ways, it is. Oh, good, I see Aldus and Gifford."

"Friends of yours?" Iago started to lead her toward the far corner of the ballroom, but she was unable to see the men he spoke of around the crowd they weaved through.

"No, friends of the marquis. He will be sure to join them when he arrives."

"Misery loves company?"

"Something like that. Oh damn."

Before Alethea could ask what had caused her uncle to grow so tense, a lovely, fulsome redhead appeared at his side. If she judged her uncle's expression correctly, he was not pleased to see this woman, and that piqued Alethea's interest. Looking more closely at the woman's classically beautiful face, Alethea saw the hint of lines about the eyes and mouth and suspected the woman was older than Iago. The look the woman gave her was a hard and assessing one. A moment later something about the woman's demeanor told Alethea that she had not measured up well in the woman's eyes, that she had just been judged as inconsequential.

"Where have you been, Iago, darling?" the woman asked. "I have not seen you for a fortnight."

"I have been very busy, Margarite," Iago replied in a cool, distant tone.

"You work too hard, my dear. And who is your little companion?"

"This is my niece, Lady Alethea Channing," Iago said, his reluctance to make the introduction a little too clear in his tone. "Alethea, this is Mrs. Margarite Dellingforth."

Alethea curtsied slightly. The curtsy Mrs. Dellingforth gave her in return was so faint she doubted the woman even bent her knees at all. She was glad Iago had glanced away at that precise moment so that he did not see the insult to his kinswoman. The tension roused by this increasingly awkward confrontation began to wear upon Alethea's already taut nerves. Any other time she knew she would have been fascinated by the subtle, and not so subtle, nuances of the conversation between her uncle and Mrs. Dellingforth, but now she just wanted the cold-eyed woman to leave. She leaned against Iago and began to fan her face.

"Uncle, I am feeling uncomfortably warm," she said in what she hoped was an appropriately weak, sickly tone of voice.

"Would you like to sit down, m'dear?" he asked.

"You should not have brought her here if she is ill," said Mrs. Dellingforth.

"Oh, I am not ill," said Alethea. "Simply a little overwhelmed."

"If you will excuse us, Margarite, I must tend to my niece," said Iago even as he began to lead Alethea toward some chairs set against the wall.

"Not a very subtle retreat, Uncle," murmured Alethea, quickening her step to keep pace with his long stride.

"I do not particularly care."

"The romance has died, has it?"

"Thoroughly, but she refuses to leave it decently buried."

"She is quite beautiful." Alethea sat down in the chair he led her to and smoothed down her skirts.

"I know—that is how I became ensnared to begin with." He collected two glasses of wine from the tray a footman paused to offer them, and handed Alethea one. "It was an extremely short affair. To be blunt, my lust was quickly satisfied, and, once it eased, I found something almost repellent about the woman."

Seeing how troubled thoughts had darkened his hazel green eyes, Alethea lightly patted his hand. "If it is any consolation, I, too, felt uneasy around her. I think there is a coldness inside her."

"Exactly what I felt." He frowned and sipped his drink. "I felt some of the same things I do when I am near someone who will soon die, yet I know that is not true of her."

"What sort of feelings?"

He grimaced. "It is hard to explain, but it is as if some piece of them is missing, has clearly left or been taken."

"The soul?"

"A bit fanciful, but, perhaps, as good an explanation as any other. Once my blind lust faded, I could not abide to even touch her, for I could sense that chilling emptiness. I muttered some pathetic excuse and fled her side. She appears unable to believe that I want no more to do with her. I think she is accustomed to being adored."

"How nice for her." Alethea sipped her drink as she watched Mrs. Dellingforth talk to a beautiful fair-haired woman. "Who is that with her now?"

"Her sister, Madame Claudette des Rouches."

"They are French?"

"Émigrés. Claudette's husband was killed for being on the wrong side in yet another struggle for power, and Margarite married an Englishman shortly after arriving."

"For shame, you rogue. A married lady? Tsk, tsk."

"A widow, you brat. Her husband died six months after the wedding."

"How convenient. Ah, well, at least Margarite did not stink of roses. If she had, I might have been forced to deal with her again."

Iago scratched his cheek as he frowned in thought. "No, Margarite does not use a rose scent. Claudette does."

Alethea stared at the two women and briefly wished she had a little of her cousin Modred's gift. There was something about the pair that unsettled her. Iago's frown told her he felt it, too. It would make solving this trouble she had been plunged into so much easier if she could just pluck the truth from the minds of the enemy. She suspected she would quickly be anxious to be rid of such a gift, however. If she and Iago both got un-settling feelings from the two women, she hated to think what poor Modred would suffer with his acute sensitivity. Although she would prefer to avoid both women, she knew she would have to at least approach the sister who favored roses at some point. There was a chance she could gain some insight, perhaps even have a vision. Since a man's life was at stake, she could not allow fear over what unsavory truths she might uncover to hold her back.

"I believe we should investigate them a little," she said.

"Because they are French and Claudette smells of roses?"

"As good a reason as any. It is also one way to help solve this problem without revealing ourselves too much."

Iago nodded. "Very true. Simple investigation. I even know a few people who can help me do it." His eyes widened slightly. "Considering some of the lovers those two women have had, I am surprised they have not already been investigated. Now that I think on it, they seem overly fond of men who would know things useful to the enemy."

"And no one has seen them as a threat because they are beautiful women."

"It galls me to say so, but you may be right about that. Of course, this is still all mere speculation. Nevertheless, they should be investigated and kept a watch on simply because they are French and have known, intimately, a number of important men."

Alethea suddenly tensed, but, for a moment, she was not sure why she was so abruptly and fiercely alert. Sipping her champagne, she forced herself to be calm and concentrate on exactly what she was feeling. To her astonishment, she realized she was feeling *him*. He was irritated, yet there was a small flicker of pleasure. She suspected that hint of pleasure came from seeing his cousin.

"Allie!"

She blinked slowly, fixing her gaze on her uncle. "Sorry. You were saying?"

"I was just wondering if you had a vision," he replied in a soft voice. "You were miles away."

"Ah, no. No vision. Just a feeling."

"A feeling?"

"Yes. He is here."

Chapter 2

Hartley Greville, seventh Marquis of Redgrave, greeted his plump cousin Lady Beatrice Bartleby with all the charm he could muster. She was a good-hearted woman, if a bit silly. In many ways she was more like some sweet, affectionate aunt than a cousin, being fifteen years his senior. When he was still a boy, she had, on several occasions, been his only source of comfort. Gratitude for those times was what brought him to her door, made him almost willingly enter into the foray of a ton event. She also only made the occasional half-hearted attempt to find a wife for him, something else he was very grateful for.

He exchanged greetings with her gruffly jovial husband, who knew far more about Hartley's life than Beatrice did. William's bluff country-squire appearance hid a brilliant mind that efficiently sorted through much of the intelligence men like Hartley gathered for the government. Hartley's smile widened briefly when William gave him a surreptitious wink. They both knew he would stay only a short time, escaping the marriage-minded mothers and their daughters as soon as courtesy allowed.

"Oh, Hartley, we have had several entertaining surprises tonight," said Beatrice. "One of those surprise guests was asking for you."

Although he tensed slightly, since there were many people he would rather not see, Hartley pleasantly asked, "And who would that be, Cousin?"

"Another one who rarely attends these functions. A bit of a recluse, but then his whole family is like that. A shame, for he is a lovely young man. He brought his niece with him."

"Him?"

Beatrice nodded. "Iago Vaughn, Baron Uppington. I did not know you were acquainted with the man."

"I am not, not truly. A nodding acquaintance at best. Did he say why he sought me out?" Since William gave him no warning sign, Hartley relaxed a little.

"No, he simply asked if you would be attending. Perhaps he wishes you to meet his niece. She is a lovely young woman. She is a widow, poor thing. As she cannot be above twenty, she must have lost her husband not long after their marriage. So sad."

Hartley nodded, thinking Bea was the only person in all of England who would think it acceptable that someone introduce him to a young widow. He only knew Baron Uppington in passing and from rumor, but he could not believe the man would dangle one of his female relations in front of him. Only a few people knew that his satyr's reputation was more rumor than fact, and if one discounted the times that seduction had been mostly a tool used to gain information for king and country, that was even more true. Baron Uppington was not one of those privileged few.

He could not make himself believe matchmaking was Baron Uppington's plan, either. Curiosity stirred within him, and he could not quell it, despite knowing the dangers it could lead him into. Then again, he mused as he excused himself from his cousins and started to make his way toward his friends Aldus and Gifford, for he was aware of all the traps matchmakers could set for a man. He had been dancing free of them for years. He could easily do so again.

Only feet away from his friends, Hartley caught the flash of motion out of the corner of his eye and saw Baron Uppington stand up from the chair he had been sitting on near the wall. Hartley next looked at his lordship's companion and abruptly halted. The sharp tug of awareness that tore through him startled Hartley. The woman standing up and looking at him so intently was not the sort he usually felt any interest in.

It took only a swift, expert glance for him to completely tally and judge her attributes. She was small, dainty, and dark. Thick black hair that held a gloss of blue beneath the candlelight was done up in a severe style, with only a few curls dangling to soften the look, but it was a style that suited her small, faintly heart-shaped face. The ivory tone of her skin next to her thick dark hair reminded him strongly of a cameo, for her features were a soft perfection, as if carved with an expert hand. Gentle dark arcs formed her brows, and even from where he stood he could see the thick length of her lashes. Her neck was long, a soft, pale throat that begged to be nuzzled by a man. She tilted her chin up as she became aware of his intent study, revealing a touch of strength in her delicate jaw. A hint of color touched the perfect line of her cheekbones, and she looked down her small, straight nose in a way that almost made him smile. The only thing that did not quite match the sweet innocence of her face was her mouth. It was slightly wide, with sinfully beckoning full lips.

Her figure was slim, almost too much so, but the swell of enticingly pale skin above the modest neckline of her gown told him that she had softness enough to please any man. He was suddenly swamped by the need to place his hands on her hips to see if they were as womanly, and inwardly shook the thought from his mind. Hartley told himself that he had no need to see if this little widow wore clothing to hide her shape, but a little voice in his mind sneered *liar*.

Then he met her steady, curious gaze, and his heart actually skipped a beat. Her eyes were of a size to appear almost too big for her face and were an intriguing silvery blue. The color was clear to see, for she met his gaze with a directness to equal his own. What made him a little uneasy was that a shiver of recognition went through him, yet he was sure he had never met the woman. Nor had he ever seen eyes like hers. Hartley was certain he would remember if he had, but the sense of recognition was not easy to shake.

"My lord, if we might beg a moment of your time?" Lord Uppington asked.

"Of course," Hartley replied, moving closer to the pair.

"Allow me to introduce my niece, Alethea Channing Lady Coulthurst. Alethea, this is Hartley Greville, Marquis of Redgrave."

"Charmed," Hartley murmured.

Alethea almost smiled as he bowed and lightly kissed the back of her hand. No polite, faint pouting of his lips for this man. She could feel the warmth of his sensuous mouth even through her gloves. A little shiver tickled its way up her arm, and the word *dangerous* whispered through her mind. He made something stir to life inside of her, something she did not recognize but which tasted like more. That was not what she had come to London for.

His was the kind of handsomeness that drove women to do something utterly reckless, but that did not surprise Alethea. She had seen enough glimpses of him over the years to suspect it. It was also a good thing that she was well accustomed to tall men, for the lean Redgrave towered over her meager height by a foot or more and even topped Iago's impressive six feet by a few inches.

She let her gaze drift over the man, finding herself a little too enamored of each perfect feature she found. His hair was a warm, mahogany brown, candlelight hinting at a touch of red in its thick depths and adding life to it. Alethea was glad he was one of the ones who had cast aside the use of powder. The fingers of her free hand flexed as she fought the urge to bury them deep into the thick hair. His face was a masterpiece of Nature's art, each feature carved with a master's hand. All clean lines from the high cheekbones to the strong jaw. Even his nose was perfect. Bold, straight, and just narrow enough to keep it from appearing too big and jutting. The rich color of his hair was matched in his brows, arched ever so slightly to follow the line of his dark amber eyes, and his lashes, thick and long enough to be the envy of women but not so lush as to look incongruous on his aristocratic face. His mouth tempted her in a way she had never been tempted before, the hint of fullness to his lips promising a woman a soft, sinful warmth.

He was, she decided, almost too much manly perfection for any woman to deal with rationally. Despite her gift, she prided herself on being a rational woman, on being able to look beneath surface charm and beauty. What troubled her was that she knew, somewhere in her heart and mind, that she would crave what lay beneath the surface of this man.

Realizing that he still held her hand in his, she gently tugged free of his grasp, vaguely irritated to notice that his expensively gloved hand was quite perfect, too. Long, elegant fingers made her wonder if he had any artistic inclinations. When Alethea found herself pondering how skillful that manly hand would be in stroking a woman's skin, she wrestled her thoughts back to the problem at that had brought her here.

"A pleasure to meet you, m'lord," she murmured, clasping her hands in front of her skirts in what she prayed was a pose of serenity and hoping that she was successfully hiding the strange but strong urge to touch him.

"Your niece?" Hartley asked, a hint of amusement in his voice.

"My eldest brother's child," explained Iago, but then he grimaced. "I also have a nephew a year older than I am." Iago suddenly turned to frown at Alethea. "Why did you not go to Gethin with this trouble?"

"He is not in London," Alethea replied.

"Just where is he?"

"America. The last word I had from him was that he

was planning to travel to the southern parts of that country because he had heard that the slaves there had some interesting beliefs and practices. I await word of what those may be."

"You had something you needed to discuss with me?" asked Hartley, interrupting what he suspected was a budding argument. "There is some trouble you think I might help you with?"

"Ah, yes and no," replied Iago, turning his attention back to Hartley. "Actually, it is Alethea who must explain to you why we have sought you out." Iago scratched his cheek. "I fear it is a difficult thing to explain."

"Good, bad, easy, or difficult, the plain truth is usually the best."

"Not always," Iago muttered, and then he cursed when he saw Claudette headed toward Hartley. "Ah, madame," he said as he moved to put himself between her and Hartley, "have you come to collect me for our dance? Such a heartless swine I am to have forced you to such an inconvenience." He kept on talking as he took her by the arm and led her away.

Alethea stood beside Hartley and watched her uncle sweep a frowning Claudette onto the dance floor with a grace and ruthlessness she had to admire. "That was very efficiently done, was it not?" she asked after a few moments of tense silence and then smiled at Lord Redgrave when he turned from frowning after Iago and Claudette to meet her gaze.

"It was an act that has certainly caught the attention of many," Hartley said, all too aware of the many curious glances sent his way. Such interest was not something a man in his position wanted.

"Ah. 'Tis a grave *faux pas* for my uncle to dance with your mistress, is it?"

Hartley frowned even more in an effort to hide his surprise over her blunt statement. In truth, many people suspected that Claudette was his mistress, but he had not taken that final step to make her so yet. The dance of seduction between him and the lovely blonde had only just begun. He was not a man to rush things, if only because too much eagerness could look suspicious. But just where, he wondered, and how, had this woman come by such information? He was confident now that she mixed with society even less than the reclusive Iago did. It was unusual, even shocking, for a woman to speak so openly of such things as well.

"And why would you think the woman is my mistress?" he asked.

"She smells strongly of roses."

"Ah, well, yes, she does." Hartley began to consider the possibility that Iago's niece had been kept out of society's eye because she was not quite right in the head.

Alethea grimaced when she saw the expression Redgrave tried to hide. It was one she was painfully familiar with, the one that said she was undoubtedly one step away from a place in Bedlam. What had seemed so simple before—come to London and warn the man—was not looking so simple now. She should have heeded Iago's words. How *did* one tell a man that he ought to avoid a beautiful lady who smelled of roses, because, by the next full moon, she would be sending him to a long, torturous death?

"My lord, I am sure you have heard a tale or two about my family, about the Vaughns," she began.

"I pay little heed to rumors." Hartley suddenly realized

that this woman was making no attempt to flirt with him and then wondered why that irritated him just a little. His duty at the moment was to seduce Claudette, not become interested in some raven-haired widow from the country.

"How very commendable of you, but that is not exactly what I asked, is it? We Vaughns, and our close relations the Wherlockes, have long been considered somewhat unusual, shall we say. Unusual in ways that cost several of our ancestors their lives, for they were tried, convicted, and executed for the practice of witchcraft."

"Ah, of course." Hartley relaxed. Now he knew what he was dealing with. Iago's niece was just a young woman who had come to believe the whispers about her family, might even think that she herself possessed some magical skill. Foolish, but not alarming.

Alethea did not like the heavy condescension she heard behind those words. The tone of his voice set her teeth on edge. "I can readily accept the disbelief of others, my lord, but condescension has a tendency to irritate me."

"My pardon, m'lady."

"Fine. I accept your apology even though there was not a dollop of sincerity behind it." She ignored his slightly raised brows. "Come now, m'lord, you would not question a man's intuition about something, would you? If that soldier at your side in battle suddenly told you he *felt* as if a trap lay ahead, you would at least heed him, would you not?"

"A telling point," he murmured.

"Thank you."

"So, you have had some intuition concerning me? How could that be possible? We have never met."

"'Tis true that *you* have never met *me*." She almost smiled at the confusion that entered his expression, but then her attention was firmly grabbed by her uncle. "Oh, no. Oh, damn and damn again."

Iago looked alarmingly ill as he strode past her. She reached out for him, but he only muttered something about the gardens and kept on moving. There had been a look in his eyes that chilled her, made her fear for his state of mind. Something far worse than a visitation by some spectre had put that look there. Alethea inwardly cursed. They did not need any more trouble.

"I must see to my uncle, m'lord," Alethea said.

"He did not look well," Hartley agreed.

"Ah, no. No, he did not. Please, m'lord, I have heard that you do not remain at these social events for very long, but I would beg of you to wait for me. I truly *must* speak with you."

Before Hartley could make any promise, Lady Alethea left him. She paused in her pursuit of her uncle only once, relieving a wide-eyed footman of a tray full of drinks. Alethea prayed that Lord Redgrave would wait for her return, that curiosity would hold him at the ball, if only to discover what odd thing she would say next. If he left, she would find him again, however, she promised herself, but now her concern was all for her uncle.

Hartley frowned after the Vaughn woman, torn between staying to discover what was going on and fleeing the odd female before he caught himself in some snare he had been too confused to see coming. Then he saw Claudette making her way through the crowd straight toward him, the gleam of a huntress in her eyes. His brief attendance at his cousin's ball was turning out to be very complicated. He was supposed to be seducing Claudette. The fact that she had twice tried to approach him tonight was a very good sign, one he should take swift advantage of. Yet his inclination at that precise moment was to chase after two people named Vaughn. When he abruptly realized he could not think of the Lady Alethea as a Channing, his curiosity grew. Anyone who had such an odd effect upon him definitely merited more investigation.

A flirtatious young man distracted Claudette in her aim to reach his side. Hartley cursed over his own indecisiveness and then gave in to a surprisingly strong urge to go after the Vaughns. It took great effort not to stride right past his friends when they hailed him. He paused to look at Aldus and Gifford, men who understood the lies and secrets he lived with, for they shared them.

"Who was the little dark beauty with Vaughn?" asked Aldus, the glint of curiosity in his dark blue eyes.

"Vaughn's niece, Lady Alethea Vaughn-Channing," Hartley replied, hastily hyphenating her last name when he began to leave off the husband's name yet again, and he had to smile at the looks of surprise and doubt on his friends' faces. "His eldest brother's child. Widow of the late, unlamented Edward Channing of Coulthurst." And why saying the man's name left a bad taste in his mouth, he had no idea.

"Damn," muttered Gifford, scowling in the direction the Vaughns had gone. "There was a man who should never have married anyone, let alone a woman as young and pretty as that one."

"Why not?" Hartley was aware of some information tickling at the edges of his mind, something he should have recalled when he had heard the name of Channing of Coulthurst, but that information was still proving elusive.

"Not one for the ladies. Never was. Never had been. Not sure he ever could be, although not certain of the why of that. No sign that he favored men or anything else, either."

"Such a waste."

"Quite so. Your current prey appears to have turned the tables and is now pursuing you, my friend," whispered Aldus as he watched Claudette extract herself from one man only to be halted in her renewed advance on Hartley by yet another. "She now makes your job easy."

"Suspiciously so," said Hartley. "Duty bids me stay and let her ensnare me, but every instinct I have is urging me to follow those Vaughns."

"Then follow them. Your instincts are usually right. I have heard that the Vaughns are an odd lot, but that they are honorable and that one can always trust the word of a Vaughn. We will wait here and keep the fair Claudette from following you, if needed."

That was comforting, Hartley thought as he made his way out to the gardens. He was curious about how Aldus would know such things about the reclusive Vaughns, however. In truth, Aldus and Gifford often astonished him with the vast amount of knowledge they had concerning the members of society. He had no doubt that, if they had not already known his secrets, they would soon have ferreted them out. If the pair ever decided to turn their hands to blackmail, they would become very rich men.

After searching his cousin's garden for several moments, Hartley began to fear that the Vaughns had fled the ball. He followed the sound of the fountain and finally saw the pair. The light from the moon and the torches encircling the area around the fountain clearly illuminated the couple. Lord Uppington was seated on a stone bench, his elbows on his knees, and his head held in his hands. Lady Channing sat by his side, lightly rubbing his shoulders. He felt his shoulders warm at the thought of her doing the same to him and quickly shook the thought out of his head.

When Lord Uppington slowly sat up straight, Hartley frowned. The man looked truly ill, and Hartley wondered if Claudette had anything to do with Vaughn's shaken condition. Although he could think of nothing the woman could have said or done in a crowded ballroom to leave the man so overset, Hartley could not ignore the fact that Lord Uppington had been with the woman when he took this strange turn. Lingering in the shelter of the shadows, Hartley hoped the couple would say something that would absolve him from turning his back on his duty and walking away from Claudette, if only for a little while.

"Here. Drink," ordered Alethea, handing Iago some wine. "You look like death warmed over."

"An apt description," Iago murmured and then sipped at the drink. "You did not have to bring so much drink. I think this one will serve."

"The rest is for me. One look at your face, and I thought I would need it."

Alethea was pleased to see him smile at her small jest.

Seeing Iago so unsettled had alarmed her. He had been able to see into the shadows all his life and was, more or less, accustomed to sights she suspected would make her swoon. For Iago to flee, to look so sick and shaken, he had to have seen something truly horrifying. She was not sure she wanted to know what it was, but then told herself not to be such a coward. Iago needed a steady, calm presence and a willing ear right now. He needed someone he could speak to openly, honestly, without fearing that listener would run screaming into the night. That need for someone who could understand, who could accept such gifts without scorn or fear, was one thing that kept the Vaughns and Wherlockes so united as a clan. Sometimes each other were all they had.

She felt an old pain stir and beat it down. It was not her fault her mother had fled, she told herself for what had to be the millionth time, and wondered if that desertion was something she would never fully get over. Her father had tried to hide his heritage, and, though doubtful of his success, the rest of the family had dutifully played along. A small child did not know how to hide such things, however. The look upon her mother's face when she had heard of a neighbor's death, a death that had occurred exactly how, when, and where Alethea had told her it would only two days earlier, still had the power to break Alethea's heart fourteen years later. Her mother had feared her then, just as she would soon fear her eldest son. When Gethin's gift had appeared, Henrietta Vaughn had not waited to see what, if any, gifts her other two sons might have, but thrust her still nursing youngest son into his father's arms and walked away. Her father had never really recovered from the desertion, either.

Forcing aside those sad memories, Alethea noticed

that Iago's color was a little improved and asked, "Lady Bartleby's house is not clean?"

"Oh, no, not as ours is," replied Iago. "Nothing horrifying or dangerous, however. I often see the others at such events. I swear, I think the music and the crowd draw them."

"Yes, I think it would me if I were lingering about some place."

"You will not pass for many, many years and will have no regrets or unfinished business. You will not linger."

That sounded very much like a command, so Alethea nodded. "It was not a normal sighting that made you get so upset, was it?"

"No." Iago shuddered and tossed back the last of his drink.

"If you would rather not speak of it," she began.

"I *would* rather forget it all, if that were even possible. I cannot. It is all tied up with the reason you have come to London, I think."

"Madame Claudette, who smells strongly of roses?"

"And death," whispered Iago.

Alethea shivered. "She is to die soon? Not before the next full moon, surely? I still believe she is there when he dies."

"No. It was not her death I saw, though retribution for her crimes must be drawing nigh." Iago shook his head slowly. "I fear I have just discovered a new twist to my gift. Madame tows about a rather large group of the others. Enraged ones, ones who want revenge, justice. She seems completely oblivious to them," he said in wonder.

"Ones whose deaths she has caused, do you think?"

Iago frowned in thought. "Mayhap, mayhap not. She is an émigré, one who fled the horrific bloodbath that has become the Revolution. These may just be sad souls who died when she was near them. Mayhap she was caught in some frenzied massacre but survived."

"Then you would have seen such sad souls before. You know several men who were soldiers, who were in battle. They would have been near death, abrupt and brutal death. Yet you say you have never seen the like of this before."

"No, I have not, not truly. Certainly not of this ilk. Not this writhing mass of fury and hate. One or two sad, confused souls. Knew who they were, too, for had heard the tale of the boyhood friend or beloved comrade dying in his arms. Even saw a Frenchman, but he was just as sad and confused as the others."

"Because it was war, a death in battle, soldier against soldier, not murder or deceit or treachery. And they died quickly, without even knowing who fired the fatal shot or swung the sword that cut them down."

"Oh, bloody hell, you are right. There lies the cause of all that anger and loathing, the whispered demands for retribution. She had something to do with their deaths. I did not see them at first. They appeared half the way through the dance, which was alarming, I might say."

"They sensed that you could see them, understand them perhaps. One can only wonder how long they have waited for just such an opportunity. That might explain why it was such a strong, violent, even upsetting visitation. They were desperately hungry for someone, anyone, to hear their pleas and so rushed at you too fast, too overwhelmingly."

"You seem to understand these things better than I do."

"'Tis not my gift. I can calmly sit back and study it."
Alethea sipped at her drink. "And you are right. This is
all connected to what I saw. She is the one who threat-
ens him."

"If what I just saw is the gathering of those whose
deaths she has caused, she is a bloody, dangerous bitch,"
Iago snapped, "and you will not have any more to do
with her."

"How forceful you sound," Alethea murmured. "I am
devastated that I cannot heed and obey."

"No, you are not." Iago cursed and dragged a hand
through his hair, disordering his neat queue. "If I tried
to send you back to Coulthurst, you would probably
just turn around and come back here the first chance
you got. On foot if you had to."

"I can be stubborn."

"Why? You do not know this man, have never even
met Lord Redgrave before this eve. This is not your
danger or your responsibility. You could leave me all I
need to properly warn him and go home."

"Uncle, we have already stomped down that path,"
she said gently. "In a rather strange way, I have known
the man since I was a small child. He is in danger. The
moment I knew that, all of this *did* become my responsibility. After what you have seen, I believe we can
assume Madame Claudette is not some honest émigré,
one fleeing for her life. Recall what else we thought
about her, about her choice of lovers, and you must see
that our responsibility grows even stronger. Not just to
the man, but, perhaps, to England herself."

"What the bloody hell do you two know?!"

Alethea looked at Lord Redgrave, startled by his
abrupt intrusion into what she had thought was a private

conversation. He looked a little pale, and his hands were clenched into tight fists at his side. He had followed them, something she had not anticipated, and had obviously overheard at least some of what she and Iago had been discussing. The look of angry suspicion he was giving them was probably justified. When she opened her mouth to reply, the sound of laughter warned her that someone was approaching and there would soon be far too many ears close by to hear what the three of them might say to each other.

Redgrave scowled toward the sound. "Later. Meet me at my house in one hour." He glared at Iago. "If I do not see you there, rest assured, I *will* hunt you down."

"Oh, dear," murmured Alethea as she watched Lord Redgrave stride away. "Do we obey?"

"I think we must," replied Iago. "He did not ask what the devil we were talking about or what we meant, did he?"

"Ah, me, no. He asked what we knew. Perhaps the danger I must warn him about will come as no surprise to him. It will just be a matter of making him believe me."

"My dear niece, if that man overheard everything we have discussed here, either he will have a few burly men waiting for us to take us off to Bedlam or he will see what you have to say as positively reasonable."

Chapter 3

"I want to know everything you two know about the Vaughns," Hartley demanded of Aldus and Gifford as he poured them each a brandy. "Everything and quickly. They will be here soon."

Hartley sat down on a plush settee facing his two friends. They had said little as he had dragged them away from his cousin's ball, brought them to his house, and ordered them into his best parlor. They had not even commented on the nearly rude way he had dismissed Madame Claudette, a woman he was supposed to be seducing for the sake of king and country. He also knew they would continue to play the game by his rules for a while longer, confident that he would eventually explain everything. Hartley was just not sure he could explain, that his friends would even understand if he tried, or that the Vaughns would clarify much when they did arrive.

He took a deep drink of his brandy to still his agitation but was not completely successful. Everything he had overheard in the garden churned in his mind despite his attempts to dismiss all but one thing—they knew about Claudette. He had considered himself a man of logic and fact, blissfully clean of superstitions, but the things the Vaughns had said had roused a few from wherever he had buried them. Worse, he had found himself listening as if they were not talking utter nonsense.

"As I have told you," said Aldus, "the Vaughns are known to be honorable and true to their word. They carry a wide variety of titles, starting with the patriarch of the clan, the Duke of Elderwood. The family seat, Chantiloup Castle, is in Cheshire, but one step from Wales. The current duke is a young man named Modred, if you can believe that. Poor sod. Do not know anyone who has met the man. Sons, cousins, nephews, and the like all seem to stumble into titles of their own, from insignificant ones to quite impressive ones. Some come from the crown for services rendered, but many come through marriages, especially from women of titled families who lack sons to inherit everything. Not all titles pass only through the sons, and a little bribery can get many a will or entail changed. There is wealth there, too, enough to make such changes. If they were not so reclusive and rumored to be odd, that family could probably wield a great deal of power. So could the other branch of the family, the Wherlockes."

"But why are they reclusive and deemed odd?" demanded Hartley.

"Well, 'tis said they can do and see things we mere mortals cannot. Such things as what got several of their ancestors tried and executed as witches, and had them all heavily persecuted for a time. That might be the cause of this lingering tendency to hide away from the world. Both sides of the family have a sad history of wives and husbands walking away never to return. The last one to do so was Lady Henrietta Vaughn, who was, I believe, Lady Alethea's mother. She left her husband and four children about fourteen or fifteen years ago. Retired to a small estate in Sussex with an aging spinster aunt and refused to speak of her marriage."

"She did occasionally let slip the opinion that her husband was in league with the devil," said Gifford. "I recall her telling my aunt once that all the Vaughns are cursed, that that curse had stained her children with the devil's mark so that she had to flee to save her own soul. My aunt said the woman was frighteningly pious. Still visits the woman from time to time when she goes to Sussex to visit her son, but claims the woman gets worse every year. Actually spoke of her children last spring, but my aunt Lily said it was all nonsense and she thinks the woman is losing her mind."

"Did she tell you what that nonsense was?" asked Hartley.

"Some of it," replied Gifford, "though Aunt Lily thinks it all delusions born of guilt over deserting her own children. The woman told my aunt that her daughter could foresee death, that at only six years of age the little girl had accurately described their closest neighbor's death two full days before it happened. Aunt Lily said she might have believed that, but that then the woman told her that her eldest son could hurl things about without lifting a finger."

"Nothing about seeing ghosts?"

"Er, no, although she has said a few things about her husband and spirits. Again, all this is according to Aunt Lily." Gifford shrugged even as he watched Hartley closely. "It is the sort of thing one always hears about the Vaughns and the Wherlockes. They can do magic, read minds, see the future, talk to the dead, and so on. Always felt that it was how people explained the family's avoidance of society."

"Do you, either of you, believe in any of those things?"

"I do not *dis*believe in them. Never seen anything to prove or disprove such things. Then again, look at Lord Iago. Young, handsome, titled, comfortably wealthy, and seems a good man. Why does he shun society so?" Gifford asked, and Aldus nodded his agreement.

"To avoid matchmaking mothers?"

"Possibly, but why does he not at least frequent any of the places bachelors do? He belongs to all the clubs, but one rarely sees him at any of them. He has a few close friends, true enough, but he is very reclusive, and I can find no reason why. No stutter, no disfigurement, no evil secret or even one of the sort the late Channing might have had, and no sign of a painful shyness, insanity, or even an unreasonable fear. All the Vaughns are like Lord Uppington to some extent. So, have you discovered their dark secret? Is that why we wait here to confront them, why you are so suddenly interested in them?"

"They know about Claudette."

"Impossible," said Aldus. "We have only just begun to suspect her ourselves. How could two recluses know about her?"

"My thoughts exactly," said Hartley, "but they do. Supposedly, if I interpret what was said correctly, Lady Alethea has come to London to warn me about Madame Claudette, that I am in danger, possibly even for my life. They know about her lovers, are suspicious of her choices in men she takes to her bed, suspect she is not the frightened, innocent émigré she claims to be, and that she has a lot of blood on her hands."

"Damnation—how?"

"Therein lies the problem. To hear them talk, all this knowledge it took us months to collect was given to them through her visions and his ghosts. Whatever I think or believe about all else I heard in that garden, one fact stands clear."

"They know too much."

"Exactly." Hartley heard someone at the front door and tensed. "And now they might explain themselves. 'Tis to be hoped that they will do so without talk of spiritual visitations."

Alethea clutched her sketchbook tightly against her chest as she and Iago were ushered into an elegant parlor to face Hartley and his two friends. The greetings and introductions were exchanged, and all the while she studied Lord Redgrave's two friends. Aldus Covington was a minor baron with a very good chance of becoming a viscount. He was about Iago's height and almost too slim, yet she suspected he had a limber strength. He was also handsome in a blue-eyed, blond, and classical way. Gifford Banning was an marquis, of an age and height with Lord Covington but broader in the shoulders, more obviously muscled, and quite startlingly handsome with his dark auburn hair and sharp green eyes.

All in all, she was standing amidst a veritable plethora of masculine beauty, wealth, and good breeding, she mused with an inner smile as she sat down on the settee Lord Redgrave led her to. The matchmaking mothers of society would tear her to pieces if they found out. She tensed slightly when Lord Redgrave sprawled on the settee at her side, leaving Iago to take the chair next to her side of the settee.

"At least there are no burly men with chains, ropes, or restraints of some sort," she said quietly to Iago as the butler and a footman set out tea and cakes, refreshment that had obviously been readied for their arrival.

"They could be lurking in another room," replied Iago in an equally quiet tone.

"We are the only ones here," said Hartley the moment the servants left. "Would you care for something stronger than tea? Either of you?" When Alethea shook her head, he looked at Iago.

"No, thank you. Too soon after the drink I downed in the gardens." He nodded when Alethea silently offered to pour him a cup of tea, and then smiled at the identical quizzical looks the other three men wore. "If you heard our entire conversation in the garden, Redgrave, then you will understand why I am cautious in my consumption of drink. It would not do at all for me to lose my, er, reticence."

"Because you might begin to speak to the spirits you claim to see, and do so in public?" Hartley asked, inwardly cursing himself for mouthing the question, one formed from his curiosity, doubt, and, worse, a strange urge to be convinced.

"My lord, I never insist anyone believe as I do, only that they give the leave to do so," Iago said.

Hartley nodded in appreciative response to that very polite set-down. It was very similar to the one Alethea had given him. He began to think they had to do it a lot.

"You truly see the dead?" asked Aldus, blithely ignoring Hartley's glare. "Even speak to them?"

"I have since I was a very small child," replied Iago. "I may have seen them from the moment I was born, but who can say? I would not be confessing such things except that it is quite obvious my secret is out, at least amongst the ones in this room."

"Are there any here? In Redgrave's home?"

"Yes, but not in this room, and none of them are malevolent."

"Can you make them show themselves or reveal themselves in some way?"

"No."

"Curse it, Aldus, we have not brought them here so that you can request parlor tricks," snapped Hartley.

"I have always been curious about such things," said Aldus, "yet I have never seen any proof."

"If you saw proof, you would soon come to regret your curiosity," Iago said in a quiet, somber voice and then turned his attention to his tea. "In fact, we would not even be having this discussion at all if the conversation between Alethea and me had not been overheard. I was too overset to take the usual precautions. I believe you can understand why we keep such things as secret as possible. History has taught us all the value of secrecy."

Hartley frowned at the Vaughns and then at his companions, who did not look as doubtful as he thought they ought to. He would never have suspected the two intelligent, well-schooled men would have a superstitious bone in their bodies. Then again, he mused, perhaps they did not, for they showed no unease at all, not as he did. They both looked simply intrigued. Hartley hated the thought that he might be the only one with a newly discovered superstitious side. He inwardly shook his head and turned his attention back to the Vaughns.

"For the moment let us say that we all accept your, er, gifts as fact," Hartley said, irritated by the glint of amusement he could see in the eyes of the Vaughns. "Just tell us how and when you came to know so much about Madame Claudette des Rouches."

"I shall begin," said Alethea, "for it was I who started it all, dragging Iago along with me, m'lord."

"One quick suggestion. We will undoubtedly have a long discussion. Shall we set aside the proprieties a little and leave off the titles? There are four m'lords here. I believe using our Christian names will help to make things a little less confusing."

"As you wish," Alethea said after a quick nod of agreement from Iago and the others. "I had a vision four days ago." She noticed Hartley looked annoyed, but his companions simply looked curious. "In it I saw you step out of a fine house. It had rather poorly carved griffins upon the posts at the base of the front steps. I could smell roses, and you looked, well, smug." Hartley looked even more irritated, but his friends briefly grinned. "Then you were accosted and dragged into a large black carriage. What followed was somewhat alarming. Swift, intense images and emotions. There was a lot of pain. Torture, I believe. Five men tried to get you to tell them your secrets. Then a sudden urgency rose amongst them, followed by your death. Your throat was cut," she whispered and then took a deep breath to steady herself. "I could not, at first, understand why they would kill you when you had yet to tell them what they wanted, but I now believe that urgency I sensed meant that they feared discovery."

"That would make sense," said Aldus.

"None of this makes much sense," snapped Hartley, "How could you have *visions* about me, Alethea? We have never met before tonight."

"True, but I do know you in a peculiar sort of way."

"Why does that not surprise me?"

She ignored that remark and handed him her sketchbook, the one she kept on hand to record her visions of him. There were a few other drawings in there, for she had, on occasion, grabbed the wrong book while still caught in the grip of the confusion and agitation that often followed one of her visions. It was, however, all she could think of to show him, holding the slim hope that it would be enough to make him take her warning seriously.

"I have been having visions of you for some time, since I was five years old." She watched Hartley's two friends move quickly to look at her sketches when Hartley cursed softly and grew pale. "'Tis why I gave you your own book. Well, mostly your own. A few times I grasped the wrong book whilst confused after a vision. I did not see you all the time, but at least once a year for the last fifteen years. Sometimes it was a vision, a strong one or just a fleeting glimpse. Occasionally I would have a dream. There were even times when I just, well, *sensed* things. I did not intentionally intrude upon your privacy, Hartley. Truly, I did not. It occurred to me that, perhaps, all these previous glimpses of you were leading to this very specific warning." She waited for his reaction, so tense that she was surprised she did not hear a bone or two crack beneath the strain.

Hartley stared at the drawings as he leafed through the book, reading the notations she had made on each page. She had a true skill: her sketches were clear, precise, and full of emotion. It was easy to see how her skill had improved over time. Her notes revealed that she had a keen, precise mind. He suspected that later he would be able to appreciate that. At the moment, however, his blood had grown cold.

He could easily recall each incident depicted in her drawings. There he stood at the graves of his mother, his father, his brother, his sister, and his dearest friend. There was the duel he had fought over that faithless jade, Cynthia. Alethea had peeked into so many of the most important moments of his life, he did not know whether to feel violated or terrified. After he went through the whole collection, he returned to the one that had briefly cut through his numb shock and studied it. When he realized why the simple drawing of him staring into the fire had so firmly grasped his interest, he abruptly shut the book and looked at her.

"Your eyes," he whispered, feeling so unsettled that he briefly feared he might swoon like some maiden.

"Pardon?" she asked, wishing that he did not look so ill. That did not bode well for her chances of getting him to listen to her.

"The drawing in which I stand staring into the fireplace, a drink in my hand. I now understand why I felt as if I should know you when we were introduced, or I think I understand. I saw your eyes that night. I decided I had had too much to drink." He handed her book back to her. "I wish I could use that excuse now. I consider myself a man of logic and science. This sort of thing is not logical. Ghosts are not logical."

"No? Do you not believe in the soul, the spirit, which leaves the body to go to heaven or hell when a person dies?"

"Well, yes, but—"

"So, if there is a soul or spirit, why can it not linger awhile when death comes unexpectedly, too soon or too violently? Why can it not be confused or in need of finishing some task or be seeking justice for a wrong done to it? And, once one accepts that there is a soul or a spirit, why would it be so illogical for some people to be able to see it?"

"You have argued this many times."

"Many, many times."

"But how do you make visions sound logical?"

"Intuition that is simply more finely honed than that possessed by others." She almost smiled at the sardonic look he gave her. "I have no wonderfully logical or scientific explanation for my gift. It just is. It has been with me for my whole life. I cannot rid myself of it and, sometimes, cannot even control it. I prefer to see it as a gift, inconvenient, sometimes annoying, and occasionally terrifying, but still a gift. Since it was given to me, I feel it is my duty to heed it. It told me that you were going to be kidnapped, tortured, and murdered. From what little I have learned this night, I still believe in what I saw. Since, I suspect, you know more than we do, I would think you would at least consider the possibility that I am right. If you will not, it does not signify. If you will do nothing, it is still my responsibility to try to ensure that my vision does not prove to be an accurate prophecy."

"Makes sense to me," said Aldus as he and Gifford retook their seats.

"You believe in all of this?" asked Hartley, astonished at the ease with which his friends accepted the idea of visions.

"Yes. And, even if I doubted, she is right. Everything we know adds weight to her warning, no matter how she came by the knowledge of the threat."

"And the ghosts?"

"Ah, I do . . . but I do not. Truth is, I do not want to believe. Then again, I have to agree with what Alethea said about souls and spirits. There are many things we believe in that we have no proof of, things that might even defy logic. God, Satan, angels, the soul, heaven, and hell. I have seen no proof of any of that, but I do believe. And, as was said by Shakespeare in *Hamlet,* '*There are more things in heaven and earth, Horatio, than are dreamt of in your philosophy.'* Aldus frowned at Iago. "I had heard that ghosts tended to stay where they died, however."

Iago nodded. "Quite true for the most part, hence so many haunted castles and dungeons. Some, however, can become attached to a person instead of a place. Some seem to just come round for a visit, the bonds of affection too strong for death to break completely."

Although Hartley did not want to have this discussion, he could not resist saying, "You did not see loved ones around Claudette, did you?"

"No. I saw fury, hatred, and a need for justice," replied Iago. "In truth, I heard the whispers demanding retribution. I did wonder if she had simply been very close at hand when the people had died, but, no, she had blood on her hands. Their blood."

"You think her guilty of murder?"

"Not by her own hand, perhaps, but she had a large

part in the deed. She may even have been close at hand when the deed was done." Iago looked at Alethea. "Although you did not mention seeing a woman in your vision."

"No, I *saw* no woman," replied Alethea, "but in the end I could smell roses."

"But you did not *see* her get into the carriage, did you?" asked Hartley, a part of him astounded that he was speaking with her as if her talk of visions was perfectly acceptable, dependable, even reasonable.

"No, but that does not mean that she did not come to the place where you were taken," Alethea replied. "I was not shown that she was there, did not hear her voice, but there was that strong scent of roses. That could mean any number of things. I took it to mean she was part of the crime done against you, and, after what Iago saw, I truly believe that she is. However, it could mean only that there are roses near the place you were taken to, or it is a repetition of the warning that your presence at her house leads you into danger. Or it could even be that the first scent of roses was so strong it lingered in the air throughout the vision." She looked at each of the three men. "But you all believe her capable of murder, I think."

"We suspect she is not what she claims to be," replied Hartley. He hesitated a moment and then decided that, between Aldus's assurances that the Vaughns could be trusted and all that they had already guessed, there was little point in being hesitant or secretive. "Her choice of lovers is too precise, always men who could give her information the government would prefer to keep secret. Men have died, ones thought to be safe and unknown to the enemy. 'Tis only a hint, but there may be deaths in

France that she is responsible for, people who should have been safe or could have escaped. Several well-planned escapes were foiled, the people killed, and she was always, well, around, shall we say."

"Your angry spirits, Iago," Alethea said to her uncle.

"Yes, undoubtedly," Iago replied. "And Claudette's sister is not so innocent, either."

"You saw spirits around her, too?" asked Aldus.

"No, but"—Iago grimaced—"she is cold, cold to the bone. I had a very brief affair with the woman. Once my blind lust eased, I felt that coldness, that emptiness, and could not abide being near her." He smiled faintly at the looks of confusion and doubt upon the faces of the other three men. "I do not possess the gift of seeing or knowing how a person thinks or feels, but I can sense approaching death. Margarite is not approaching death, yet there is about her a similar feeling, a chilling emptiness, as if some part of her has died or left her spirit."

"Her conscience?"

"Possibly. If she has been responsible for any deaths, those who have died may not have suspected her. She might just help her sister in some small way. What I sense, however, is the soulless chill of a killer. She might not do the killing with her own hands, but she does not, or will not, hesitate to see it done or care who is killed. Or how."

Alethea could see that Hartley was made uncomfortable by such talk, and a sharp pang of disappointment struck her heart. After seeing him in visions and dreams for so many years, she had obviously nurtured the hope that he would be the one who would understand, would believe in her and not fear her as her husband had. Despite the fact that he had seen her eyes that night she had seen him staring into the fireplace, he was stubbornly hanging on to his disbelief. The meeting lasted barely a half hour longer, and, after arranging another, she left with Iago.

"I think they actually begin to believe us," Alethea said as Iago's carriage began to move along the busy streets.

"More or less," agreed Iago, "but Hartley did not want to. There is no denying the proof held in that sketchbook you brought, but Hartley was struggling mightily to do so. Aldus and Gifford believe. I am certain of it."

"They are both very curious men, and that probably makes them more accepting of new ideas, more prepared to accept strange things without fear or unease. I got the feeling that your gift, and mine, were ones Aldus has long been intrigued by."

"True. Of course, none of them have met Modred. The tolerance we met with tonight might fade quickly when faced with his particular gift."

"Sadly true, even amongst our own family. His gift does tend to make people very uneasy. What do you think their lordships will do next?"

"I have no idea. The only thing I can be sure of is that they no longer think we are in league with the enemy."

"For the moment, I suppose that is enough," Alethea murmured and fiercely beat down that part of her which tried to ask for more, a great deal more, from a certain golden-eyed man.

"Do you believe all that?" Hartley asked his companions the moment he was certain the Vaughns had left.

"Yes," replied Gifford, and Aldus nodded.

"Damnation, we cannot accept talk of spirits and visions. Are we not men of science, logic, and education?"

"Of course we are, but what difference does that make?" asked Aldus. "Did you not see logic in what Lady Alethea said when she explained, even defended, such gifts? And what of the fact that you saw her eyes in your fire at the same time she saw you in her fire?"

"She is simply well-practiced in mouthing logical explanations for things that are *not* logical. As for the fire, the eyes, and all of that, I am sure there is a logical explanation for that, too."

"Come, Hartley, there are many, many things we accept as truth that are not logical in the least. We have all accepted a fellow soldier's intuition, even his prophetic belief that he will not survive a certain battle."

"She said that," Hartley muttered.

Aldus ignored him and continued. "We have all felt that moment of blind intuition ourselves, that certain sense about something or someone, and we heed it without question, or nearly so. And have we not all, at some time, felt that chill, that tickle of suspicion, even fear, that we are suddenly not alone? Why is it so difficult to believe that some people may have a keener sense of such things, a true gift for seeing and knowing things we cannot?"

"Because it is strange?" Hartley drawled, but found himself very much in accord with his friend's opinion.

"Very strange indeed. However, one cannot deny the truth of her sketchbook. Nor are the Vaughns out to wrest money from anyone. It would certainly explain why the Vaughns are all such recluses. I would certainly be wary about where I went and who I accepted as a friend if I were burdened with such a gift."

"Can you not imagine what value such gifts would have in our work?" asked Gifford.

The three men stared at each other and then frowned in thought. The value of such gifts was all too easy to see. Hartley suspected they would be thought mad if they presented the idea to their superiors, however.

"Iago said he did not have the gift of how a man thought or felt," murmured Gifford. "It makes one wonder if one of that clan actually does possess such a skill."

"Bloody hell, just imagine what one could make of that." Aldus shook his head and then looked at Hartley. "Is that what you intend to do? Use them? Is that why we will be meeting with them again?"

"Yes." Hartley dragged his hand through his hair, making a mess of his neat queue. "I may waver in believing *how* they came to know so much about those cursed sisters, but the fact is, they *do* know a lot. They might also learn more. Right now, I would accept anything, even some pagan ritual done under a full moon, if it will halt the killing."

Chapter 4

"That was unpleasant," Iago said as he finished off the brandy a concerned Alethea had served him.

Alethea sat next to her uncle on the thickly cushioned settee where he had collapsed after Margarite and Claudette had left. He had made use of her sketchbook, but she had not yet found the courage to look at what he had drawn. After what he had seen clinging to Claudette, she knew the images would be sad, even dark. Instead, she had busied herself in getting him a drink in the hope of putting a little color back into his cheeks. Her venture into London may have been prompted by the best of intentions, but it was proving to have a lot of frightening pitfalls she had not anticipated.

"Perhaps we should step aside," she said. "The warning has been given. 'Tis enough, is it not?"

"No, and in your heart, you know that to be true. You were right to say it has become our responsibility." Iago smiled weakly and patted her hands where they lay tightly clenched together in her lap. "I was prepared this time, but you must give me leave to suffer a moment's weakness after the ordeal. And the two of them together was very much an ordeal." He shook his head. "It seems a sin to have such beauty encase such evil. Evil as they have within them should give some sign of its presence, and not just to ones like us."

"A large, hairy wart, perhaps," she murmured and was pleased to hear Iago laugh. "Why did they come here?"

"I do not mean to sound vain, but Margarite wants me."

"Ah, of course, and she is not a woman who likes to be denied or cast aside. For a moment, I feared they knew about us."

"No, for if they did, they would never risk drawing so close to us."

"True. Do you think Margarite could be a danger to you?"

"She *is* angry, so quite possibly, but I am aware of the threat she poses to me and others. We must see this through to the end, Alethea. You know that, as I do. You said so before I did. Your visions demand it of you, and what I have seen concerning these two women compels me. What use are such gifts if they are never used for something worthy?"

"And using them against the enemies of one's country is worthy. I know it. I just had not anticipated that the danger I saw reaching out for Lord Redgrave would also try to reach out for you. And me."

"I am not at ease with the fact that there is any risk for you, but I will do my best to see that such risk is minimal. I believe we will both be well guarded. Despite their unease, those lordlings believed us, and they are smart enough to see that we, and our particular talents, could be of some use." Iago stood up. "Our reluctant allies will soon arrive, and I wish to show them a list I made last evening."

"A list of what?"

"The men I know of who have shared the beds of Margarite and, or, Claudette. I suspect they already have such information, but one never knows."

Before Alethea could ask how Iago had come by such knowledge himself, he was gone. She sighed and slumped down in her seat. It was naïve to have thought she only needed to warn Lord Redgrave and not only would he heed her, but that her part in it all would then be done. Her uncle seemed almost pleased to have become a part of the secretive battle against England's enemies, but she sorely regretted pulling him into her mess.

If she was honest with herself, she, too, experienced a touch of pleasure, even excitement, over the chance to help her country. She felt the same over the opportunity to be close to the Marquis of Redgrave. There was a strong possibility, however, that he could prove a greater danger to her than the French spies.

When she had first set eyes on the living, breathing form of the man who had haunted her dreams for so long, she had been spellbound. If not for the importance of what she had come to London to tell him, she feared she might have fawned over him like some love-struck schoolgirl. The more she had thought about her reaction to the man, the more she began to fear that all those years of visions and dreams had not only been leading up to this very important warning. There was a very good chance that she had been connected to him for so long, bound to a man she had never met and knew nothing about, because he was the one she was fated for.

"And that is a grossly unkind twist of fate if ever there was one," she muttered, sitting up straight and rubbing at her temples in an attempt to banish a beginning headache.

The man was far above her touch. Too thin, oddly shaped ladies with coal black hair and strange eyes did not capture the attentions of men like Lord Redgrave. Oh, she had bosoms full enough for a man and rounded hips, but she was built on very lean lines everywhere else. But such men were meant for the Claudettes of the world, for the beautiful, worldly women. He was also a rake, a sophisticated seducer of women. She had not the faintest idea how to play that game, even if, by some miracle, he wanted to play it with her. If Hartley revealed an interest in her, a part of her was already more than willing to cast aside all caution and let him lead her down the primrose path. The problem was that with her body would go her heart, and when he walked away, as a man like him surely would, he would take her heart with him.

Then again, she mused, if fate had chosen this man for her, there was not a great deal she could do about it. She would do what she could not to play the fool, but suspected that was all she would ever have control of with that man. It seemed weak to be so resigned to fate, she decided as she noticed a lacy handkerchief on the floor, but she was not sure anyone could be anything but resigned. Fate was a very strong force to fight.

Discarding that problem for the moment, Alethea reached for the handkerchief. A little voice in her head told her she did not want to touch it, but her curiosity proved stronger. The moment she grasped hold of the expensive handkerchief, she wished she had listened to that little voice. She cried out as she was swept into a whirlpool of frightening images, dark visions of death and hate. Unable to pull free, she screamed for her uncle before she lost all ability to do so, and then became a prisoner of her own gift.

Iago entered the hall just as his butler let in the lords Hartley, Aldus, and Gifford. So punctual, he thought with an inner smile as he greeted them. It was hard to hide his smile as he looked at a scowling Hartley. *And one of them so very reluctant to be here.* He could not quibble over that reluctance, however. The confrontation and all its revelations had gone far better than he had expected.

"Welcome, my lords," he said and then quietly instructed his butler to have some refreshments brought to the parlor for his guests. "You *are* welcome," he continued as the butler left to do as he had been ordered, "even though I am not quite sure how much more help we can be."

"Neither am I," muttered Hartley and ignored the scowls his companions sent him.

"Actually, we did have some interesting callers today," Iago began.

"Iago!"

The scream sent a chill down Hartley's spine. Instinct told him it had come from Alethea. He was astounded at how quickly Iago reacted, turning and racing down the hall without hesitation. Hartley ran after him, his friends but a step behind. He could hear the rapid approach of others and suspected there would be anxious or alarmed servants to deal with soon.

He stumbled to a halt a few feet inside the room Iago had rushed into, his friends flanking him. Alethea knelt on the floor, slowly rocking back and forth. She clutched a lacy handkerchief in her hand. Her complexion was gray, tears ran down her cheeks, and she was staring blindly at something that deeply horrified her, something he could not see. Just as Iago reached for the handkerchief Alethea held, a plump maid, Iago's butler, and another man who closely resembled the butler rushed into the room.

"No, m'lord," cried the maid. "Leave it be!" She ran to Alethea's side and knelt down beside her.

"But, Kate, 'tis that which upsets her," said Iago.

"I can see that, but she is deep into a powerful seeing. Might not be good to pull her free of it too quick like." Kate gently stroked Alethea's hair. "Best we wait for a sign that she knows we are here, I be thinking."

Hartley watched the servant who so closely resembled Iago's butler crouch down behind Alethea. He heard movement in the doorway behind him, and, after a brief glance over his shoulder to make sure no one was in the way, Hartley shut the door on the curious servants peering into the room. When he looked back at Alethea, Kate was gently dabbing the tears from Alethea's cheeks with her apron and murmuring softly into the woman's ear. Hartley could see complete acceptance upon the faces of the servants tending to Alethea. Their actions indicated that they were accustomed to this. They only looked concerned for the well-being of Alethea.

This was real, he thought, staring at the small woman caught tight in some waking nightmare. This was no game, no trick or show. No one could act this well. He was sure of it. And, if Alethea had *seeings,* as the maid called them, then that meant that Lord Iago Vaughn saw ghosts. Hartley wondered just what he had gotten himself tangled up in. It was beyond strange. It was beyond his comprehension. It left him feeling uncertain, uneasy. In truth, Hartley was certain of only one thing—he did not like this.

"Kate," Alethea whispered as the tight grip of her vision began to ease.

"I be here, m'lady," said Kate, and then she asked, "Can ye leave go of the linen?"

"No. Take it away. Please."

Iago snatched the lacy handkerchief from her hand. Alethea collapsed, but Alfred's strong grip kept her from sprawling on the floor. A strange look came over Iago's face, and Alethea tried to tell him to drop it. Kate cursed softly and yanked the handkerchief from his hand, tossing it toward the fireplace.

"None of you touch that again," Kate ordered. "'Tis cursed!" She looked at Iago's butler. "Hot, sweet tea, Ethelred. Alfred, help me," she ordered the man steadying Alethea.

"My sketchbook," Alethea said in a hoarse voice as she crawled toward a table set between the two settees.

Hartley cautiously moved closer, his companions matching his steps, as an ashen Alethea made frantic sketches in her book. The two servants gently steadied her still-trembling body. A pale Iago slowly hoisted himself up from the floor and collapsed in a chair. The moment Alethea ceased her drawing, Kate and Alfred helped her onto one of the settees. Hartley quickly claimed the spot next to her, Aldus and Gifford taking seats on the settee facing him.

Iago's butler arrived with the tea for Alethea, and Kate stood by as she drank it. Right behind Ethelred came two footmen with trays heavily laden with food, wine, and more tea. Kate shooed the other servants away, ordered Alfred to serve the drinks, and fruitlessly tried to convince Alethea to seek her bed. After a few minutes, Iago told both Alfred and Kate to leave. Hartley gulped down the wine he had been served and hastily refilled his glass.

"You can trust the Pughs to say nothing," Iago said as he helped himself to a lemon tart.

"Poos? Your servants are called Poos?" Hartley tried to clear his head of the numbing effects of shock.

"No." Iago briefly grinned. "Pughs. P-U-G-H. I think it was once Ap-Hugh, son of Hugh, but over the years it degenerated into simply Pugh. Pughs, Davies, and Jones. The three families have served the Vaughns and the Wherlockes for centuries. Not a whisper of what is done or said here will ever leave these walls."

"So, the Welsh connection is strong."

"Very strong. Stand on the walls of Chantiloup and you can spit into Wales. Have a few holdings in Wales as well." He looked at Alethea. "Better?"

"Yes," she replied. "It was rather"—she hesitated as she searched for the right word but found none—"unpleasant. I knew, even as I reached for the handkerchief, that it was a mistake. The smell of roses warned me, but I was already in the act of picking it up."

"May I look?" Iago began to reach for the sketchbook.

"Please do." Alethea glanced at the other three men. "All of you. One of you may be able to understand what I saw. I fear the images came so quickly and so fiercely it will be a while ere I can puzzle it all out. And, the faces . . ." She shivered a little and quickly moved to pour herself another cup of heavily sweetened tea. "I do not recognize any of them."

Hartley moved quickly to join his friends in studying the sketches along with Lord Iago. He was stunned by what he saw. Lady Alethea had filled the page with hastily but superbly drawn images. If her mind had been crowded with so many dark images, it was no wonder that she had been so badly overset.

"I see Peterson there," Aldus said in a soft, unsteady voice.

"And Rogers," said Gifford in a similar tone.

"And the Compte de Laceau and his lady," whispered Hartley.

"They must be the strongest ones." Iago pointed to his own sketching done on the facing page. "I saw the same earlier, saw their faces in the miasma surrounding Madame Claudette."

Lord Uppington was also very skilled at drawing, Hartley decided as he studied the man's sketches, although his work lacked the emotional impact of Alethea's. Yet it was still chilling to think this man could see such things. Even more chilling to think that Iago saw it all around a woman Hartley had planned to bed. He was going to have to change his plans. It would prove impossible to feel any desire for Madame Claudette now. Despite his strong need to deny all he was seeing now, he knew he would forever see these images in his head when he looked at Claudette. The fact that he felt relieved over the possibility of ending his seduction of Claudette was something he would have to examine later.

Turning his study to the words Alethea had written by each drawing, Hartley frowned slightly. The word *roses* was very easy to understand. Alethea had already made it clear that the scent was Claudette's signature. The other words troubled him, however. As he retook his seat by her side, he was relieved to see that she looked less pale.

"Why did you put the word *laudanum* next to Peterson?" he asked her. "He was not killed by that."

"In a way, he was, I think," replied Alethea. "I saw him dragged from a rose garden. He knew what was to happen. There was fury and fear, but his mind was clouded, and his body would not heed his commands. He could not save himself, and he was enraged."

"Peterson exactly," murmured Aldus as he and Gifford retook their seats.

"And the word *hate* written below the drawings?" Hartley asked.

"It came from many of them. The Rose was the most infected with it, however. Greed, too. That came only from The Rose." She took a deep breath to steady herself, still trying to dispel the taint of all the ugly emotions carried within the vision. "Bloodlust and power. The Rose savors both, one feeding the other. The killing makes her feel strong."

"The couple, the compte and his lady, were betrayed? That is the word you wrote next to their picture."

"Yes. Betrayal, utter despair, and then a demand for vengeance was what I felt from them." She frowned slightly. "There was something else. No, someone else. Two someones sheltered behind them, but I could not see them."

Iago nodded. "I felt the same. The compte and his lady are now very clear to me, but they are not alone. There are two essences with them, clinging and shielded."

"The children," whispered Hartley, the sting of grief

that seared through him telling him that he no longer doubted the gifts of the Vaughns. "But there were four children."

"Only two others were with them," said Iago.

Pushing aside her horror over the realization that Madame Claudette had sent children to their deaths, Alethea mentally reviewed her vision and nodded. "Yes, only two others were with them." She struggled to recall exactly what she had seen and sensed concerning the French couple. "Young. Very young. One young enough to struggle with his words. *His* words? Ah, a small boy, then." She shook her head. "Not enough seen or sensed for me to know for certain which two children were there."

"But young?"

"Yes. Of that I *am* certain."

"As am I," said Iago.

"They had four children," said Hartley. "Andre, who was but two years of age, Blanche, who was five, Bayard, the heir, and eleven, and Germaine, who was fifteen. The older children are from his first marriage. To my sister Margaret."

Alethea sighed, knowing there was nothing one could say to ease the pain of such a loss. "I am sorry, Hartley. I did not see or sense the older children. Were they quiet children?"

"No. Bayard was quite spirited, and Germaine was a complete hoyden."

Iago frowned. "I felt nothing . . . Yet, a girl so close to womanhood? And spirited? I think she would not be hiding." He shook his head. "If you seek some clue that they still live, I am afraid we can give you none. I did not feel their presence, and Alethea has not yet seen them in her visions. It could mean that they yet live. Sadly, it could also mean that they, well, moved on, shall we say."

"And there is no way you can seek them out?" Hartley asked.

"Not really. Alethea's visions cannot be that well controlled, if at all. You just saw how she fell victim to it by simply picking up a handkerchief. If I see the spirits who cling to Claudette's skirts again, I might seek them, might have a chance to gain some information from the strongest of them. I can promise nothing, however. Spirits are not always cooperative. The ones about Claudette are most specific about what they want, but they may ne'er be clear about why, or who they are. How long ago would they have died?"

"Nearly three years ago. That was when the escape was all planned, yet they never made it." He mumbled a curse and dragged a hand over his hair. "I cannot believe I am accepting this, even suggesting more, and yet . . ." He waved a hand toward the sketchbook.

"Exactly," said Aldus. "And yet. A shame it cannot all be controlled and used as one wishes, when one wishes it." He looked at Hartley. "Give it a little more time, see if more comes forth, and then we will set our people on it."

"But they have been looking for the de Laceaux for three years."

"Yes, for a family, for the compte and his lady and *four* children. That could be blinding them. Once we can offer more than, er, visions to explain how we know only the two eldest children may have survived, we will do so."

Hartley nodded and helped himself to an apple tart.

"Bayard would be fourteen now and Germaine a young woman of eighteen. That would, indeed, alter the search that has been ongoing." He struggled to temper the hope surging to life inside of him, but it was difficult. Although reluctant, he knew he was rapidly becoming a believer in what the Vaughns could do.

"If you have anything from that time," began Alethea, and then she shook her head. "It would have to be something personal, something that was there when the deaths occurred or the danger was present." She looked at the handkerchief still lying on the floor near the fireplace. "I could try to see if that stirs another vision."

"But not today," Iago said firmly. "We shall both have a go at it on the morrow, under the proper conditions. 'Tis possible Claudette had it with her and that she was there when the de Laceaux family was set upon. 'Tis also possible it but held some memories from those who cling to her. I favor the latter, for what woman keeps a handkerchief for three years?"

"One who was once very poor," Alethea said as she poured herself yet another cup of tea. The harsher the vision, the more thirsty it left her. "One who has suffered the sting of poverty and the scorn that can come with it. The handkerchief is of the finest linen and the most expensive lace, things she never had the coin for. She will not rid herself of it until it is stained beyond cleaning or tattered." She noticed all four men were staring at her, thought over what she had just said, and frowned. "I wonder how I knew that. Ah, and she was raised in a poor tenant's cottage."

"How do you know *that*?" asked Hartley.

"I have no idea. Something about chickens. Odd that that should come forth now."

"It was probably overshadowed by all the more upsetting images," said Iago.

"That must be it. Perhaps more will come to me later." She smiled faintly at Hartley, heartsore that she could not provide him with something he could immediately make use of. "None of it is much help, is it?"

"It confirms a lot of our suspicions," he replied.

"And gave us some information concerning the deaths that we had not had before," said Aldus. "The sort of information that could be very useful if we get our hands on one of the ones who was involved. A mention of such details, the sort only those involved could know, can make a prisoner think you know it all, that one of his own has or is betraying him."

"And it assures us that we are on the right path, have not been wasting our time," said Gifford. "We do that too often in this game."

Alethea smiled, relieved and pleased. "I know you cannot tell people *how* you came by the information and were concerned that that made it all useless. It is good to know that it can serve some purpose, be of some help to you. As Iago said earlier today, what is the worth of such gifts if they cannot be put to some use?"

"I, for one, wish we could put them to even greater use," said Aldus. "The possibilities are endless, and both time and work could be saved, used more profitably elsewhere. And lives could be saved as well, many lives. Unfortunately, acceptance of such things is not widespread, as you well know."

"Even those who do believe can be most reluctant to deal with such gifts in even the smallest way."

"Or can begin to wish one could still pile kindling around your feet," drawled Iago.

Everyone winced, and the conversation turned back to what little they had learned. Sensing that the Vaughns were in need of some time to recover from their ordeals, Hartley soon brought an end to the meeting. He still found it all unsettling, but he could no longer deny the truth. Alethea Vaughn had visions, and Iago Vaughn saw the dead. Part of the birth of his new belief was because of the Vaughns themselves. He realized he trusted them implicitly, and there were few people he could say that about.

"Damn my eyes, but I wish we could use this information openly, without fear of ridicule over how it was obtained," said Aldus as their carriage started on its way back to Hartley's home.

"We shall just have to think of some clever story to explain how we know what we know." Hartley thought of the possibility that his sister's children were still alive and fought against the surge of hope that tried to rise up within him. "And soon."

"You think your niece and nephew may still live?" asked Aldus.

The man had always been able to sense what was on his mind, Hartley thought and sighed. "'Tis a possibility, a small one. They were just children. Yet Germaine was always a strong, clever girl. If any young girl could survive such a tragedy, survive on the streets of the madhouse that is now France, it would be Germaine."

"Even with a young boy to protect and care for?"

Hartley nodded, absolutely confident in his opinion of his niece. "Even then. In fact, that would make her even fiercer and more determined to survive. I fear having my hopes raised, but I cannot stop it from happening."

"Perhaps seducing Claudette—"

"No. A woman who kills so easily will not be brought down by seduction and pillow talk." Hartley grimaced. "I would also fail in seducing her now, I fear. I will never be able to look at her, touch her, without seeing the faces of Peterson, Rogers, the compte and his lady, and those two innocent babes." He silently admitted to himself that even his baser lust had stopped being tempted by the woman from the moment he had stared into a pair of silvery blue eyes.

Gifford nodded. "Just do not tell our superiors that."

"Why not?" Hartley asked. "I shall need to explain why I am turning away from her."

"Oh, you will still be able to do that, but I think we shall say that our knowledge comes from a careless slip made by Claudette as you worked your magic upon her."

Hartley hesitated for only a moment and then nodded in agreement. It was a good plan. Unease tickled at him, however, and he suddenly realized it was because he did not want Alethea to hear that he was still sniffing after Claudette. He inwardly shook his head when he next realized that the only woman he wanted now was Alethea Vaughn, a woman who had a gift that sent chills down his spine.

Chapter 5

Biting the inside of her cheek to curb the urge to smile, Alethea greeted Hartley as he was shown into the small blue salon. He looked nervous, a look that did not sit well on his strong, handsome face. She doubted it was because he found himself alone with her. He paced the room until Ethelred brought in some tea, wine, and cakes. The moment the butler left, Hartley sat down on the settee facing her.

"Is Iago home?" Hartley asked, nodding his agreement when she silently gestured toward the teapot.

"No," Alethea replied as she poured them each a cup of tea. "This is the night he goes off with his friends. If it is important that you speak with him now, I believe Ethelred could tell you where to look or send a message to him."

"Ah, no. Do not do that." He grimaced, a little surprised at how concerned he suddenly was with the proprieties. He had spent a lot of time in rooms alone with a lot of women and never fretted, but, then, those women had not been Alethea. "I did not expect to find you all alone."

"I am not a young maiden, Hartley. A maid will be chaperone enough."

"There is no maid here."

"There is, if anyone has the temerity to ask or imply otherwise." She smiled faintly. "Do not fear. If you call for help, Ethelred and Alfred will immediately rush to your aid." She ignored the disgusted look he gave her. "Why are you here?"

Hartley took a bracing sip of the strong tea. "After what you told us two nights ago, after hearing all you had learned from simply holding that scrap of linen and lace, I began to think on what you might discover if you did touch something else, something that belonged to the prey instead of the predator." He struggled to keep the image of her pale, tear-streaked face from his mind, because he needed her to do this, needed to find the truth.

"As I told you, I cannot promise anything."

Alethea could understand what drove him to make the request. He needed to know what had happened to his niece and nephew. She could see the hunger for that knowledge in his eyes. Considering what might have happened to them, she was not eager to touch anything that might have been with the children that day, but she could not bring herself to refuse him. This was what her gift was for. If those children were alive, and she was, even in the smallest of ways, able to help him find them, then it was worth whatever unpleasantness she might have to suffer.

When Hartley saw the faint look of unease on her face, the memory of how upsetting it had been for her to hold that handkerchief, the grim images she had been forced to see, slipped free of the bonds he had put on it.

He hesitated to add to that, to chance giving her new, even more upsetting images, but only for a moment. For three long years he had wondered what had happened to his niece and nephew, had searched and worried. Although he had also worried about the compte, his wife, and their two children, it was Bayard and Germaine he had been desperate to find. Aside from a few distant cousins, they were all the family he had left. He could not fully discard what he had seen two nights ago, could not make himself dispute Alethea and Iago's claims that the compte, his wife, and their two children were dead. His need to know the fate of his sister's two children had grown with each hour since then. Hartley pulled Germaine's locket out of his waistcoat pocket and stared at it for a moment before fixing his gaze on Alethea.

"I bought this for Germaine when she was but ten," he said. "It was one of the few things found at the place where the whole family was to meet with me and my men." He frowned at her and then glanced toward the door. "Should we call your maid in case you will be needing her aid?"

After considering that, Alethea shook her head. "You were here that night and saw what she did."

"She stroked your hair and spoke softly to you until you recognized she was there. Only then did she take away the handkerchief. Then you drew those chilling pictures, and, once done, she had you drink tea."

"Sweet tea. At least four lumps of sugar." Bracing herself for what she might face, she held her hand out for the locket.

"I *have* to know," he muttered when he still hesitated, both in apology to her and encouragement to himself, and then he placed the locket in her hand.

For a brief moment, Alethea thought nothing was going to happen. She was both relieved and heartily disappointed. She truly wished to help Lord Redgrave, to help those lost children, but she was not that fond of her visions, especially when they were of dark, frightening things. Just as she saw the hope Hartley tried to hide begin to fade, she was caught up in a dizzying barrage of images and emotions. Her whole body rocked with the force of its arrival. She saw it all, just as if she were one with the young girl who had worn the locket while her world had been decimated by violence. She experienced all the terror, the grief, and the rage. Then, ever so slowly, the mist began to clear. Alethea became aware of a pair of strong arms around her and a deep, melodious voice. Her senses returned, lured back by the scent of him. She was strongly tempted to wallow in that comfort for a moment, to soak up the warmth of the big, strong body so close to hers. The urge to record what she had seen prevailed, however.

She pushed free of Hartley's grasp, ignoring the sharp pang of regret for doing so, and fell to her knees by the table. A heartbeat later she was sketching out her vision with a strong touch of desperation, as if she could pull it out of her mind by putting it to paper. There was too much, however, so she restricted herself to those things she felt certain would stir her memory each time she looked at them.

It touched her heart when Hartley tended to her first. She knew he was desperate to learn what she had seen, but he helped her sit down when she was done and stayed by her side as she drank the hot, sweet tea he had poured. When he picked up the locket she had dropped on the floor and glanced anxiously toward her sketchbook, she put her hand over his. She was not sure what to say to prepare him, however.

"It was bad?" he asked in a soft voice and then cursed and shook his head. "Of course it was. I could see it in your face. They are dead?"

"I cannot say. At the time your niece had the locket with her, no, she did not die. In the following years?" She shrugged then tightened her grip on his hand before he could reach for the drawings. "Wait. Let me tell you what I saw first."

"There is no need. I can just look at your drawings. Do not torment yourself with speaking of all you saw."

"I believe this vision will linger for quite a while no matter what I do. The drawings do not tell all I saw. There was too much. It was as if I was seeing it all as she saw it, suffering as she suffered." When he put his arm around her, she did not hesitate to lean against him, savoring his warmth, for she was chilled to the bone. "I can only tell you what happened up until your niece lost that locket."

"It will be more than I know now."

Alethea nodded and took a deep breath to steady herself. "They were all waiting for you on the shore as planned. They had packed lightly but carefully, a few clothes, all the money they could gather, and all of their jewels. Bayard needed to, er, visit the bushes, and Germaine went to guard him. She heard shots. The marchioness screamed. Germaine started back, moving swiftly but keeping out of sight. She saw six men. The two youngest children were already dead, the marchioness on her knees wailing over the bodies. Her father cried out that they had killed his only children, and Germaine knew he was telling her to get away, to get Bayard away. She caught her brother trying to go back and fled with him. She heard the marchioness's wailing abruptly stop as she pushed and pulled Bayard up a steep, rocky slope. She heard her father curse the men before he, too, was abruptly silenced. At the top of the rise, she saw a coach. When she saw who stepped out of it, she shoved her brother down and lay down beside him. It was as she scrambled along, pulling Bayard and trying to keep out of sight until she could get them away from that part of the road, that she lost the locket."

Hartley sighed, saddened by the wanton killing of a good man and his innocent family, yet hopeful that his niece and nephew had survived. Cautiously, he moved to look at what Alethea had drawn. The images were stark, chilling, and he was horrified by what his niece had seen and suffered. A drawing of Germaine's face held him spellbound, the girl's expression fascinating him even as it alarmed him. This was not the sweet, funny, laughing girl he had known.

"Germaine looks as if she wants to kill someone," he murmured.

"She does. That was the last clear thing I saw and felt, and then the locket was lost. Germaine recognized the person getting out of the carriage." Alethea pointed to the rose she had drawn.

Staring at that and knowing whom it represented, Hartley felt nauseous. He had touched that woman, kissed her, would even have bedded her had not the Vaughns intruded. It had been bad enough to know she had had something to do with the death of his compatriots, but the proof of that had been so thin, it had been easy to doubt it all. But Germaine had seen the woman at the site of her family's deaths. It was still not proof he could use, and he did not understand how Alethea could see such things, but he believed it all.

"They escaped," he whispered as he returned to his seat next to Alethea, blindly accepting the tea she gave him. "They did not die with the rest of them."

"No. They fled," said Alethea. "Unfortunately, the locket was lost before your niece had any plan of action aside from keeping her brother alive. Oh, and killing that woman."

"If she tried to kill the woman, she would have died there with her family, simply done so a little later."

"True, and I grasped no sense of such a plan. Your niece was thinking coldly, clearly, and only of saving Bayard. I believe she would have chosen duty over emotion. There was no sense of immediacy to her thoughts of killing the woman. It was simply a fact."

Hartley cursed, rubbed a hand over his face, and then took a drink of his tea to steady himself. He would have liked something a great deal stronger but decided it was for the best if he stayed with tea. "Germaine was only fifteen, more child than woman, and Bayard was still more infant than child. So young. Too young to survive in the rabid air of France, alone, for three years."

Alethea sighed. "It would seem so, and yet, it was truly as if I were there with her, Hartley. No, within her, seeing and feeling all that she did. There is a deep core of strength in your niece, Hartley. Think on it all. She saw her siblings dead, heard her stepmother die, and then her father. Yet she never faltered, never hesitated to act as she knew her father meant her to. She heard his last command, subtle as it was, and acted immediately. There was such pain and grief within her, a roaring agony of it, but she kept that boy moving, hiding, silent.

Even when she heard the shots and the marchioness's first scream, she did not run blindly toward her family, but moved toward them with the ever-present thought of the need to stay out of sight. I know, truly know, that the girl was desperate to go to her family, but she did not. That girl has hard steel in her spine, and, now, a deep need to avenge her murdered family. I wish I *could* tell you what happened after that moment on the beach, but once the locket fell from her neck, I lost touch with her. I do feel, however, that she has an indomitable will to survive, and to keep her brother alive."

He nodded and stared at the drawing of Germaine as he sipped the last of his tea. Alethea suddenly found her attention pulled away from him, which surprised her a little, as she took a dangerous delight in watching him, being close to him, even taking subtle deep breaths so that she could fill her head with the crisp smell of him. She stared down at her hands and allowed her mind to wander where it wished, to pick through the flood of images and emotions she had just experienced. There was something there demanding her attention, and she had experienced such a thing often enough to know it was best not to ignore it or fight it. Breathing slowly and evenly, she let her thoughts flow.

When Hartley turned to speak to Alethea, he frowned and set down his cup. She looked half-asleep. He softly called her name, but she did not respond. Afraid she had slipped into some kind of trance, he gently stroked her arm and tried to decide what to do next. He was just thinking he ought to call for her servants when she suddenly sat up straighter, her body tense and her eyes wide. It startled him a little when she turned and grabbed his hands in hers. This gift of hers was going to take some getting used to, he thought and then wondered why he was concerned with that.

"The jewels," Alethea said, struggling not to allow her excitement to overrule the lessons she had been taught by other Vaughns about how to best use her gift.

"What about the jewels?" Hartley asked. "Have you seen something else?"

"No, nothing new. I but carefully looked over all that I saw. When a vision is as strong as this one, the images coming so fast and the emotions so intense, it sometimes takes a while to recall the small, often very important, details. Something was pestering me, as if some piece of information was demanding I take note of it. The compte and his family brought a casket of jewels with them, yet you said very little was found upon the beach."

"I suspected anything of any value was taken and has been sold by now."

"Some of the things, most surely. But not all, I think. I was blinded by Germaine's emotions when she saw the Black Rose—"

"The Black Rose?"

Alethea blushed faintly. "The name I decided to call the woman, I fear."

A quick glance down at her drawings revealed that the rose she used to indicate Claudette was indeed black, that she had shaded in the petals with her charcoal instead of leaving it as just the outline of a rose. "A good choice." He looked back her, trying hard not to be infected by the excitement he could see sparkling in her beautiful eyes. "Go on. What have you remembered?"

"Germaine saw the woman get out of the carriage and"—she pointed at the drawing of Germaine—"you can see how she felt, so you can surely guess how

strong that emotion was. Then the need to flee, to hide,
returned, and I now realize that she saw a little more
than the woman, even looked back once. A man came
up from the beach and handed the woman a casket. She
opened it and smiled, briefly lifting a lovely ruby pen-
dant up to look more closely at it before stuffing the
whole casket into the carriage. Just before Germaine
lost her locket, she had the thought that she could find
the woman through those jewels. Germaine was certain
the woman would try to keep most of them, if not all
of them. Could you not do the same?"

"I will need to make a list of what jewels I am aware
of," Hartley murmured, beginning to allow himself to
share a little of Alethea's excitement. "There may even
be a listing amongst the papers the compte left behind
with my solicitor. He knew it was dangerous despite the
truce, but felt compelled to see if any others of his
family still survived and if there was any chance of re-
gaining at least a few of his holdings." Hartley sighed.
"I tried to keep Germaine and Bayard here, with me,
but they wanted to be with their father as much as he
wished them to see his homeland."

"There is one other thing that may help in your
search." Suddenly aware of how she had grabbed hold
of his hands, Alethea subtly tried to pull away from him,
but he ever so slightly tightened his grip, and it was
enough of an invitation that she stopped. "Germaine
was dressed as a boy." She nodded at his look of astonishment. "Her father must have thought it safer for her
to do so. Even her hair was cut short, like a boy's."

Hartley stared at her in shock for a moment, then
abruptly yanked her into his arms and kissed her. He
had the fleeting thought that this was unwise, before

he lost himself in the sweetness of her kiss. It was not a gentle kiss, either. Startled by his action, she had gasped, and he had taken swift advantage of that, plunging his tongue into her mouth and savoring the heat of her, the taste of her. She tasted like more. He wanted to feel her soft pale skin rub against his and her body wrapped tightly around him.

It took more effort than he thought it should to end the kiss. Hartley took one look at her flushed, wide-eyed face, and quickly stood up to pace the room, forcing his thoughts back to the important matter of Germaine and Bayard and off the compelling urge to indulge in more kisses. Knowing that he would soon want far more than kisses, no matter how stirring and sweet they were, alarmed him enough to help him regain his senses. Not only would seducing Alethea after all she had done for him be churlish, instinct told him it could prove very difficult to maintain the usual detachment he employed with his lovers.

"I was so transfixed by her face, I missed seeing how short her hair was. I feel certain Germaine would contrive to continue that disguise," he said, breaking the heavy silence that surrounded them.

Alethea blinked, inwardly shaking free of the bemusement his kiss had caused. She clenched her hands together in her lap to repress the urge to touch her lips, lips that still held the warmth of his, lips that actually tingled slightly. The warmth of his kiss had spread rapidly through her body and was slow to dissipate. She wished he would leave for a few moments so that she could contemplate her first real kiss, and recover from it at her leisure. Sternly telling herself it had been no more than an impulsive act stemming from Hartley's joy and raised hopes over all she had told him, Alethea fixed her attention upon the matter at hand—his lost family.

"As do I," she replied, pleased at how calm her voice sounded, for inside she was a tumultuous mass of emotion. "She would undoubtedly see the advantages of it."

His composure restored, Hartley turned to look at her. He briefly considered apologizing for taking such liberties with her person, but hastily decided against it. For one thing—it would be a lie to say he regretted the kiss. It also appeared that she was going to ignore it as well, excusing his actions as an impulsive response to the hope she had just given him, something that both relieved and annoyed him. He did not like the idea that she could ignore what had just happened or, even worse, put it out of her thoughts. Hartley shook away such strange thoughts and fixed his mind on the most important matter—rescue of his niece and nephew.

"So, I shall have to send word that it is not a family of six we seek, but two children. Actually, a young woman and a boy, *and* that the young woman may well be disguised as a boy. This will narrow the searching yet also make it much more difficult."

"Is there nothing particularly distinguishable about her features? She looked a pretty girl." Alethea stared at the sketch she had made and struggled to recall hair and eye color. "I doubt her features have changed all that much."

"Probably not, but all I have is a miniature painted when she was much younger, barely more than an infant."

"A problem easily solved." Alethea took up her sketchbook. "I will do a sketch of how she looked three years ago." Even as she began to sketch the girl's face, softening the hard, murderous expression a little, Alethea could suddenly see Germaine as clearly as if the girl were standing in front of her. "She has blue eyes," she murmured.

"Yes, like my sister's. She has my mother's eyes," he said as he retook his seat at her side.

"Hartley, for a connoisseur of women, that was a very dull description."

"I would not call myself such," he muttered, a little shocked to discover that he did not want this woman to think him some heartless rogue who seduced and discarded women. How completely absurd, he mused, since he had worked hard on just that reputation for several years.

Alethea ignored him and the look of male bafflement he was giving her. "Germaine has very distinctive blue eyes. She may be able to hide everything else, but she could never, never completely hide those eyes." She carefully tore the page from her sketchbook. "Her eyes are the clearest, brightest blue, like a beautiful summer sky or bluebells. Very, very blue, but not a dark one like mine or a pale one. Boy's clothes, cropped hair, and all of that can never hide eyes like those. Her hair is a lovely golden brown, but that only helps if she is not covering it or it is not dulled with dirt. Ah, but those eyes, they mean that all your searchers have to do is get her to look at them."

Hartley stared at her sketch of Germaine. "You have a true talent. I am glad you eased that look of hatred and anger on her face."

"Will that be enough? I could make more if needed."

"I believe this will do. I will send it with the next man going into France, and he can show it to our men there." He looked at her and fought the urge to stroke her cheek, to feel the soft warmth of her lovely skin beneath his fingertips, to taste those full lips again. "This is all very difficult for you, is it not?"

"Yes and no. I do not usually—oh, how can I put this?—connect or bond with the person in my vision so strongly. I think Germaine's emotions were so very intense they pulled me in. Seeing the murders through her eyes, feeling the fear and grief and fury that she felt, was difficult, but knowing I may have given you a clue that will help you find her and the boy? That makes it all worthwhile. There is hope in it all."

"True, yet why has she not made it back to England? Surely she would try to come here."

"Of course she would, but she fled that beach with nothing save the clothes on her back and Bayard. Also, the truce or lull in the madness has ended. She is stuck in a country at war, with itself as well as with other countries. I would not be surprised if she is managing to do little more than keep herself and Bayard alive, something that would take all of her strength and time. And whom could she trust? Whom could she *dare* to trust?"

Hartley nodded. "You are right. I was not thinking straight. Damn, not only are they half English; they are also half old-French aristocracy. The bloody riots have eased, but not the hatred. Or the mistrust, for many of the aristocracy who survived that insanity now oppose the government." He stood up, took her hand in his, and brushed a kiss over her knuckles. "You have been most helpful, and kind. I know it is an ordeal for you."

"Oh, no, I . . ." she began, trying to think of what to say despite the fact that the warm touch of his lips against her skin had apparently caused every thought in her head to scatter to the four winds.

"It *is*. I doubted it all at first, but when I saw you as you held that handkerchief"—he shook his head—"I could no longer argue away all the things you had said and shown me with your drawings." He looked at the locket. "To me, this is but a pretty little trinket. Knowing where it was found, I could guess some tragedy had occurred, but it does not speak to me as it does to you."

When he stepped back and tucked the locket back into the pocket of his waistcoat, Alethea stood up and lightly touched his arm. "It did speak to you in a way. You *knew* something was wrong. I suspect you got some feeling each time you touched it, that sense of danger and tragedy. It just speaks more loudly to me. If you had handed this to me before your niece went to France, it probably would have been no more to me than a pretty trinket as well. I might have sensed a few simple things such as the youth of the wearer, but nothing more. But, you see, she was wearing it against her skin when all those horrible things happened, when her world was shattered. It is as if her emotions soaked into the very metal, became trapped inside it. That is what gives me the vision."

"You never touched anything of mine, had never even met me."

Alethea grimaced. "I know. I do not understand why I have had visions of you for so long, dreams as well, and even felt your presence at times. It makes no sense. It never has. All too many times I was wretched, for I felt as if I had trespassed, bursting uninvited into your private moments." She sighed. "'Tis a weak explanation, but I still wonder if it was all done to ready myself for this. I thought it happened so that I could save you, but now I begin to wonder if saving those two lost children was the reason, or a big part of it." She briefly touched the pocket of his waistcoat where the locket rested. "After all, what were the chances that someone would find the locket Germaine lost and return it to you?"

Hartley thought that over for a moment. "Very small. It was found when the area was searched for some sign of them. It could be as you say. You were sent to save me because it is only through me that you can save Germaine and Bayard. Hah, just listen to us trying to make sense of the miraculous." He also touched the pocket of his vest where the locket now rested. "I know it will be difficult to find my sister's children, that they may well have died sometime during the three years they have been trapped in France. But now I have some hope."

"I pray that hope is rewarded," she whispered and put her hand over his where it still rested over the locket.

The warmth of her touch, of her honest concern and hope for him, flowed through Hartley's body. He had never reacted so fiercely to the mere touch of a woman's hand and was a little startled. Even as he told himself he should step away, should not give in to the growing attraction he felt for her, he reached out with his free hand and stroked her cheek. Her skin was soft and warm, a delight to touch, and he ached to touch more of it. Her eyes darkened to a rich blue, and he knew she felt the same craving he did. Pushing aside all thought of the consequences and ignoring his own resolutions of but moments before, he lowered his mouth to hers. He had to have another taste.

She tasted sweet, hot, and willing, he thought as he slid an arm around her slim waist and pulled her closer.

Just as he feared, she still tasted like more—more than kisses and a few gentle caresses. The way she fit against him made him wild with need, and he struggled against the fierce urge to tumble her down on the carpet. Alethea was a widow, but all his instincts, honed through years of playing love's games, told him that she was far from an experienced one. The way she again seemed so startled when he slipped his tongue into her mouth simply confirmed that opinion. That taste of innocence only made his hunger for her more intense. He wanted to be the one to show her all the pleasure a man and woman could share.

Alethea was both thrilled and frightened by the desire Hartley stirred within her. A timid part of her wanted to pull away and flee the room. She silenced it and pressed closer to his hard body. Aside from a few light brushes of her husband's lips across hers, Alethea had never been truly kissed, and she was not about to run from a second taste of this delight. The fact that it was Hartley introducing her to this pleasure only made her want it more. When he caressed her, moving his big hand down her back and over her bottom, she shivered, his bold touch firing her desire to even greater heights. The clothes that separated them became an irritation instead of the shield she should see them as.

"Ahem!"

If someone had poured a bucket of icy water over her head, Alethea doubted she could have been more startled. The passion that had been heating her blood faded so abruptly she nearly cried out in protest. Hartley tensed and pulled away, a chill distance eradicating the last of the warmth they had been sharing. She looked toward the doorway, where her uncle stood scowling at them, and bit back the urge to tell Iago to get out and be sure to shut the door behind him.

Taking a step away from Hartley and trying to look utterly innocent and unembarrassed, Alethea said, "We believe we know how to find his sister's children."

She immediately began to tell her uncle the tale of the locket and what she had seen. Iago's attention and interest were quickly caught, just as she had hoped. Alethea was relieved when nothing was said about the embrace Iago had seen. She hoped her uncle had decided it was not worthy of causing a scene. She prayed her luck would hold.

Chapter 6

"He just wants an affair, you know."

Alethea sighed as she looked at Iago, who sprawled elegantly on the carriage seat facing her. A whole night and a day had passed since he had caught her and Hartley embracing. She had thought Iago had decided to just let the matter pass without mention. He had obviously not done so, had instead spent that time pondering the matter. Or perhaps, she thought as she studied his dark expression, brooding would be the better word.

"Mayhap that is all I wish as well," she said and nearly smiled at his dark scowl.

"You may be a widow, but you are not experienced. A man like him could easily hurt a woman like you."

"Physically?" She knew in her heart that Hartley would never harm her that way but was curious as to what her uncle thought.

"Never, but emotionally he could tear you apart."

She could not argue with that, for every instinct she possessed had already warned her of that possibility. Good sense, however, appeared to have fled the moment Hartley had kissed her. She wanted more kisses. She wanted much more than kisses, too. Her dreams last night had been filled with all the scandalous possibilities of how he could give her the pleasure his kisses promised. What she had to decide was whether it would be worth the pain of being no more than a fleeting lust for him. Alethea feared she was more than willing to take that risk. The desire his kisses had aroused within her offered her a temptation she doubted she could resist.

"If I allow him to hurt me in that way, 'tis my folly, is it not? My foolishness to give my heart to a reputed rake, a man whose interest in and passion for women is well known to be as fleeting as a fine summer day."

Iago grunted and then sighed. "Since you understand what such a man is like, why risk that trouble at all?"

"Would you ask a man the same question?"

"Clever wench," he muttered and briefly smiled. "No, and well you know it. Men are expected to sow their wild oats, as many say. I do not quite understand why a man who seduces many women, has repeated affairs, and becomes marked a rake is smiled upon and accepted, considering how protective men are of the women in their family, but there it is. A man has to do some extraordinarily shameful things ere he is shunned. A man who is a rich, unwed marquis, handsome and young, has to do even more before the matchmaking mothers will allow him to be refused entry to any and all ton events. A woman, on the other hand, can find herself shunned and whispered about for simply dancing with and smiling at the wrong man."

"How grossly unfair. Iago, I am a Vaughn despite my married name. If not for the fact that you are young, titled, and unwed, I would not be invited to these events anyway."

"If people knew you—"

"If people truly knew me, I would never be invited anywhere save for a few small teas or salons where I would be expected to tell someone if their husband is faithful or whom they might wed. I would be the entertainment. I am not even an heiress some mother might wish to grasp for her son. I am just a young widow with enough of a portion to live in a small manor on a small acreage several days' journey from London. What I am is the sort of woman men like Redgrave want as a lover."

"Alethea—"

"No, Iago. This must be my decision. If 'tis folly, then so be it. If I end up heartbroken, then so be it. When this trouble ends, I go back to Coulthurst with Kate and Alfred. That is my future as it stands now. Would you begrudge me a short time of pleasure, of testing my wings?"

Iago sighed and shook his head. "No. As you say, you are a widow. Few know that you had no true marriage, and widows are allowed some freedom as long as they are discrete. Redgrave is discrete."

"Then how does everyone know he is a rake?"

"Discrete just means that no one can *confirm* what is going on save for the ones directly involved, that the affair is not flaunted before one and all."

"I do not think I will ever fully understand society."

"Do not even try."

"And this discussion may prove moot anyway. Hartley must continue his attempt to seduce secrets from Madame Claudette." Alethea was surprised at how it hurt to even state that cold fact, but only a little. She had already guessed that she was in grave danger of losing more than her innocence to the far-too-handsome Marquis of Redgrave.

"I would be most surprised if he could even stomach being in the same room as that woman now. How could he not see the blood on her hands, mayhap even that of his niece and nephew, simply because she cast them out alone in France when she had their family murdered? He must be trying to think of a way to escape that duty even now, having lost all urge to do it."

"Not even for king and country?"

"Ah. Forgot that. Will that trouble you?"

"I cannot say I will enjoy watching him ply his charms on another woman when I should very much like him to ply them on me, but I want her brought to justice. Not only for the lives she has already taken, but for the ones she plans to take."

"Such as Redgrave's."

"Exactly. Remember, I saw her when I had the vision as I held Germaine's locket. The woman had two small children, a good man, and his young wife slaughtered so she could have jewels. There may have even been some petty need for revenge for some imagined insult. If not for Germaine's wit and strength, four children would have died on that beach. She did it all for gain, and that sickens me. Oh, yes, she may have had more reasons than simple robbery and revenge, but I know, deep in my heart, I know, none of those reasons go beyond her own greed and vanity."

"Somehow, I do not believe seduction will work to get information out of such a woman."

"No, it will not, but Hartley's superiors think it will,

and Hartley is, above all else, a good soldier. Since he cannot tell his superiors how he knows what he now does about Claudette, I think he will have to continue the game."

"We shall see *how* he plays it soon," said Iago as their carriage pulled to a halt before an elegant townhouse well lit by torches. "Both he and Madame Claudette will be here tonight."

As Alethea allowed her uncle to escort her into the Lorings' home, where the grand ball had already begun, she fought the urge to turn and flee. Her mind knew Hartley but played a game with Claudette, that he had been ordered to woo the woman and that in doing so he might find clues to lead him to his sister's children, but she knew her heart would not understand. It would bleed a little with every smile he gave that woman. What should have been yet another lovely night of seeing how London society comported itself could easily turn into a painful nightmare.

"I see you responded to Madame's coy invitation," said Aldus.

Hartley grimaced and nodded even as he made certain Claudette was still immersed in conversation with her sister several feet away. Her note may have been coy, but the demand for his escort tonight had been very clear. Even if he would step away from her, he began to see that she would not allow him to do so easily. Her previous successes had made her arrogant, and arrogant people were not good losers.

So, he would flirt and smile. He would escort her places if he had to. He might even promise her more with an occasional kiss or caress. What he knew he would not do, could never do, was bed her. The mere thought of doing so turned his stomach.

"She will not give me the information we seek," he said with utter conviction. "She plays this game for her own purposes, Aldus, and not just because she seeks me as her lover."

"I know," Gifford said as he handed Hartley a drink. "The more we learn of her, the more certain I am that she is not one to betray herself between the sheets. She hopes you will do so, however, as I fear others have. Peterson and Rogers died because some fool allowed his wits to flee whilst caught up in passion's snare. The best you could do is let slip some false information that would lead her into a trap, but such tricks are not often successful. Yet how do we tell our superior Willsett that this is a waste of your time?"

"We will think of something ere you *have* to bed her, Hartley," Aldus assured him.

"I cannot and will not bed that woman," Hartley stated in a voice so hard and fierce it surprised even him. "My gorge rises when I simply kiss her hand, for I know how stained with innocent blood it is. I feel certain nothing else will rise even if she does her skillful best to make it so. My revulsion for her holds its own dangers. She may be a murderous viper, but she is also a survivor, and cunning. Soon she will notice that my ardor is false, that something has changed in me, and not to her favor. It would be best if I get away from her as soon as possible."

Aldus nodded. "Understood and understandable. I am working on it."

"Maybe we should just go to Willsett and tell him

we are certain seduction will not work with this woman, that it might even make her suspicious." Gifford shrugged when his friends just stared at him. "Just a thought. He has always trusted our judgment about such things."

"It is a good thought, Gifford," said Hartley, knowing that the man was right about their direct superior's trust in them. "Willsett would heed our opinion, and we might not have to thoroughly explain how we came by it. Unfortunately, Willsett has gone home to Hampshire because his wife is due to birth their first child."

"I could ride to his home and speak with him."

"We will both go," said Aldus.

Hartley opened his mouth to say no, that they should not trouble Willsett at such a time. Then he looked at Claudette, who smiled at him. He smiled back but knew by the slight narrowing of her eyes that his expression was not quite right. She was already growing suspicious, sensing the change in him that he was struggling to hide. Over the years he had become expert at hiding his feelings and suspicions, but this time it was all too personal. It would be safer for all of them if he could step away from her before that suspicion could grow into a hard certainty.

"Yes," he said. "Go. I see now that I already falter in my act of ardently wooing her to my bed. I feel certain that, even now, she can sense the change in me. I realized last evening that, before we met the Vaughns, even though I did not like Claudette, I thought her no more than a seller of information, a greedy woman who gave no thought to the lives lost because of what she did. Now I spend all the time I am near her fighting the urge to put my hands around her neck and try to choke the truth from her."

Aldus cleared his throat. "Most assuredly *not* lover-like." He briefly grinned. "Do restrain yourself, old friend. And I only say that because it would gain us nothing. The woman has too many allies with the power to set her free if we try to question her without the proof needed to make them back away from her. She also has the cunning to know who can or cannot fulfill such a threat. You cannot. Not with your thoughts clear and your blood cold. You will not hesitate to bring her to the justice she so richly deserves to face, but you are no torturer. Certainly not of a woman."

Hartley was not as confident of that as Aldus sounded. He could almost smell the blood on Claudette. Worse, he could see the fury and grief that had aged young Germaine's face. Claudette was responsible for the loss of his sister's children, of their innocence. If they had survived the past three years alone in France, he could only imagine what they had suffered. Such thoughts darkened his dreams and robbed him of his sleep.

"I do not know what you are thinking, Hart, but best you shake it out of your head," said Gifford. "If Claudette sees that look on your face, she will flee the country."

Hartley took a deep breath and struggled to calm the fury boiling in his veins. "Better?"

"Some. Leastwise you no longer look as if you wish to kill someone. Ah, and here are the Vaughns."

Alethea. The name whispered through his mind, igniting his senses, and Hartley nearly cursed. She was another reason he was not sleeping well. He would wake in the night, his mouth full of the rich, sweet promise of her kiss, and his body hard with wanting. Instinct warned him that the little seer could change his life, and he was not ready for change. At least that is what his stubborn mind kept saying. The rest of him was ready to leap into it with both feet and a cheer.

He looked at the Vaughns, who were slowly making their way through the crowd. Alethea was dressed in a gown of a deep burgundy, one that enhanced the soft curves of her body and touched the delicate ivory of her skin with a hint of warm color. His body tightened with need, and he had to smother a groan. The neckline of her gown was lower than what she usually wore, and he could see the soft swells of her breasts more clearly. He had a sharp vision of burying his face in that silken flesh and clenched his fists. The urge to go over and yank up the neck of her gown or find a shawl to throw around her shoulders was very strong. Control had never been so difficult to claim before.

"There is one sure way to push Claudette aside," said Aldus when the Vaughns paused to speak to an older woman and her young, blushing daughter.

Hartley saw how intently Aldus was studying Alethea and immediately guessed his friend's plan. "No."

"Claudette would not wish to be in competition with any woman. She would hunt new prey. It would also explain to all the gossips why you turned away from her."

"Alethea is in this too deeply as it is. And what surety do you have that Claudette would just step aside? We now know the woman is a cold-blooded killer. And that she takes insult at the smallest things. Mayhap she would even decide she still needed to gain information from me. If I put Alethea between us, Claudette could simply decide to have her removed."

"Ah. I had not considered that. You must continue to remain acquaintances and no more, then."

"Exactly. Let us hope Claudette has not heard the

rumors about the Vaughns and, even more, does not believe them if she has."

"Yes, that could cause trouble. Might be an idea to keep a close guard on them."

"It might. We will just have to think of some reason it is needed, some reason they feel the need to add such guards."

"Or a very good reason for them to have gained some extra burly, well-armed servants."

Just as the Vaughns stepped up to him, Hartley felt a slim arm slide into the crook of his. The cold touch of a small hand on his forearm told him who it was even before he looked, as did the strong scent of roses. Claudette had returned to his side. Something about her posture told him that she was staking a claim on him. He glanced at the small, gloved hand clutching his arm, idly wondering why, despite the layers of cloth between them, that delicate hand burned his skin with cold. Death's touch was cold, he thought, and then decided his imagination was obviously a lot stronger that he had known it was.

It was not until Aldus began speaking, politely making certain that everyone knew each other, that Hartley realized how deeply he had fallen into his own thoughts. The faint tightening of Claudette's hand on his arm revealed that she had noticed his slip in manners. One thing he had learned about the woman at his side was that she was easily offended, seeing scorn or insult at every turn. He needed to keep his head clear and just try to accomplish his mission as best he could until he was officially relieved of the duty. He did not want to join Roberts and Peterson in the crowd of furious spirits clinging to Claudette.

Claudette began to flirt with Iago, and Hartley almost smiled. Did she think to make him jealous? It was several moments before unease began to creep over him. Claudette was not flirting; she was digging for information. She could be doing so for her sister's sake, attempting to discover why Iago no longer visited Margarite's bed, but Hartley doubted anything Claudette did was so innocent. He began to fear that he had already pulled the Vaughns into dangerous waters. Considering what Iago claimed he saw around Claudette, the man was holding up well, but Hartley wanted to warn him. When the small orchestra began to play a minuet, he saw a chance to do so. In as fulsome a manner as he could manage, hoping to soothe any stung vanity the woman might suffer, he parted from Claudette and led Alethea into the dance.

Dancing was not something Alethea did often and was not sure she could do well, but she made no protest when Hartley led her into the crowd assembling for the dance. She had decided it might be best if she avoided as many of these affairs as possible. Just seeing Claudette at his side, clinging to his arm with an obvious air of possessiveness, was enough to make her want to flee the ballroom. She was certain now that she could not endure watching him work to seduce the woman, at least not without revealing how much it pained her to do so. She had no wish to make a fool of herself.

"You must warn Iago to be very careful around Claudette," Hartley said in a low voice as he led her through the steps of the dance with an easy grace that made her look good.

"I think my uncle is all too aware of what a viper that woman is," Alethea said, frowning as she looked at his face, and wondered how he could look so calm when she could sense how troubled he was. "He sees the death around her, if you recall."

"I know, but how skilled is he at playing the games of spies and traitors, at deceit?"

"Not very, I think. It is not one he has played before. Why? Need he be?"

"She is trying to pry information out of him."

"I thought she was trying to discover why he had turned away from her sister."

"That is just what she wants us to think. I did so for a little while. Vain fool that I am, I even thought she was trying to make me jealous. But then I began to listen more closely, more carefully. She seeks information. I fear that, because you and he now appear to be our friends, she may well think that Iago knows far more than he does. After all, she knows what we are, that we are working for the government. It is why she turned her attention my way."

Alethea tensed and fought the urge to run to her uncle and drag him away, far away, from that woman. "Iago is neither stupid nor foolish. I do not think you need to worry that he will disclose any information she seeks. I say again, do not forget, he sees far more clearly than anyone how soaked in innocent blood she is."

"So I thought, but I would feel remiss if I did not at least issue some warning."

"Accepted, and I will be sure to tell him of it at the first opportunity."

"We think it might be time to put a guard on you and Iago."

"That is something you will need to discuss with him, but I will be sure to tell him of your wishes."

Alethea wondered if she sounded as coolly polite to
him as she did to herself.

They finished the dance in silence, one that held a
hint of discomfort, as if they both wished to say something but could not. Every touch of Alethea's hand,
every brush of her body against his, had Hartley fighting for control. Even the reminder that she had visions,
had a gift he did not understand, did not dim his growing need to hold her close, to taste her passion.

When the music ended and she looked up at him,
he was caught fast in the warmth of her silvery blue
eyes. Each time he looked at her, she grew more beautiful to him. He started to lean toward her, giving in to
the need to taste her lips once more, and hastily caught
himself, stepping back and politely offering her his
arm. She was causing chaos in his life, his mind, and,
he feared, his heart, but he did not know what to do
about it. There was even a part of him that did not want
to do anything to stop it, and that part was gaining
strength daily.

It was difficult to restrain a loud, childish tantrum
when Hartley left her at her uncle's side and took a sick-
eningly coy Claudette away to dance. Alethea knew she
had seen a hunger in Hartley's eyes, a wanting that
matched her own, but he had pulled back from her. Her
lips had tingled with the promise of the kiss she
had seen in his expression, in the way he had begun to
bend toward her. She sternly reminded herself that
they were in public, that he had a job to do, a duty to
king and country, but a large part of her wanted to tell
king and country to go to the devil and take Claudette
with them. Hartley was dancing with and smiling at
Claudette when he should be dancing with and smiling

at *her*. In the hope of distracting herself from her own
tumultuous emotions, she accepted Aldus's request for
a dance.

Two hours later, Alethea had had enough. More than
enough. She was desperate to go home. As if to com-
pensate for his ever-so-brief lapse with her, Hartley
was wooing Claudette with what appeared to be true
ardor, and Alethea was sick to death of watching them.
Iago was deep in a conversation about investments
with Lord Dansing, however, so Alethea decided she
would take a stroll in the gardens. A little night air
might be just what she needed to clear her head before
she gave in to the jealousy gnawing at her heart and did
something foolish. In the game they were all caught up
in at the moment, doing something foolish could easily
prove deadly.

The crisp night air was like a much-needed slap, and
Alethea breathed deeply of it as she meandered along
the torchlit paths. The Lorings had an extensive garden,
and she wished it were daylight so that she could enjoy
the full effect of it. Gardens had always worked to calm
her, their beauty a true balm for her soul.

And she sorely needed that calm, she mused as she
paused to enjoy the quiet music made by the tumbling
water of an elaborate fountain. She had entered the
dangerous world of spies and traitors, lies and secrets.
Her visions had shown her how evil that world could
be. Events could not proceed as she wished them to in
such a dark world. It did seem grossly unfair, however,
that when she finally met a man she actually wanted,
one who gave her the hope of finally tasting the passion poets rhapsodized over, he was out of her reach.

Even if she and Hartley became lovers, it would not

stop his pursuit of Claudette. Alethea could not give her body to a man who was trying his best to climb into another woman's bed, no matter how honorable and understandable his reasons for doing so. Having an affair with a man, knowing the passion and delight he gave her would be a fleeting thing, was acceptable, no matter how much pain she suffered when he left her. Having an affair with a man who openly wooed and bedded another woman was not.

The sound of footsteps on the ground-shell path drew her from her moody thoughts. Alethea turned to see who else walked in the garden, and tensed. A large man was walking straight toward her. She stepped aside, hoping he was only exploring the garden as she was, even though her pounding heart told her otherwise. He just smiled, a cold, vicious smile that caused fear to rush up and choke her. Suddenly she knew why he was there.

She hiked up her skirts and started to run. A sharp cry of alarm escaped her when he grabbed her by the hair and yanked her back toward him. When she had looked into his eyes, she had cursed her gift for being so slow to warn her of any danger to herself. It told her so many things, why could it not have warned her of this in time for her to avoid it? She struggled as best she could, but his tight grasp on her hair, his strength and size, and her heavy, restrictive clothing all worked against her.

"You are making some people very angry," he said.

Alethea shuddered when he wrapped his arms around her, pinning her arms to her side, and his hot breath brushed against her cheek. He smelled of smoke and ale, but strong as those scents were, they could not disguise the fact that the man badly needed a bath. Even though too many people still shied away from bathing regularly, this man smelled bad in a different way from the ones in the ballroom. He smelled of the streets and alleys of the city. There was another scent there, but she could not grasp what it was even though her mind told her it was important. He was also dressed fine enough to mix in, but she was certain he was not of the ton. Then he idly rubbed his big hands over her breasts, and she gagged, the sense of defilement the touch brought almost more than she could bear.

"I have no idea what you are talking about," she said, pleased that her voice remained steady, revealing none of the bone-deep terror she felt.

"I am to tell you to go home, to take your fine self far away from Lord Redgrave."

Claudette, she thought as he turned her around and held her in place with one big hand wrapped tightly around her wrists. He also stood just far enough away that kicking him was not an option open to her. Alethea did not know what she or Hartley had done to anger the woman, yet something had obviously warned Claudette that Hartley was not falling into her snare.

"How ridiculous," she said. "I am no threat to any woman."

"Oh, I think you are. Now, I would much rather be tossing up your skirts and having a turn with you, but I have my orders. Not this time, she said. So I am hoping you do not heed this warning."

As she watched his large fist move toward her face, Alethea found herself thinking that she much preferred a beating to what this man said he would rather be doing to her. And then pain exploded in her head.

Chapter 7

Hartley marched into Lord Loring's snug library and helped himself to the brandy he knew the man kept there. The heat of the potent liquor quickly spread through his body, and he knew he would soon regain the control he had been losing in Claudette's presence. Over the years the game of seduction had become second nature to him, but, with Claudette, he was struggling mightily to produce even a cool smile, let alone one that promised heated delights to tempt her into his bed.

So why was she looking so smug? he suddenly wondered. He had already been told, with charming subtlety, that she was not yet inviting him to be her lover, yet she had acted as if she had won the game already. One moment she was watching him with a definite glint of suspicion in her eyes, and the next she behaved as if he was hers for the taking. Even at his best he had never given a woman that amount of certainty about what he was going to do. It made no sense, and that worried him. In the business of intrigue, things that made no sense could prove fatal.

Just as he was about to pour himself another brandy, idly thinking that being a little drunk might make the rest of the night pass more easily, Iago strode into the room. The tense look on the younger man's face sent a faint thrill of alarm through Hartley. He carefully set down his glass.

"Have you seen Alethea?" asked Iago. "I was hoping she was here with you."

Hartley did not ask why Iago would think his niece would have slipped away with him to tryst in Loring's library. Iago had caught him and Alethea in a heated embrace, after all. The news that Alethea was missing was too alarming to care about that indiscretion and how Iago might feel about it. She rarely moved from her uncle's side during such events, and Hartley doubted she had gained any added confidence or acquaintances in the short time she had been in London. He tried to tell himself that he had not known her long enough to be so certain of that, but the certainty lingered.

"Where did you last see her?" he demanded.

"She was standing near me while Lord Dansing and I discussed some investments. I thought she may have been asked to dance, but she is not in the ballroom. Not in the refreshment room, either. Or the lady's retiring room, or, as I now know, here with you. I am beginning to get concerned."

"Are all the other players in this game accounted for?"

Iago nodded. "I made sure of that first, although, surely, 'tis too soon for anyone to see Alethea as a threat."

"Perhaps not. Aldus, Gifford, and I have been to your house several times. I went there alone once. If we are all being watched closely, as I now believe we are, the danger we are playing with may already have reached out to you and Alethea."

"You think someone has taken her?"

"Let us not race ahead of ourselves. Have you searched the gardens? The Lorings have a large, well-lit garden, easy to reach for the guests who wish a breath of fresh air."

"I was going there next."

"We will collect Gifford and Aldus on the way. They can help us search for her."

Hartley strode out of the room, Iago close at his heels. Alethea could have just wandered off, tired of standing near Iago as he and Dansing talked, but Hartley's gut told him it was more than that. His instincts had kept him alive in the dangerous world of intrigue he had walked through for years, and he was not about to ignore them now. Something was wrong. Somehow Alethea had stumbled into danger; he was certain of it.

What he was not certain of was the how or the why. The possible reason for Alethea's disappearance came to him so suddenly and clearly that he nearly stumbled over his own feet. Claudette. Now he understood her sudden smugness. Somehow the woman had come to see Alethea as a threat to her plan to seduce secrets out of him. It could be a matter of simple stung vanity, but with a woman like Claudette, even that could be dangerous.

His gut twisted as he had to accept that this might be his fault. If Alethea was in danger or hurt, it was because he had given Claudette some reason to see her as a threat. He had erred somewhere, and it could be Alethea who paid the price for that.

He signaled to Aldus and Gifford as he and Iago walked through the ballroom toward the doors leading out into the gardens. Hartley's certainty grew with each step he took. Somehow he had revealed his interest in Alethea, and Claudette had seen it. The woman had then acted quickly to remove the obstacle to what she wanted. The question that kept nagging at the edge of his mind, and caused what little doubt remained, was how had Alethea not foreseen the danger she was in.

Once outside he sent the other three men off in three different directions. He went straight, along the widest path that he knew led to an elaborate fountain. It was the site of many a tryst. The thought that Alethea may have disappeared because she was rendezvousing with some rogue caused him a sharp pain. He decided it had to be aggravation, that he was annoyed that she would do something so foolish and make them all afraid for her.

The sound of a man's voice coming from the direction of the fountain caused Hartley to hesitate. If Alethea was trysting with another man, he really did not wish to see it. Shaking free of his hesitation, he moved closer with as much stealth as he could muster. Rage roared through him when he saw a man holding Alethea in a brutal embrace. It took all of his willpower to stop himself from racing over there to yank the man away from her and beat him into the ground. Caution was needed, he sternly reminded himself, and some of the red haze of fury eased. He could not yet be sure if the man had a weapon at hand, one he could quickly use against Alethea.

"You are making some people very angry," the man said, his speech correct but the hint of an accent revealing it was only a thin veneer over a rougher, darker form.

"I have no idea what you are talking about," Alethea said, and Hartley felt a definite sense of pride over how calm she sounded even though he knew she had to be badly frightened.

When the man groped Alethea's breasts, Hartley barely smothered the growl that erupted deep in his throat. He wanted to kill the man for touching her so. The soft sound of Alethea gagging in revulsion only added to that fury.

"I am to tell you to go home, to take your fine self far away from Lord Redgrave."

The man turned Alethea around, holding her by the wrists at a distance that told Hartley the man had done this sort of thing before and knew how to protect himself.

"How ridiculous. I am no threat to any woman."

"Oh, I think you are. Now, I would much rather be tossing up your skirts and having a turn with you, but I have my orders. Not this time, she said. So I am hoping you do not heed this warning."

Almost there, Hartley thought and cursed the ground shells and other garden detritus that made his progress so slow. Trying to remain in the shadows also slowed him down. His fists were clenched in anticipation of making the man pay dearly for touching Alethea. Then the man punched her. Hartley gave up all attempts at stealth, save for swallowing the urge to bellow out his rage. He ran, but even as he forced himself to as great a speed as possible, the man hit her again, tossed her alarmingly limp body to the ground, and kicked her. He was just pulling his foot back to kick her again when he finally noticed Hartley.

Hartley cursed long and viciously when the man bolted just as he was within a hairsbreadth of grabbing him. He started to follow, but the sight of Alethea sprawled on the ground halted his pursuit. She looked like a broken doll. He could not leave her like that.

A sharp whistle brought Aldus into view, and Hartley sent him off after the man. When Gifford and Iago arrived a heartbeat later, he sent Gifford after the man as well. Iago moved toward him as Hartley knelt by Alethea's side. He slipped an arm beneath her to gently lift her upper body off the ground, careful to fully support her head even as Iago reached his side.

"I do not think they will be able to catch him," Iago said as he dampened a handkerchief in the fountain, crouched at Alethea's other side, and began to tenderly wipe the dirt and blood from her face. "Why would anyone beat her?" He looked her over carefully. "Obviously not because she said no to his advances. Her gown shows no sign of that sort of attack."

"This was a warning," said Hartley. "I heard him say so. It was a warning to stay away from me." And the guilt that roused in him nearly choked him.

"Are you saying Claudette had this done to Alethea?"

"I did not hear the man say Claudette's name, but he did say *she*. From almost the moment you said Alethea was missing I began to fear it, even though I could not understand the why of it all."

"The why? The why is because you have kissed Alethea, and you have been sniffing around her skirts."

Hartley wanted to respond angrily but knew the man had a right to accuse him. "First, there is no way on earth Claudette could know that I kissed Alethea, for that was done inside your home. Unless your servants—"

"Never."

"Then there are only three of us who know of that kiss. I wondered if it was because we came to your home several times, as I said, but I only came there alone once, so that does not make much sense. Yet, this is Claudette's doing. I *am* certain of that. I must have given Claudette some reason, in some way, to think that Alethea was a threat to her making me her lover."

"Wait—I thought *you* were seducing *her*."

"I allowed her to think that is what I thought."

Iago sighed and rinsed out his handkerchief in the fountain before returning to the work of cleaning Alethea's badly abraded face. "I should have considered that possibility. Claudette must have caught sight of the way you look at Alethea."

"What are you talking about? I was most careful."

"Not careful enough. Your wanting is clear to see in your eyes, and it takes no special gift to see it. Cold face, hot eyes. Each time your gaze rests upon my niece, I fight the urge to call you out. 'Tis that hot, that carnal. Claudette must have seen it, too."

Hartley was not about to waste time arguing that, for he suspected he might have looked at Alethea with wanting in his gaze. He certainly suffered from that wanting far too much and too often. "Why the devil did Alethea have no warning of this? No vision telling her of the danger she was about to face? Something to tell her not to walk into the garden alone."

"I cannot say for certain, but it appears that a seer cannot foresee her own future. Many of the ones in our family who have the same gift complain of that limitation. 'Tis most rare for one of them to foresee anything in their own future, good or bad, and often they cannot even see the futures of the ones closest to their hearts. It is an unwritten rule within the family not to allow all the seers to become too close to each other."

"So then at least one might foresee the danger to another one or those close to that other seer?" When Iago nodded in response, Hartley had to ask, "Does that work?"

"More or less. I believe she is waking up now." Iago sat back on his heels as Alethea's eyes fluttered open.

Alethea saw two shadowy figures leaning over her, one holding her in his arms, and tensed in fear. It took the clearing of her vision, recognizing the men at her side, to smother her rising panic. The moment her fear receded, pain swept over her, and she groaned. She placed a hand over her right side and wondered why she felt pain there. Her last clear memory was that of the man's fist swinging toward her head.

"My side hurts," she murmured and looked from Iago up at Hartley. "Why does my side hurt? He hit me in the face."

"He also kicked you when you were down," Hartley replied.

The urge to cry was so strong Alethea had to swallow hard, twice, to conquer it. She did not wish to appear weak before the two worried men leaning over her, even if she did hurt everywhere. The presence of Hartley and Iago took away her fear for the moment, and she tried to find some strength in that.

"He said he was giving me a warning." It hurt to talk, but Alethea suspected it would hurt even more so very soon. There was so much pain in her face; she suspected her attacker had hit her again even as she was sinking into unconsciousness from the first blow. She was sure it was already swelling and had the brief, vain thought that she must look terrible.

"I know. I heard him. I was trying to slip up behind him, as I was not sure if he had a weapon."

"Just his fists." She started to sit up on her own, fighting the inclination to stay in Hartley's arms, and gasped aloud at the pain that shot through her side. "I am going to look like a walking mass of bruises tomorrow," she said when she finally caught her breath.

She could tell by the looks on their faces, fleeting though the expressions were, that they thought she looked that way now. Before she could say anything, Aldus and Gifford ran up to them. The way those two men winced when they looked at her made Alethea feel like crying all over again. She hoped Kate had some wondrous salve that would help lessen her bruises and the swelling she knew had already begun by the increasing tightness of the skin on her face.

"The man got away," said Gifford. "We did not even get a good look at his face, either."

"I did," Alethea said. "I can draw you a picture. I just do not understand why he did this to me." She had a very good idea of who ordered it done, but the why of it was puzzling. How could a woman like Claudette see her as any sort of threat?

"We can discuss that later," Hartley said as he settled her more firmly in his arms and stood up.

"I can walk," she protested despite the fact that she wanted to stay right where she was.

"Not after two blows to the head and a kick in the ribs." Hartley looked at Iago. "Can you bring your carriage around to the street side of the garden wall? There is a gate there. I can bring Alethea out that way."

"It may take me a few moments, as I have to go through the ballroom and may be momentarily detained here and there," said Iago as he stood up and brushed off his clothes. "I will tell whoever I meet that

I must leave because Alethea has fallen ill. That will explain her sudden disappearance, her slipping away unseen, and the fact that she will not be seen until her bruises fade."

Aldus watched Iago leave and then looked at Hartley. "I will devise some emergency to explain your sudden disappearance as well. Mayhap Gifford should go with you so that what I say carries some weight and will not have people wondering why you and Alethea disappeared at the same time. I will also offer to take Claudette home and then meet you at the Vaughns as soon as possible." He looked at Alethea. "I think the woman begins to believe herself untouchable. This is her work, is it not?"

"I have no proof of that, but, yes, I think it is," replied Hartley. "We can talk about it later. Alethea needs to get home, and a doctor needs to be summoned."

"No doctor," Alethea protested. "Kate can tend to me."

Aldus just grinned and left. Gifford fell into step beside Hartley as he started to make his way through the gardens to the gate where he was to meet Iago. The guilt Hartley suffered for what had happened to Alethea was a heavy weight upon his heart. She had been drawn into this trouble because she had wanted to save his life. She stayed because she wished to help him find his sister's children. Yet because he could not control his growing desire for her, even in the way he looked at her, she was now hurt and in danger.

"It is not your fault, Hartley," Alethea said quietly.

"And whose fault is it? Is it not because of me that you are here at all?"

"No one but the five of us knows that. As far as the world and its mother is concerned, I am but visiting my uncle. I doubt anyone thinks I know anything about spies and intrigue and all of that. I am only a simple country widow. If Claudette had this done to me, it was the act of a vain, spiteful woman. How she got the idea that I was a threat to the success of her seduction of you, I do not know."

"Oh, I have an idea or two about that," said Gifford, but he quickly pressed his lips together when Hartley glared at him.

Alethea laughed and immediately regretted it. Her laugh turned into a groan as pain tore through her body. She was not sure which hurt the worst, her side or her head, but she was certain she would be doing her best not to laugh for a while. It was evident that Hartley blamed himself for what had happened to her, but the pain clouding her thoughts made it difficult for her to form any reasonable argument against that. It, too, would have to wait until later.

The move into the carriage was an agony she hoped to never have to endure again. Alethea knew Hartley and Iago were doing their best to move her gently, but the pain became a continuous ripple beneath her skin. She had only a moment to recover after she was settled on the carriage seat with her head in Hartley's lap, and then the carriage began to move. Alethea gave up her fight to remain conscious.

"She has swooned," said Hartley.

"Best thing for her," said Iago. "I do not think any ribs are broken, for she is breathing well, but they are certainly badly bruised. Until her ribs are wrapped and the pain from the blows to her head eases, she will have to lie still." He watched as Hartley did his best to keep her steady in his hold as the carriage rolled along. "I am not a violent man, but I dearly wish I could get my hands on the bastard who did this to her. I think I could kill him and never lose a night's sleep over it."

"Wait to kill him until we get the name of the one who ordered him to do this," said Hartley.

"We know who did this."

"We need a name. Never forget that Claudette has some power and a lot of allies with power. As you yourself noted, she has been very selective in her lovers, and, if only to protect themselves, those men could be called upon to help her against such an allegation."

"Fools. The whole lot of them. And the ones who gave her the information she needed to kill those men of yours are as guilty of murder as she is."

Hartley could only agree. Although Claudette had not done the actually killing of anyone, as far as he knew, she was a killer. She tossed people's lives aside as if they were worth nothing, only her needs and wants of any concern to her. The men who had allowed passion to blind them to what she was and let slip some of the country's secrets were almost as guilty as she was. They should have known better, should have thought of the dire consequences of even one weak moment.

Before he could say anything, the carriage stopped before the Vaughns' home. "We need to send someone for a doctor," Hartley said as he helped get a still-unconscious Alethea out of the carriage.

"No need," said Iago. "Kate will see to her."

"Kate is no doctor."

"She may be common born, uneducated in the finer schools, and all of that, but she can fix near any injury and cure most illnesses. If she cannot, she is the first to call for a surgeon. I do not believe Alethea's injuries require a surgeon, however. And, if Kate sees to her, the less chance there is of any of this becoming fodder for the gossips."

Hartley's chance to argue that opinion was stolen away the moment Iago's butler opened the door for them. Chaos ensued as Alfred and Kate came running at his call of alarm. Although he was allowed to carry Alethea to her room, Hartley was quickly pushed aside by a worried, and thoroughly outraged, Kate. He finally allowed Iago to lead him down to the drawing room, where Gifford was already comfortably settled with wine and food.

"Does Kate know she is a servant?" Hartley asked quietly as he helped himself to some wine and food, still stinging a little from being so summarily dismissed by a maid.

Iago laughed as he sprawled in a chair, but the heavy mood that had dogged him since he had found Alethea missing quickly returned. "She knows, but she has been with Alethea since they were both children. Kate is only a few years older. Five, mayhap six. Kate is one of those retainers who become almost part of the family."

Hartley slowly nodded, thinking of the kindly Mrs. Huxley, his housekeeper in his London home. "If Kate decides a doctor is needed, I know a good one. Skilled and, most important, discrete."

"Thank you. The Vaughns have one like that as well. A kinsman whose gift is in healing. Unlike some others who have that gift, he can control it."

"Why would anyone want to control the gift of healing?"

"It drains the life out of the healer if he uses it too

much or on the very sick, trying to cure them in one sitting. Archimedes has learned how to be careful, how to use his gift little by little, so that he is never exhausted by its demands."

"Archimedes?" Gifford shook his head. "Your family has a gift for odd names as well as for other things."

"True. I have never actually understood why that is. Some ancestor began it, and we all dutifully follow tradition."

They talked idly about useless subjects, fighting to keep their minds off what was happening with Alethea, until Aldus arrived. Hartley had to fight the urge to jump on the man and shake him for information as Aldus helped himself to some food and drink. He knew a lot of his tense agitation was due to concern for Alethea, but he realized that he no longer appreciated how slowly the business of intrigue was conducted. Gathering information on traitors or the enemy was a slow, tedious business occasionally broken with periods of extreme danger.

"Did Claudette say anything when you told her I had been called away?" he asked the moment Aldus had settled himself comfortably beside Gifford.

"Nothing precise, of course," Aldus replied. "She did act surprised when I told her you had left on an emergency. I also noticed that she looked around the ballroom most carefully. It did not please her to see no sign of the Vaughns. I believe she realized you had all left at the same time and, perhaps, guessed that that was your emergency."

"Did she expect Alethea to come staggering back into the ballroom?" asked Iago. "Surely she must have realized that someone would take Alethea home once she was found. Unless she had hope that someone would find a body."

"This was just a warning," said Hartley. "The man that accosted Alethea said so himself. Claudette was probably displeased that her act of anger had actually worked to her disadvantage. Both Iago and I were now gone."

"Me?" Iago did not even try to hide his surprise. "What on earth would the woman want with me? I have no ties to the government."

"I believe you do have, through a few cousins," replied Hartley and noticed how Aldus nodded. "You are also now tied to us, and to a woman Claudette is seeing as a rival or, at the very least, an impediment to her plans."

"Ah, of course. It astounds me that one vain, coldly selfish woman could be so much trouble and so dangerous. There has to be a way to stop her."

"We are close, very close. Unfortunately, the ones who know enough about her to get her hanged soon end up dead. Claudette has also gathered together a small cadre of very lethal men. I believe she has her escape route all carefully planned out, too. It will not be easy to bring her down, and it will definitely be a very dangerous job."

"It has already proven to be so. Do not forget Rogers and Peterson," said Gifford.

"Never." Hartley thought of his sister's children as well, and the rage he constantly battled to control shifted inside of him, eager to get out and find some target. "We have long suspected the woman and have spent many hours gathering up all the information we can." He nodded toward Iago. "And now we have you and Alethea."

"But you said you could not openly use what we have told you," Iago said.

"No, but it points us in the right direction and that is no small thing. We will get this bitch, and she will hang. We just need the right proof to make even her lovers back away, more afraid of being touched by the blood on her than for their good names."

"Why have you not gone after some of the men she has slept with? Why not try to find a weak point there? I doubt any of them actually sat there and told her exactly what she sought, handed her secret papers or the like. Yet, although they fear being tainted by her crimes now, if you can get them to believe it, just one of them, *and* swore to keep whatever slip they made a complete secret, they could be of some help."

Hartley sighed and slowly nodded. "I had wished to avoid confronting any of them simply because of the utter aggravation of such a process, but I think the time for catering to their position in society or the government must end. Good people are dying, and our secrets are being sent to our enemies, and all by a woman society allows into their homes. God alone knows what she has found in those homes, or pilfered to send to her compatriots. Even if we cannot get enough proof to hang her, I think it is past time we start to close all those doors and make her games impossible to play."

"Try to disarm her in a way," murmured Gifford.

"Exactly," agreed Hartley. "Disarm and break down the shields she hides behind, one by one."

"It should be done slowly," said Iago, and he smiled when all three men looked at him. "Slowly done it will take her a little while to notice, then it will begin to make her uneasy, and then it will be too late for her to do anything about it. A sudden rush to cut her off will make people listen if she cries foul. A slow picking away at her connections to society, done subtly and secretively, will leave people to believe that she has done the injury to herself, and her claims of slander, or whatever else she may try, will not be heeded by enough people to matter."

"Are you certain you do not work for the government?" Aldus asked after a moment of heavy silence from the ones experienced in intrigue.

Iago chuckled. "No, I do not, but I have always been fascinated by strategy. Bold and daring will gain honor and have songs sung about you. Sleek, quiet, and slow will gain you little recognition but most often works. It will, however, make her increasingly dangerous."

"We will be ready for that," Hartley said with a confidence he did not wholeheartedly feel. Claudette had been fooling them for a long time, playing them all for fools, and he could not discount her skills at that game too easily.

"M'lord," Kate called as she entered the room, pausing for a brief curtsey to the men. "I thought you might be interested in Lady Alethea."

"Of course," replied Iago. "You can speak freely, Kate. How is my niece?"

"Naught was broken. She will be sore and bruised for a while, though, and I be thinking that does not surprise any of you. Her ribs were wrapped, but they are only bruised. I have put cool cloths on her poor battered face, so I be hoping the swelling will not be too bad. My salve will be helping, too. But she is not to be getting out of that bed for at least three days, and after that she needs to be very careful."

"I will be certain to help you keep her to that regimen," said Iago. "Thank you, Kate."

"You want to thank me, m'lord, you find the bastard what did that to my missus, and you cut his bloody hands off, then hang him up by his feet until he bleeds out like the beastie he is. Then you find that vicious whore—"

Iago had her by the arm and was ushering her out of the room before she could finish that sentence. "Quite. I will keep your wishes in mind, Kate. Why not go to the kitchens and see what sort of tasty broths and healthy drinks you can plan for Alethea's recuperation?"

"Aye, I will, but you best not let the fact that that viperous bitch is a woman stop you from treating her as she deserves."

After shutting the door behind Kate, Iago looked at the other men in the room and shrugged. "Kate loves Alethea, and God help anyone who hurts her."

"I rather liked the cutting the hands off and hanging him up like a beastie," murmured Gifford and then laughed along with the other men.

Hartley found that he was able to laugh with them. Alethea was going to be all right this time. And now they had a firmer plan in mind to insure that there would not be a next time.

Chapter 8

"It is too soon for you to be out of bed."

Alethea blinked at Hartley as he strode into her drawing room. He had become a regular visitor to the house over the last week, while she had been healing from the beating. The way he went straight to the drinks table and helped himself to some of Iago's fine brandy told her that he had also begun to feel right at home. Since no one had announced his arrival or even asked if she was *at home* to him, it was evident that the servants also saw him as almost family, him and his two companions in intrigue.

That made her both happy and uneasy. She was pleased that he had fallen into such an easy, comfortable companionship with her and Iago, but she did not want him to be too easy with her. Alethea did not want Hartley thinking of her as family.

"Hello," she said. "How pleasant to see you, too."

Hartley rolled his eyes and sat down beside her, taking a deep drink of the brandy Iago kept on hand and savoring the slight burn as it went down his throat. During his many visits with Alethea as she had been recovering from the attack, he had discovered that she could be decidedly pert, her humor dry but rarely sharp or cruel. Too many women he had known had thought unkind remarks about others constituted humor or wit. Hartley doubted Alethea often, if ever, said anything truly unkind or cruel about anyone. Nor did she gossip much. He found that yet another thing he appreciated about her. Too few people within society knew the important difference between gossip and actual news or information. In the work he did for the government, he had to listen closely to all gossip, rumor, and salacious whisper, but he had never liked it.

He was beginning to think it was time, far past time, that he took an interest in a woman beyond what she could give him in the bedroom. He needed an heir, and he could not get one without a wife. The first time the word *marriage* had tiptoed through his brain he had shuddered in horror and hastily pushed it aside, even made the futile attempt to avoid Alethea as if it was her fault he had had such a chilling thought.

The thought would not stay away, however. For a man in his position, marriage was a necessary step to take. Alethea was the first woman he had ever thought of in that way, the only one he could actually see himself married to. She would give him passion, loyalty, and, most of all, companionship. He felt comfortable with her, when he was not lusting after her. Such talk would have to wait for a while longer. It was too soon. If nothing else, he needed to do some wooing of her first. With visions, murderous rogues, traitors, and a coldly evil woman to deal with, there had not been much time left to do any wooing.

"I beg your pardon for the abrupt arrival," he said

as he draped his arm over her shoulders, liking the way she accepted the light embrace without any hint of coyness, even shifting closer to him. "It has been a long, tiresome day. But—you are looking much better."

The bruises that had marred her pretty face had faded to the point where a little powder could hide them. Each time he had looked upon her injuries, first the livid swelling and then the equally livid bruises left behind after the swelling eased, he had ached to hunt down her attacker and beat him into the ground. Every soft gasp or moan of pain that had passed her lips had plucked at the rage that burned inside him. He had even admitted to himself that, like Iago, if the beating he hoped to deliver killed the man, he would not lose a moment's sleep over it.

Now Alethea moved with no sign of pain from her badly bruised ribs and spoke easily, the stiffness in her jaw gone. He had balked at leaving her in Kate's care, at not summoning a doctor, but it was clear to see that the Vaughns' trust in the maid's healing skills was fully justified. Despite her improvement, despite how the evidence of what had been done to her was fading from view, his rage lingered. He suspected it would do so until he had made someone pay for her pain.

"Thank you, kind sir."

Alethea smiled at him, knowing he was sadly lagging in charming flatteries when he spoke to her. But she took that as a good sign. He was not playing his seductive games, using well-practiced moves, touches, or words. With her, Hartley was just Hartley. She was not fool enough to think it meant he had developed any deeper feelings for her, but it did mean that he did not see her as he had seen all of the other women in his life. That could only be a good thing.

"My pleasure." He lightly kissed her cheek, fighting back the need to kiss a lot more than that soft, decorous spot. "I have officially been given permission to cease chasing after Claudette. Willsett believed us when we told him that there would be no seducing secrets out of a woman like Claudette, but it took a little longer for him to then convince his superiors that we knew what we were talking about. Once Willsett agreed, however, I began to step away from the woman, slowly ending the dance we had been involved in."

No news could have been more welcome to Alethea than that. As she had healed, confined to bed and the house, she had suffered too many dreams of him holding Claudette, kissing her, sharing passionate moments with her. She had begun to think that not knowing exactly what was happening between him and Claudette was as bad, if not worse, as knowing and watching it all go on right in front of her eyes.

"And how has she taken your withdrawal of attention?" she asked.

"The withdrawal is not complete yet, and she already shows signs of not taking it well. When I consider what she had done to you just because she thought she saw me look at you with interest, I begin to wonder if it might be best if you returned to Coulthurst." He had to struggle just to voice the suggestion, as he did not want her to leave, something he knew he ought to examine very closely.

"No." She met his scowl with a smile. "I stepped into this business because of my vision, and I mean to stay until it is done. *And,*" she added hastily when he opened his mouth to start what she was sure would be an argument, "I am still needed. We have yet to discover what happened to your niece and nephew. Has there been any news of them?"

"'Tis too soon." He set his drink down on the table in front of them and took her hands in his. "There is a lot of danger circling round you now, Alethea. I would have you clear of it."

"Forewarned is forearmed. We know the danger is there and can watch for it. And how can we be sure the danger will not follow me to Coulthurst? I am now marked, as you have said, so I cannot see that leaving London would change that."

"No, probably not." He kissed her on the forehead and then rested his cheek against her hair, praying he was not letting his need to have her close at hand force him to agree with her.

Alethea's heart raced as he held her close. She sighed her pleasure out loud as she savored the feel of his strong arms around her. Such embraces as well as light caresses and sweet, too-innocent kisses had grown more frequent during her convalescence. It made her hope even as it frustrated the desire he had awakened in her.

Daringly, she moved her hand over his broad chest up to his neck. The touch of a thin gold chain beneath her fingers when she reached the edge of his neckcloth caught her attention. Just as she opened her mouth to ask what it was, an all-too-familiar feeling swept over her. Alethea had only enough time to clutch at Hartley's arms before she sank into the swirling montage of images and impressions.

Hartley tightened his hold on Alethea when her whole body spasmed in his arms. One look at her face, into her wide, storm-cloud eyes, and he knew she was having a vision. He prayed it was not another one foretelling of danger or, worse, the death of one of his friends. He held her close, murmuring soothing nonsense and stroking her back as he waited for her to come to her senses enough to realize he was there at her side.

Searching his heart, he discovered a complete lack of unease or fear. All he found within himself was concern for Alethea, worry that she was still too weak from her injuries to endure a fearsome vision. The moment she came back from wherever her vision took her, she pulled free of his hold, grabbed her sketchbook, and began to rapidly draw what she had seen. He hurried to the door, called for the butler, and ordered tea. He was back in his seat and ready to hold her again when she stumbled back into his arms, her frantic drawing done. A *gift* should not be so hard on the one it was given to, he thought as he held her trembling body close while Alfred rushed in and set the tray with tea and light cakes on the table in front of them.

"Just ready the tea, Alfred," he said. "I will make certain she drinks it and eats something."

Alethea took several deep, slow breaths to still the excitement bubbling inside her as she reluctantly eased away from Hartley. She did not wish to fill Hartley with a hope that could easily remain unfulfilled, but she knew she had to tell him everything. Although she was certain she had just seen what *had* happened, it had done so only recently; it had not been a vision of the now or of the future. Matters could have taken a turn for the worse since what she had seen had happened. France moved from calm to boiling to murderous and back again with alarming regularity.

"Was it a bad one?" Hartley asked as he handed her the heavily sweetened tea.

She took a bracing sip of the tea before trying to answer him. Selfish though it was, she wanted to enjoy the gentle way he rubbed her back, the concern he revealed for her well-being. Once she told him about her vision and he looked at her drawings, his mind and heart would be taken up with the plight of his sister's children. Then a pang of guilt pushed aside all thought for herself. Hartley needed to hear about his niece and nephew more than she needed to be held and soothed.

"Hard, fierce, but not bad," she replied and pointed to her book. "It was a vision of something that occurred recently, not of the now or the will be. I think it may help you find the children."

She was not surprised when he snatched up her sketchbook like a starving man would a crust of bread tossed aside by a rich man. She knew the two children were all he had left of his family save for a few very distant cousins. For all that a family could be a torment at times, one missed it when it was gone. She knew herself fortunate to have such a large, caring collection of relatives, for it meant she was never really alone. Hartley was completely alone.

"What did you see?" he asked as he studied the pictures she had drawn on the paper.

"A farm, a few cows, and an old horse," she replied. "Probably a poor farm. I think they are working there." She frowned. "I think the older couple I saw took them in years ago, mayhap even shortly after they fled the beach. They may not have had to struggle too much to survive, at least not for too long."

"Yet you still drew her as a lad."

Alethea stared at the picture she had drawn of Germaine. "So I have. Then that is what she must be. There may be a good reason for that. She and Bayard are, after all, two aristocratic, English children in France."

"Any sense of where or when?"

Alethea slumped in her seat, resting her head against the back of the settee. She closed her eyes and tried to drag up any and all memory of her vision. Hartley lightly caressed her clenched hands where they lay in her lap, and it calmed her enough that the memories came more easily.

"South," she murmured. "Yes, the south of France. Two days' ride in from the beach." She frowned as she strained to grasp an elusive thread of information.

"There are a lot of beaches in the south of France."

"The beach where her family was murdered, where they had gone to be saved. Two days' ride east, and a little north. Moyne."

"There is no Moyne in that area. I confess I do not know every village and town in France, but that one just does not sound familiar."

Alethea opened her eyes to look at him. "I think it is a name, not a place exactly. The name of the farm, the creek running nearby, the family, even the largest landholder. Moyne. Just saying the word feels right. Yes, Moyne. A name. It might not be the full name, but it has something to do with where they are and who they are with." She gave him a sympathetic smile. "I may recall something later, but that is all I have for now."

"It is a lot. A place, a name, a farm with a few cows and an old, swaybacked horse. Even better, I can get this news to France quickly, as a few men are slipping over there tonight."

"I pray you can find them, Hartley. They need to come home. I think Germaine has tried to get them out of France a few times, and the failure weighs heavy on her."

Hartley took her in his arms and kissed her. Alethea sank into the kiss, savoring the taste of him and the heat he stirred within her. She was not surprised when he ended the embrace too soon, however. She could sense the tense excitement in him, the hope that he struggled to keep under control.

"I need to get this information to those men," he said as he forced himself to release her and not give in to the need clawing at his insides. "May I take the picture? Your drawing of the farmhouse may help them."

"Of course. Hartley? What is that chain that is sticking out of your neckcloth? I think that is what brought on the vision."

Hartley knew he was blushing a little, for his cheeks tingled with the heat of it as he quickly shoved the chain beneath his neckcloth. "Germaine's locket. I did not think, have only just begun to wear it in the hope that it would give me some luck in the search for her and Bayard. I am sorry. I could have brought on that horrific vision you had before when you touched it."

"No. Whatever held that vision in that locket has passed. It must be because it is Germaine's that I had this vision, however. There is obviously still some faint connection to her through it." She leaned forward and kissed him gently. "Godspeed, Hartley." She watched him hurry out of the room and sent up a prayer that this time her vision would lead his men to the children and bring them home where they belonged.

* * *

Hartley paced the morning room in Aldus's small townhouse as he waited for his friends to join him. Gifford often stayed at Aldus's home to escape his mother and sisters. For once Hartley's luck had been good, and Gifford was there as well.

He could have gone to the men headed to France himself, but he suddenly realized he would need a good reason for having this new information. The men who slipped in and out of France were a hard, suspicious sort. His hope was running so high and his excitement was so intense that he doubted he would be able to concoct anything that made sense or did not make him look like a madman. For a glib tongue, he needed Aldus.

It annoyed him that he needed some clever explanation, and Hartley almost smiled at how far he had come from thinking the Vaughns were charlatans or madmen to now resenting the fact that they had to be so careful. Their gifts had many good uses, ones that could help the country. Instead, the Vaughns, and their kinsmen the Wherlockes, stayed mostly in the shadows. He might not like the idea that there was no true scientific explanation for what Iago and Alethea could do, but he did not fear it all as some trick of Satan.

A grunt drew his attention, and he watched a bleary-eyed Gifford shuffle over to the sideboard. The man piled his plate high with food and shuffled to the table to slump into a chair. A silent servant poured Gifford some rich-smelling coffee. Suddenly, Hartley was starving. He picked out what he wanted from an impressive assortment of food and joined Gifford at the table just as Aldus walked in. Aldus looked almost as bad as Gifford did.

"Rough night?" he asked as he poured himself some of the strong coffee Aldus always served.

"I was chasing down the bastard who hurt Alethea," said Aldus, already beginning to look more awake after drinking some of the coffee.

"And I was following that damned woman," said Gifford. "She never sleeps, and I do not believe she meant to be faithful to you, Hartley." He grinned slightly before stuffing his face with sausage.

"I am devastated." He pushed aside the moment of humor and asked, "Did you get the man, Aldus?"

"No, curse it twice," grumbled Aldus. "He is a slippery devil. Do have some information on him, however, that will make the hunt easier. I think he may be some relation to Claudette. Pierre Leon. Has few allies in the city, as he is a cheat, a liar, and a bully. Someone will give him up soon."

"Good. I want him, and not just for what he did to Alethea. We will need him to help prove Claudette is what we claim she is. I have been slowly compiling a list of the men she has slept with, and it will take all we can find to get her to pay for her crimes. But I did not come here and roust the two of you out of bed just to discuss Claudette and her minions."

"No? What else are we working on?"

"Finding my niece and nephew."

Aldus grimaced and rubbed a hand over his hair. "Damn me. Sorry, Hart. I am not completely awake yet."

"Quite all right. There is a lot on our plates at the moment, and this is not your family."

"Still, children lost in that morass in France should be remembered. Have you heard some news?"

"Not exactly. Alethea had another vision." In between

sips of coffee, Hartley told his friends all Alethea had told him. He then cleared the table enough to set out the pictures she had drawn. "I think they have been hiding as laborers all this time, or as part of a family. Both of them spoke excellent French, so that would be no problem for them."

"But did she tell you how they are now? 'Tis little help to us if this vision was of, let us say, a month or more ago. They could have moved."

"Or been hurt or captured. I know all that, Aldus, much as I would like to ignore that cruel truth. But this is the first time we have been given any idea of where in France they might be. Even a name or part of a name. I thought I might give this to the men leaving for France tonight so that they can pass it along to my men. It might aid them in their search."

Aldus studied the pictures Alethea had drawn as he finished his food and then pushed his plate aside. "I am still astonished by how well she draws. I feel as though I should recognize that little farmhouse, yet I do not understand why I should."

"Mayhap you can think of the reason as we go to find those men."

It took them an hour to leave the house as both Aldus and Gifford took time to tidy their appearance. By the time they headed out in his carriage, Hartley's good mood was a little frayed around the edges. It only got worse as they tried to find the two men who would be slipping away to France that very night.

Hartley was muttering that it would be faster if he found a ship to France and took the message to his men himself, when Aldus had the carriage stop and leapt out. The stink of the docks slapped Hartley in the face as he followed his friend, Gifford close on his heels. They wove their way through the crowds until Aldus quickly approached two men. Hartley slowed to a halt, Gifford at his side, and let Aldus do the talking. He had no doubt that these were the men they sought. He did not recognize them, but that was no surprise. There were too many men and too many different branches of the government for anyone to know everyone, especially when some did not wish to be known. The men who slipped in and out of France most certainly did not want to be known. Aldus did better than most. It was obvious that Aldus had known exactly which two men were headed over to France.

When Aldus waved them forward, Hartley was hard-pressed not to run up to the men. His need to get the new information he had to his men was so strong it was an ache in his bones. Both men were tall, though one was a lot slimmer than the other, both had dark hair, and both watched him with faint smiles on their faces. Hartley frowned at Aldus when he reached his friend's side, wondering just what Aldus had told the men.

"Hartley, allow me to introduce the Baron of Starkley, Sir Leopold Wherlocke, and his cousin, Bened Vaughn." Aldus quickly told the men who Hartley and Gifford were and grinned as they all shook hands. "You did not need my glib tongue today, Hart."

"Let us see what our little cousin Alethea has drawn," said Leopold. "If I recall, she always had an astonishing gift at drawing."

"She still does," Hartley said and handed them the drawings.

He waited with ill-disguised impatience as the two men studied the drawings. It was surprisingly difficult to suppress the urge to ask them what *gifts* they possessed. The fact that Leopold was knighted and a baron, yet Hartley had never met the man, added a lot of weight to the rumor that the Vaughns and the Wherlockes were a reclusive group. He wondered if the man's superiors knew and accepted whatever gifts the men did possess.

"She *has* honed her art," Leopold said as he rolled up the drawing and stuck it inside the long coat he wore. "If you will allow, we will assist your men before we begin our work."

"You know my men?"

"We have bumped into each other several times over the last three years."

"How many of your family work for the government?"

"Only a few, and those who do often enlist the aid of others. And, ere you ask, no, we do not freely express our various gifts. Such honesty could soon hinder us in our work. I am pleased that you men so easily accepted what our cousins can do."

Hartley sighed. "I would not say *easily*, but belief came soon after we met them. For me it came when I saw Alethea gripped by a vision, and then she told us things she could not possibly have known." He smiled faintly. "As for Iago and his ghosts, I believe he sees them and thank God that I cannot."

Bened nodded. "Always grateful I was never cursed with the gift of seeing the dead."

Hartley wanted to ask just what gift the big man had, but bit back the question. There was a glint of amusement in Sir Leopold's eyes that told him the man knew how Hartley fought against his own curiosity. They spoke of how to contact Hartley's men and the intricate plans that had been made to get his niece and nephew home, and then the two men left.

"How did you know exactly who we were looking for?" Hartley asked Aldus as they walked back to the carriage.

"Did not know the names, only the where and what they looked like," Aldus answered. "I started telling my tale, and Leopold told me to cease trying to lie and just tell him the truth. Then he introduced himself and Bened, and I saw no reason not to tell the truth."

"How did he know you were lying?" asked Gifford. "No one is ever sure when you are lying. You are disturbingly good at, always have been."

"So that is his gift," said Hartley before Aldus could answer. "He can scent a lie no matter how skilled the liar. Very useful. I wonder if his superiors know that."

"They may guess it," said Aldus. "Just as Willsett guessed that we got our information on Claudette from some *gift* the moment I mentioned the Vaughns. I am thinking there are a lot in our government, at least the ones we work for, who know about the Vaughns and the Wherlockes already."

"You did not say you had told him about Alethea and Iago."

"I did not tell him much, just mentioned their names, and after I did, all of his doubt disappeared. I could see that he knew how we got so much knowledge about Claudette, but he did not ask and I did not say. It is obviously not just the family that keeps the secret." Aldus shrugged and climbed into the carriage. "Mayhap it is one of those things that no one wants to be the first to admit to believing in."

"I think I can understand that. Too many disbelieve

or are frightened of it all. No man wanting to better his position in any branch of government would want it known that he not only believed in such things, he was ready to make use of them. He would soon be crushed by the ridicule and find himself no more than a secretary."

"True. I certainly do not intend to boast of my wife's ability to have visions."

Hartley had to bite back a laugh as he watched his friends' faces. First puzzlement and then open-mouthed shock. It was several moments before anyone spoke, and he was not surprised when the first one to say anything was Aldus.

"You have asked Alethea to marry you?" Aldus asked.

"Not yet, but soon," replied Hartley. "I am the last of the Grevilles save for a few very distant cousins. If Bayard is still alive, he cannot be my heir, not as the entailment is written now. I need a wife. I knew that from the day I buried my brother. I just decided I did not need one too soon. Never met a woman who even made the word enter my head."

"Until Alethea."

"Yes, until Alethea. And, yes, I know there is a good chance that any child we have will have some sort of gift, but, after having met her and Iago and now two of her cousins, that does not worry me. I will admit that when the thought of marriage first entered my head I pushed it out as fast as I could. But it came back again and again. I am comfortable with her in a way I have never been comfortable with another woman."

"Not very romantic," murmured Gifford.

"No, and I have decided I need to woo her. I have done none of that, especially since I was still trapped in that business with Claudette." He laughed and shook his head. "I realized I know seduction but have never truly wooed a woman. And now that I might have Germaine and Bayard coming home, God willing, I feel an even more urgent need for a wife."

"She is a bit young to act as mother to your niece and nephew."

"And I would never ask her to. But she can help both of them in many ways, even if only to aid them in their eventual return to the society they were born into."

"Do you care for her?" asked Gifford.

"Ah, yes, I do in my own way. I like her and I want her. I also enjoy her company and trust her. Since I plan on being a faithful husband, I believe those things are far more important than some emotion no two people describe in the same way twice and which seems to be used all too often to hurt or entrap."

"I suggest you do not tell her how you feel about love."

"I do not intend to speak of that at all."

Aldus grinned and winked at Gifford. "This should be very interesting."

Hartley just scowled at his friends, who kept right on grinning.

Chapter 9

Alethea briefly wondered if she could claim her injuries still pained her and that she needed to go home as she looked around the crowded ballroom. Then she cursed softly, causing an older woman to frown at her and move away. She had neither a twinge of pain nor the shadow of a bruise left and had been complaining about being trapped in the house for over two weeks. A walk through the park on a cold, rainy, windy day would be preferable to this torture, however, she mused.

The room was hot from the press of too many over-dressed bodies and too many candles. A multitude of scents crowded the air, not all of them pleasant. The heavy perfumes some used to hide the smell of an un-washed body were the worst. It did not hide anything, mixing instead with the odor of the body to create a completely different, nose-wrinkling smell. She wondered how the ones who indulged in such things could be so blind to their own rank scent.

Sipping at a glass of watery lemonade, Alethea watched Hartley dance with the daughter of one of his father's old friends. The old friend stood on the side

of the room watching them with a benevolent smile.
He knew this dance with Hartley would be enough to
get his child the notice she needed to find a husband.
The daughter looked as if she wished she could melt
away into the highly polished floor. Alethea felt badly
for the girl, understanding all too well the heady mix
of Hartley and the music. She hoped, for the girl's
sake, that no one noticed how poorly she danced.

At least he is no longer fawning all over Claudette,
she thought with a surge of relief. Hartley did not
ignore the woman, but he did make it very clear that
her many charms were not enough to lure him into her
bed. Claudette might still be smiling and flirting as
if nothing troubled her, and acting oh so very polite,
but there was no ignoring the hard glint of fury in the
woman's eyes.

When the woman suddenly looked at Alethea, it was
as if sharp, icy knives were piercing her skin, and
Alethea looked around for her uncle. As usual, he was
discussing ways to increase his fortune with Lord Dansing, but Alethea moved to stand by his side anyway.
It was a little cowardly to use him as a shield, but she
decided she would rather be cowardly then face a furious Claudette.

She was soon bored, but, for once, she did not care.
Claudette gave her the chills, truly frightened her. And
that fear was not all caused by the ghosts of her bruises
whenever she looked at the woman. There was a dark
madness in Claudette. Alethea also suspected that the
woman had committed so many crimes and eluded justice for so long that she believed herself invincible, or
simply so much cleverer than the rest of the world. It
was not cowardly to try to protect herself from such a

woman; it was wise. From this moment on, until that woman was imprisoned or dead, Alethea had no intention of going anywhere alone.

Her attention fixed upon making certain her skirts were smoothed and straightened, Alethea stepped out from behind the screens shielding the chamber pots and closestools in the lady's retiring room. A chill swept over her, and she shivered despite the warmth of the room. She tensed, and her heart began to beat a little faster. It was a warning of some kind: she was certain of it. Lifting her gaze, she met the hard, cold stare of Madame Claudette des Rouches. For a second time, her gift had warned her of a danger to herself. Alethea just wished it would learn to do so in time for her to escape. Warning her of danger when it was standing only a few feet away was useless.

"I have discovered a few things about you, m'lady," said Claudette.

Alethea did not think she had ever heard the word *m'lady* spoken with such venom, as if it was the foulest of dockside curses. "And what would those things be, madame?"

"You are one of the Vaughns, blood related to the Wherlockes, worshippers of the devil."

"What rot!" she snapped, her fear pushed aside by her instinctive need to defend her family.

"Is it? I think, mayhap, you have bewitched my marquis. *Oui,* it is the only explanation for why a man like him would be sniffing around the skirts of a woman like you. He has no need of some mousy little country widow. And rumor has it that, even though you are a widow, you are not experienced enough to satisfy such a man."

That stung, but Alethea did not betray the pinch she suffered by even the faintest of winces. "I have not noticed any of this, er, *sniffing*. You imagine things." Alethea needed all of her willpower not to step back when Claudette curled her fingers in such a way that, with her long nails, it made them look more like talons than fingers. "Lord Redgrave is an unwed man. I suspect he looks at many women, all very beautiful, as I am not, yet you show no inclination to accost them in the lady's retiring room."

"Do not try to play such games with me, m'lady. I have played them far longer and am much, much better than you at them."

"How very nice for you." Alethea suspected that Claudette was a mere breath away from attacking her and wondered why she continued to goad the woman. "I play no games. I leave them to the experts, such as you claim to be. Lord Redgrave is a free man and can do precisely as he pleases. I sincerely doubt he would appreciate you interfering with his life."

"Heed me, witch. Cease drawing him to your side. I want him, and I shall have him. Being a marchioness would suit me very well, and I mean to be one. If you do not run home to your little farm soon, you will regret it. Trust me on that. And cease spreading tales about me, and cease it right now! Or soon there will be many a tale whispered about you and your cursed family."

"There have been whispers about my family spread about the ton for centuries. No one will heed your lies."

"Oh, I will not bother with the ton. They have proven that they care not that witches and sorcerers walk freely amongst them. *Non,* I speak of the common folk. They are not so enlightened, *oui?* They still believe in demons, witches, and sorcerers, and hate them. Fear them as they should. And I think you have heard how easily a mob can be stirred up, eh? So leave and shut your mouth or you will not be the only one who suffers my wrath."

Claudette was gone before Alethea had the chance to respond to the threat. It hung in the air, a miasma of pure evil. Alethea was not sure what she should do. It was one thing to refuse to run from a threat to herself, but Claudette had just threatened her whole family. Every Wherlocke and Vaughn child had grown up with tales of the past and warnings about letting too many people know what they could do, and would recognize the force of the threat. The early years of both families were littered by the horrific deaths of their ancestors at the hands of angry mobs.

Alethea was not surprised to see her hand shaking as she reached for the door latch. She would have to go back to Coulthurst. She could not allow Claudette to fulfill her threat to her family. There were too many Vaughns and Wherlockes in the city, and London was notorious for the ease with which its citizens could be roused into riots and destruction. She needed to find Hartley or Iago to take her home so that she could begin packing for Coulthurst.

She hated to leave before she could see Hartley reunited with the last of his family. She especially hated to leave before she could see Claudette pay, and pay dearly, for her crimes. But Alethea knew she had no choice now. It was not just her life and safety that was at stake any more.

* * *

Hartley meandered back inside the Hitchmoughs' home after enjoying a smoke with some friends and contemplated dancing with Alethea. His connection with Claudette was as good as severed, having dwindled to no more than a cool, polite acquaintance, at least on his part. Although he loathed gossip, the whispers he and his friends had carefully seeded through the fertile fields of the ton were beginning to bear fruit, and that was something that pleased him.

Claudette was slowly being pushed out of the hunting grounds she needed to survive. He soothed his distaste for the scheme by reminding himself that the whispers held hints of the full ugly truth about Madame Claudette des Rouches and thus were not complete gossip. In a way, it was also a just retribution, for she had ruined the names and reputations of many a man and woman with her gossip and lies.

The only thing that worried him was that he could see the fury building in Claudette. It glittered in her eyes and tightened her features, stealing some of the beauty she used to such ruthless advantage. Hartley could not begin to guess how she would react when she realized how fully she had lost in the game, but he knew it boded ill for someone.

He was just wondering if he should have even more men shadowing her and her sister when he turned a corner and bumped into Alethea. Hartley quickly caught hold of her when she started to fall backward. He began to chuckle as he steadied her, but his humor died a swift death when he saw her face. She looked terrified, her skin too pale and her eyes slightly glazed.

"What has happened, Alethea?" he asked. "Are you hurt?"

"No. No, I have not been hurt, but I need to get home," she replied as she gripped his arms tightly. "Take me home now, Hartley. Please."

"You are shaking, love. Tell me what has happened."

Alethea looked around quickly and saw no one, but shook her head. "No. Not here. Home. Get me home."

"I will need to call for a carriage, but I do not wish to leave you alone when you are so upset."

Hartley was wondering if he dared take her through the ballroom when she was in such a state when Aldus strolled up to them. The man had been outside with him and a half dozen other men sharing a smoke when Hartley had returned to the house. He did not think he had ever been so glad to see Aldus.

"Aldus, can you call me a carriage and then tell Iago that I have taken Alethea home?" said Hartley.

Aldus looked at the way a trembling Alethea clung to Hartley and frowned. "What has happened?"

"I will tell you when I know. She is not harmed. That is enough for now."

"How will you get her out of here?"

"Out through the servants' entrance. Do not forget to tell Iago that she is *not* hurt, just upset."

Hartley stared at his friend, hoping that Aldus would understand what he was not saying. He wanted to take care of Alethea himself, did not want Iago rushing home. It had been days since he was last alone with Alethea, and, even if the time was spent soothing her, he wanted to be alone with her now. Hartley had not even realized how tense he had become until Aldus nodded and he relaxed. Aldus gave him a wink, patted Alethea gently on the back, and then strode away.

"I am being such a craven coward," Alethea muttered as Hartley wrapped his arm around her waist and began to lead her to the servant's entrance of the house.

"Do not be foolish," he said. "You are no coward, love. No one who can see the things you can and then act on them could be a coward. I will get you home, you can have something to drink, and then you are going to tell me why you are so upset. If you recover sooner, you may tell me what has happened as we ride in the carriage."

Alethea said nothing as he ushered her out to the front of the house and helped her into the waiting carriage. She settled herself into his arms with a sigh, needing to luxuriate in his warmth and strength. He calmed her without saying a word, but she did not change her mind about what she planned to do. Claudette had threatened her family, and she could not let her need to stay near Hartley sway her in her decision to leave.

"What happened to frighten you so, Alethea?" Hartley asked when he felt her trembling begin to ease. He stroked her back and struggled not to let his hunger for her change his attempt to comfort her into a seductive caress.

"Madame Claudette confronted me in the lady's retiring room," she replied, and his whole body tensed against her. "She has decided that she wishes to be a marchioness and wanted me to get out of her way."

"Good God! Even if I had no hint of what she has done, I would never consider making such a woman my marchioness. I think she has bedded half the House of Lords."

"That *would* be awkward." She ignored his badly muffled laugh. "She told me to go back to Coulthurst and threatened dire retributions if I did not do so, and soon."

"I will increase the guard around you."

"More guards will not help. She also threatened my family. The Vaughns *and* the Wherlockes. You cannot guard us all, Hartley." She eased out of his hold a little and was not surprised to see him scowling at her in the dim light of the carriage lamps. "Her threat cannot be defeated with sword or fist. It cannot even be spoken of because it would only hurt my family more if we had to prove that the threat had any teeth to it. She plans to spread the whispers of our being witches, demons, devil worshippers, and all that. I told her that my family has been whispered about in the ton for centuries, scoffing at her threat at first."

"And rightly so. Even if she could get someone to heed her, the ton would shrug off her tales as they have shrugged off such tales before."

"And so I told her, but that is when her threat became truly frightening. She will not spread her tales through the ton, but through the common folk. As she said, they are not so enlightened as to laugh it away. They still believe in demons, devils, and witches, still fear them. She said she would stir up a mob against my family, and we both know how easily that could be achieved."

"It has been a long time since there was any persecution of witches," he said as the carriage pulled to a halt in front of Iago's townhouse.

"So many think because they have not had the superstitious amongst us turn on them and their loved ones."

Hartley helped her out of the carriage and escorted

her to the door, thinking hard on a way to convince her that she did not need to fear this latest attempt by Claudette to frighten her away. Ethelred opened the door just as their feet touched the top of the steps. Hartley noticed that Alethea looked a lot calmer, but he suspected it was because she had come to a decision and one he would not like.

"Ethelred, have my trunks brought to my room, please," Alethea said and then turned to Hartley the moment the butler walked away. "I will leave for Coulthurst in the morning." She kissed him on the cheek and started up the stairs, fighting the urge to turn and run into his arms with every step she took.

"Oh, no, you will not," said Hartley and started up the stairs right behind her.

"'Tis what I must do. Kate," she called, "I need you to help me pack for the journey back to Coulthurst."

"Kate, she is *not* packing," Hartley yelled. Catching her by the arm, he dragged her off to her room. "And tell Ethelred she needs no trunks," he added as he saw Kate standing only a few feet away as he pushed Alethea into her bedchamber.

"Hartley! Do not order my servants around. I *have* to leave. Kate!" Alethea caught a brief glimpse of Kate hurrying down the stairs to the foyer just before Hartley closed the door and latched it. Kate had obviously decided to try her hand at a little matchmaking, and Alethea promised to make her pay for that. "Damn it, Hartley, I cannot risk my family. I told you, there are a lot of Vaughns and Wherlockes in the city right now."

"Then warn them. I suspect they are well aware of what to do about such a threat."

"They are, but they should not have to worry about it just because I have tangled myself up with a madwoman."

She moved toward her wardrobe only to find his big body blocking the door. He did the same when she darted toward her dressing table. How did a man of his size move so quickly? she thought angrily. Alethea stopped, put her hands on her hips, and glared at him.

"You cannot expect me to take the chance that she can do as she threatened to. I have to leave."

"No."

"Why? Why are you being so difficult about this? I am no soldier or spy. Already you waste valuable men in the protecting of me, men who would be better used to help bring that woman down. If I have a vision, I can always send word to you. Why must I stay here?"

A squeak escaped her when he grabbed her, picked her up, and carried her to her bed. Surprise stole her breath when he tossed her down on it. When he sprawled on top of her, she feared she would never regain that much-needed breath. A heady warmth flowed through her as his hard, strong body pressed against hers. Alethea fought against the cloud of desire that began to encircle her mind. She wanted what he was offering, wanted it badly, but she had no time for it now.

"What do you think you are doing?" she asked, unable to keep all of her sudden breathlessness out of her voice.

"I am about to show you why you cannot leave." Hartley moved so that he could easily remove her shoes and then ran a hand up one slim leg.

"You think you can seduce me out of doing what is necessary?"

Alethea knew she ought to stop the man. He was

taking her clothes off, pausing only to shed a piece of his own clothing now and again. It would not be long before they were both naked. That should shock her and bring a stern protest to her lips. Instead, it made her heart skip with glee in her chest and her blood run hot. By the time she was stripped to her shift and he wore only his breeches, Alethea knew that protesting was the very last thing she wanted to do.

The Marquis of Redgrave was a very handsome man in all ways, she decided as she tried not to pant. She had seen men with their shirts off before but not one of them had made her so short of breath just from looking at them. Hartley was all lean, elegant muscle and taut, smooth skin. She wanted to put her mouth on that skin, to taste him everywhere. That thought should also have shocked her right down to her toes, but it just made her more eager for what he planned.

"This could prove to be a complication," she forced herself to say, knowing full well that it would be one for her and hoping it might be for him as well.

"No, I think not."

Hartley removed her shift and caught his breath so quickly he nearly choked. He had suspected that Alethea dressed in a way that disguised most of her curves, but his imagination had not come close to the reality. Her breasts were full and round, almost too much for her otherwise slim shape to hold, and they were tipped with large, dark rose aureoles, her nipples already hard and inviting. Her hips flared out invitingly from her small waist; he already knew she had a firm, well-rounded backside, but her legs were long and slender. That shapely body was covered by soft ivory skin that only enhanced the tidy vee of black curls at the juncture of her strong, slim thighs. Despite the fact that she had a wealth of thick black hair on her head, the rest of her body was surprisingly lacking in hair. Hartley found that intoxicating.

His blood pounding with need, he yanked off the last of his clothing and tossed it aside. The way her eyes widened as her gaze settled on his erection, the way they darkened with desire, made him want to strut around the room. Need overpowered that strange urge, and he quickly settled his body over hers. He groaned with pleasure when his flesh touched hers, her soft gasp of delight music to his ears.

"Hartley." Alethea found it a struggle to talk but forced a sliver of clarity into her desire-fogged mind. "There is something you need to know about me."

"Your husband never touched you."

"How could you know that?"

He kissed her, growling his approval when her tongue tangled with his. "There were rumors that Channing was not, well, he had little appreciation of women. Am I right? Are you untouched?"

"Yes. Channing never did more than give me the occasional kiss, brief and closed. I do not know much about all this, and you are used to women with experience—"

He stopped her words with another kiss. "It is going to be a pleasure beyond words to teach you about all a man and woman can share."

Alethea had the fleeting thought that he sounded annoyingly arrogant, but his kiss banished it. She wrapped her arms around him, caressing the smooth, taut skin of his broad back. Just the feel of his flesh against hers, the warmth of it beneath her hands, sent desire tearing through her veins with a strength that was almost frightening in its intensity. She could not get close enough, could not touch him enough to satisfy the craving that grew within her.

She tilted her head back in welcome as he kissed his way down her throat. When he covered her breasts with his hands, she gasped at the pleasure the caress brought, the faint calluses on his fingers making her nipples ache as he caressed them. Then his warm lips followed the path of his hands, and her body filled with an aching demand.

"Hartley!" she cried when he licked the aching tip of her breast, and even she did not know if it was a cry of protest over such an intimate caress or a cry of utter delight. All interest in which it was disappeared completely when he took the swollen tip of one breast into the damp heat of his mouth and sucked.

Hartley savored the way her small hands clenched on his body, her nails scraping against his skin. Her lushly curved yet lithe little body shifted against him in a silent demand he was struggling to ignore. She was searing fire in his arms, her passion running as fierce and hot as his own. He ached to bury himself deep within her and ride her, hard, until they both cried out in release, but he fought to chain that urge. Alethea was untried, and he was determined to make her first time with a man, her first time with *him,* as enjoyable as every time to follow would be.

Greedily enjoying the taste of her on his mouth, the scent of her desire perfuming the air, and the silken warmth of her skin beneath his hands, Hartley worked to build her passion up so high and so hot that she would not even flinch when he took her maidenhead. Just the thought of her innocence caused him a twinge of unease, so he ruthlessly banished it from his mind. He caressed every inch of her body with his hands as he feasted upon her full breasts, pausing in that sublime chore only to kiss her now and then. She was fulsome, well-rounded in all of the places a woman should be, yet slender as a reed everyplace else. It was a heady mix. Delighting in her every gasp and soft moan, he slid his hand between her legs, stroking her, and was pleased to find that she was already weeping in welcome for him, readying her body to receive him. Her shock over such a deeply intimate caress was so fleeting, Hartley knew she was more than ready for the next step in their erotic dance.

Hartley kissed her as he began to join their bodies, her tight heat making him so eager and hungry that he had to grit his teeth to stop himself from moving too quickly. The moment he reached her maidenhead, he grasped her by the hips and thrust home. He groaned with relief to discover the shield of her innocence was a thin one, easily breeched, and eliciting only one soft gasp from her. She quickly arched her body up toward his, helping him to sink even deeper into her heat.

Alethea was startled out of the haze of passion she had sunk into by Hartley's abrupt entrance into her body. Only a brief twinge of a shadowy pain told her of her lost innocence. She felt uncomfortably full, however, and shifted her legs a little farther up his body. Alethea then arched against him and all discomfort eased, the sense of being filled becoming a pure delight. He kissed her, his tongue mimicking the slow, deep thrusts of his body. She clutched at his back as something within her began to tighten in a way that was a mix of pleasure and pain. It was as if every drop of desire in her blood was rushing toward the place where her body was joined with his.

"Hartley?" she called softly, a sliver of fear trying to cut through the heat of her passion. "I feel . . . There is something." Alethea almost cursed aloud at her inability to explain what she was experiencing.

"Do not fight it, love," he said and nipped at her earlobe. "Flow with it, give in to its pull."

A heartbeat later she did, crying out his name as the knot of blazing hunger split apart, sending waves of blinding passion through her veins. Alethea was faintly aware of Hartley pounding into her, once, twice, and then his whole body tensed as he growled out her name. The sound was feral, fierce, and it added to the swirl of heat and beauty she was caught up in. The hot surge of his seed spilled inside her just before she became completely lost in the maelstrom of desire gripping her mind and body.

The cool, damp movement of a cloth over her nether regions yanked Alethea out of the daze she had slipped into with a shocked gasp on her lips. She raised her hand to push away whatever assaulted her so intimately only to hear Hartley chuckle. The heat of a blush stung her cheeks when she realized he had just been washing away the signs of their lovemaking on her body.

And it had been lovemaking, at least on her part, she realized when he climbed back into bed and pulled her into his arms. She looked into his slumberous golden brown eyes and nearly sighed like some love-struck girl right out of the schoolroom. Alethea inwardly straightened her spine, squared her shoulders, and pushed that moonstruck chit into a dark corner of her mind. This was an affair; that was all Hartley wanted. To pine for more was foolish; to let him see clearly that she pined for more would put a swift end to this affair. She was going to have a shattered heart no matter when he walked away from her, and she was determined to make every moment with him count, as well as gather as many of those moments as possible.

"I was prepared for pain," she said as she rested her cheek against his chest and idly circled her palm over his taut stomach, "but there was so little it barely made me blink."

"Your innocence was but lightly protected, love, and I am grateful for that. It allowed you to enjoy the full measure of pleasure."

Her heart skipped with joy when he called her *love,* but she ignored it, knowing what an empty endearment it could be, and sighed. "I should still leave. It is my duty to protect my family."

Hartley kissed the top of her head, regretting the fact that he could not stay with her longer, could not hold her through the night and make love to her again and again. "Trust me, Claudette's threat is troublesome, but that trouble can be averted now that we know of it. We have men working all over the city, and they will be told the why of such rumors and ordered to smother them. To succeed, her voice needs to be the only one, or at least the loudest and clearest, and it will not be."

"I do trust you, Hartley. I shall try to put aside my fear for my family."

"Good, for I would rather do something other than lie here and talk of your family in the short time I have left. I would like nothing better than to spend the night, to wake at your side in the morning, but I will have to slip away soon."

"How soon?"

"In an hour or two."

Alethea rubbed her body against his, watching as a flush of renewed desire touched his cheeks. "Why, however shall we pass the time until then?"

Hartley laughed and turned until she was sprawled beneath him, more than ready for a second taste of the fire she shared with him.

Chapter 10

"I wish you would cease glaring at me, Iago. It is quite spoiling my appetite."

Iago looked at Alethea's full plate and nearly snickered. He doubted she even realized how much she was eating. A night of illicit passion had obviously stirred up her appetite, he thought, and then glared at her some more. She looked disgustingly content, while he felt an utter failure as her uncle and protector.

"Why did you leave the ball last night, aside from the need to rush home and take a lover to your bed?" He smirked when she glared at him, experiencing a hint of triumph over spoiling her good mood.

Alethea considered pouring her porridge over her uncle's head. Laden with honey and cream, it would make a satisfying mess. Then she sighed. He was undoubtedly all tangled up in some manly sense of failure. His niece had been seduced beneath his very roof, and he had done nothing to stop it or to challenge the man who had seduced her. Alethea was not sure how she could cure him of something she did not really understand. After all, she was a grown woman, a widow, and she had already explained to him that she wanted Hartley and would have him if he showed any interest. This start of an affair could be no great surprise to Iago.

"Iago, I told you that—"

"Yes, yes, I know what you told me." He sighed. "I suppose I just never expected you to actually do it."

"Well, I did. I wanted him, he wanted me." She shrugged.

"Do not try to make it all sound so simple, as if it were no more than the act of a spoiled child—or children. You love him."

"I fear I do." She slathered honey on a piece of toast and struggled not to reveal how much that worried her. "But I might be mistaking lust for love. Men do it all the time. I do not think so, but what do I know about it all? I went from an isolated childhood into an isolated marriage, which was no marriage at all."

"True, and I am sorry that your family did not investigate that fool more closely. You did not deserve to be locked into such an empty marriage. It would not have taken us long to discover the truth about the man. Your husband's preferences had been whispered about and speculated upon for a long time."

"His preferences?" Alethea frowned as she tried to guess what Iago meant and then suddenly smiled as comprehension came to her. "Oh, you mean that he preferred men. No, I think not. I do not believe my husband ever preferred men to women. I think he had no preferences at all, actually. He had no passion in him at all, not for anything or anyone. What I had seen as a calm, even-tempered man was actually a man who was, well, dead inside. Something was missing in him, that something that makes us cry, laugh, hate, love, even fear and rage. Whether something happened to him to make him that way, we shall never know, but he may have even been born that way."

"Oh. The one time I met him, I thought him a pleasant, gentlemanly sort."

"Pleasant, gentlemanly, and empty. He was empty, Iago. He never even blinked when I had a vision. Nothing moved him, absolutely nothing. What I saw as kind was only good manners performed blindly. I had to accept that truth when a child was killed in the village, trampled by horses. Channing looked at that poor, mangled little body, and there was nothing in his eyes, not even revulsion at the sight of the body. But he did all that he should, from arranging for the body to be moved and properly buried to speaking to the grief-stricken parents. And then went on to have his lunch—always served at precisely the same time every day."

"I do not believe I have ever met anyone like that."

"Be thankful for it. It is chilling. And, mayhap, that is why I am so drawn to Hartley. He does not realize it, I think, but he is a man of very strong emotion. I confess, I soak it up, revel in it. In some ways, living with Channing smothered me, and now I can breathe."

Iago drummed his fingers on the table. "I nearly confronted you last night, but Kate stopped me."

Alethea blushed. "That could have been very embarrassing."

He grinned. "For all of us, I think." Then he grew serious again. "It pricks at my pride that I am just standing back while Redgrave has an affair with my niece, but so be it. As you have said, you are a widow, a grown woman. But if he shames you, sullies your name, or treats you unkindly, I will not allow you to stop me from doing as I must."

"Fair enough," she agreed, although she knew she would do everything in her power to stop her uncle and her lover from fighting.

"Now, tell me, what was it that upset you so badly last night?"

Alethea told him everything about the confrontation between her and Claudette, including her decision to leave. She waited patiently while her uncle muttered a long string of curses before saying, "Hartley assures me that, if she tries such a thing, it can be stopped before it goes too far."

"I suspect it can, but I will still send word to any of our family residing in the city."

"That is what Hartley told me to do, yet Claudette's threat made my blood run cold. I immediately remembered every terrifying tale from our family's past." She took a bracing sip of tea. "I am still not certain I should stay, and wonder if I allowed him to convince me to do so just because I do not wish to leave him."

"That is probably some of it, but you cannot bow down to threats, and everyone in our family would agree with me on that. That woman will soon be gone. She is very diligently digging her own grave. I just worry that, once she fully realizes how much power she has lost, she will lash out at one of us, at Hartley, or at you. There is a cold madness in that woman."

"I know. I have felt it. 'Tis there to see in her eyes. When you see it, you have to wonder how she was able to seduce so many men."

"The men who sought her out, bedded her, were not particularly interested in her eyes."

"Wretch."

Alethea's amusement faded quickly, however. Madame Claudette could not remain blissfully ignorant of the banishment rolling toward her for long. When the acceptance of society was finally, firmly pulled away, all her lethal games would come to an end. So, too, Alethea mused, would Claudette's source of income and comfortable life, as well as whatever power she had managed to grasp. Alethea did not *worry* that the woman would strike out when that happened—she was sure of it. She knew it as well as she knew her own name.

Hartley finished the last of his breakfast, pushed his plate aside, and began to drink his tea. He would like to have shared a breakfast with Alethea but knew that would have been pushing Iago too hard up against the wall. It did not surprise him that he wanted to do something he had never done before—wake up beside a lover—either. He was becoming accustomed to acting unusually around Alethea. Since he had made the decision that he would make her his marchioness, wanting to share breakfast with her was just more proof that he had made the right decision.

He watched the footmen clear the table and thought on the threat Claudette had made. Alethea had been terrified, and for that alone he wanted Claudette to pay dearly. He did not fully understand Alethea's fear, however, and intended to gather as much information on her family's history as possible. There was no doubt in his mind that some of her ancestors had paid dearly, horrifically, for their gifts. Iago and Alethea had made reference to that dark past and those troubled times, but he had shrugged their remarks aside. He would do so no longer. That deep fear Alethea revealed could be used against her, as Claudette had shown, and he needed facts if he was to ever be able to ease that fear in his wife.

Wife. The word used to terrify him. Now he was eager to make Alethea his in all ways. He did not want to creep out of her bed again, slipping away in the dark of night like some thief. Hartley had thoroughly disliked waking up in his bed—alone. And that was yet another drastic change in his ways. He knew there would be more, yet felt no resentment over that fact. He was ready to be married, ready to be married to Alethea.

The sound of men hurrying toward the door pulled Hartley from his thoughts. He stared at his friends in surprise as Aldus and Gifford rushed up to the table. For a moment he suffered the sharp stab of fear that something had happened to Alethea. Then he saw that their expressions were ones of excitement, not alarm.

"What is it?" he asked, sitting up straight. "What has happened?"

"They found them," said Aldus, and he held out a crumpled, dirty piece of paper.

"Them?" Hartley reluctantly took hold of the paper even though he did not understand his hesitation to do so.

"The children. Germaine and Bayard. They found them alive and are bringing them home." Aldus patted a stunned Hartley on the back and then moved to see what food was left on the sideboard, Gifford following suit.

Hartley was not surprised to see his hands shaking as he held the message. For three long years he had searched and hoped for some sign that his sister's children had not died on that beach. Alethea had renewed his waning hope, but years of failure and fear had taken their toll, and he had tried not to let his hopes rise too high. Now he held word that Germaine and Bayard had survived, that they would soon be home with him, and he found himself frozen in fear and indecision. It was almost laughable, as if now that the prize was within reach, he did not know what to do with it.

"Are you all right, Hartley?" asked Aldus as he sat down on Hartley's right, his plate heavy with food.

"Yes, I think so." Hartley shook his head as Gifford sat on his left. "It must be shock that it has happened so quickly. After three long years of nothing, Alethea has a vision, her cousins go to France with that information, and a week later I hold the news that my niece and nephew have been found and will soon be home. My mind is finding that hard to accept." He read the message again. "Someone must have rushed this to the ship the moment the children were seen."

"Or near to. Leo does say that it took some time to convince your niece that he was who he said he was, and that they had tried to run at first. Seems that fellow Bened is a tracker, a very good one, and he soon caught them."

"It does trouble me that the couple who kept them hidden demanded some payment for all their trouble."

"You would have given them some anyway," said Gifford.

"I would have," agreed Hartley, "but the fact that they demanded it leaves me wondering just what place my niece and nephew held at that farm."

"Ah, yes," agreed Aldus. "Something to consider."

"And Leo says nothing about their health, just that they are alive, and he will make sure they get on the ship home. I had not realized that the baron and his cousin would join the hunt."

"He said they would be pleased to assist."

"It sounds like they did far more than that, yet they had other business to do in France, and, even though they implied it would not start the moment they landed, I doubt they had days to spare. Still, I am grateful beyond words."

"So, soon you will have the care of your sister's children."

Hartley grimaced. "They are not truly children any more. Bayard is rapidly approaching manhood. Germaine is eighteen now, a young woman. If life had taken the route intended for her, she would be attending balls and hunting for a husband now. My sister would have enjoyed that," he added softly and then shook away a faint pang of remembered grief. "I think I must push forward my plans to marry."

"What are you going to do? Go to Alethea and say that your niece and nephew are coming home and could she marry you now so that there is someone there to help care for them? I am sure that will make her heart beat faster."

"I will certainly not phrase it that way, but neither will I hide the fact that I wish her to help me with the children. They will need a woman's guidance, her sympathy and understanding."

"I think you might want to say a few words about caring and passion and all," said Gifford and then filled his mouth with sausage.

"I am not without skill with the ladies, you know,"

said Hartley, although their words began to make him uneasy about how Alethea might respond to his proposal.

"With experienced women who look for lovers and like to be seduced," said Aldus. "This is a gently born country lass. Not a London lady. I hate to tell you this, Hartley, but a practical proposal will probably gain you a hearty refusal. You need to dress it up with a few warm words."

What Hartley had no intention of telling his friends was that he and Alethea had already shared enough warmth to heat every Londoner's home. He would remind her of that. It might be wise, however, to plan what he would say to her even as he got the special license he would need. What he would not do was claim an undying love for her; he would not start his marriage with a lie. He almost smiled. Considering the family he was marrying into, that could prove to be a huge mistake anyway.

"Eat up," he ordered his friends. "I need to secure a special license, and witnesses to the marriage will be needed." He ignored the grumblings of his friends and turned his thoughts to the proposal he was about to make.

Alethea looked up from her needlework and smiled as Hartley, Aldus, and Gifford were escorted into the family parlor. Hartley stepped over to her and kissed her on the lips right in front of his friends and her uncle. She blushed and wondered what he was up to. There was an air of excitement about him, but he asked Iago if he could talk to him for a moment, and the two

of them left. She set aside her needlework and looked
at Aldus and Gifford.

Before she could begin to question them, Alfred and
Ethelred arrived with food and drink. She sighed and
began her role as hostess. The minute the servants left,
however, she returned her full attention to the two men
now seated across from her. They were acting as if all
that interested them was the food on the table, but she
was not fooled for a minute. There was a tension in
the men that told her they knew what was going on.

"What has happened?" she asked and frowned at the
suspicious way the two men exchanged looks before
meeting her gaze.

"Germaine and Bayard have been found," said Aldus.

"Alive?" she asked in a voice that was close to a
whisper, her heart beating hard with fear that there had
been bad news.

"Very much so."

Before Alethea could ask a single question, Aldus
launched into a long, convoluted tale of meeting up with
her cousins and how they had offered to help. She knew
they were trying to keep her diverted so she would ask
no more questions. Alethea inwardly sighed. Considering what work these men did for the government, it
would undoubtedly have been a waste of time to try to
pry information out of them. She turned her attention
to the tale they told and decided to wait for Hartley.

"What can I do for you?" asked Iago as he led Hartley into his private study and sat down at his desk.

Hartley took the seat facing the desk and carefully
weighed his words. He could sense a coolness in Iago

and knew the man had found out about him and Alethea. Hartley hoped a marriage proposal would ease the sense of insult and anger the man felt, for he liked Iago.

"My niece and nephew have been found alive and will soon come home," he said.

"Wonderful!" Iago reached over the desk and shook Hartley's hand. "Damn, 'tis near a miracle after having been lost in France for three years."

"It certainly feels so. I had planned to woo your niece—"

"I think you have done more than that," muttered Iago.

"I may have overstepped my bounds"—he ignored the way Iago raised one eyebrow and almost smirked—"but I had already decided that I wanted to make her my marchioness."

"You want to marry Alethea?"

"Yes, I do."

"Why?"

"I like her, I desire her, and I trust her. And, ere you ask, I have no trouble with her gift. My first hesitation concerning that was born of doubt—utter disbelief, in truth. This was not a sudden decision despite how little time we have really known each other. The word *marriage* started to slip into my mind almost from the beginning, however."

Iago grinned. "Pushed it out of there fast, I suspect."

"That I did, but it would not stay away." Unable to sit still, Hartley stood up and began to pace the room. "I wanted her from the beginning, and that, too, got stronger. When she was injured, I was afraid as much as I was enraged by what had been done to her. I wanted to lock her up somewhere safe. When Claudette's threats so upset her, all I could think of was comforting her, and when she spoke of leaving, I was adamant in refusing to let her do so."

"Do you love her, then?"

Hartley faced Iago and shrugged. "I am not sure I believe in such a thing. What I do believe in is that I want to have breakfast with her, I want her in my bed at night, and I want to wake up to her in the morning. And I want her to be the woman who gives me children." He stood straight beneath Iago's close scrutiny.

"And you now need a mother for your sister's children," Iago said.

"I would be a liar if I said the return of my sister's children has nothing to do with this. They do not need a mother, however. A woman's softness, a kind heart and willing ear, mayhap, but not a mother. All this has done has made me want to marry Alethea immediately instead of taking some more time to woo her."

"I would have preferred it if you claimed to love her. Alethea deserves better than a marriage of convenience."

"It is no marriage of convenience that I offer." He smiled faintly. "And telling a lie in this family would be most unwise, so I will claim no emotion I am not certain I feel." He was pleased when Iago smiled back, that coolness gone. "I want a true marriage. There will be no other women. I might question the validity of love, but I believe in honoring vows taken and come from a home where that was done. I mean to build a home and family. Those requirements and beliefs are why I have been hesitant about marrying despite my need for an heir. I do not want what appears to be the common ton marriage."

"You mean the heir and the spare, and then go your own way."

"Exactly. I do not believe you can build a strong family that way. So, do I have your permission to marry your niece?"

"Yes, although you do not really need it. She is a widow. However, if she says yes, we can then sit down and discuss the finances of the whole matter. She handles most of her finances herself, but the law requires that a man be involved, and I was chosen as executor by her late husband."

"Fine, then. We will talk after she accepts me." Hartley refused to think that she would refuse. "I have a special license and would like to put it to use right away. Her family?"

"It would take weeks to arrange anything that would bring them together. We can see to some kind of celebration when all this trouble with Claudette is done." Iago stood up and shook Hartley's hand. "I will send her in here. Good luck."

For the first time in his life, Hartley felt nervous. He paced, tapped his fingers against his leg, and practiced his speech as he waited for Alethea. He reminded himself that she had been a virgin and yet had given herself to him with a passion that he knew he would crave for a long time. Despite that assurance, he tensed when she entered the room.

"What is it, Hartley?" she asked as she hurried to his side, sensing his nervousness. "Aldus told me the wonderful news. Are you troubled by how much the children you once knew may have changed?"

"Marry me."

Alethea stared at him in open-mouthed surprise, and

Hartley silently cursed his sudden lost of tact and charm. He tried to tell himself that it was because marriage was such a big step, that it was a bond meant to last a lifetime, but he knew he was lying to himself. His ineptitude was due to the fact that he was afraid she would say no and would not be able to find the words to convince her to say yes.

"Did you just ask me to marry you?" Alethea asked, not surprised by the tremor in her voice, because her heart was pounding so hard she feared it might leap free of her chest. "No, did you just *order* me to marry you?"

"Yes, although my intention was to ask, and I am doing a damned poor job of it." He reached out and took her hands in his. "Let me try again. Will you do me the honor of becoming my wife?"

"Is this because I was a virgin?"

"No, although I cannot say I am not pleased that my future marchioness has known no other man. Alethea, I have been thinking about marriage almost since the day I met you. I want you, I like you, and I think we are very compatible. As I told your uncle, I want to see you at the breakfast table, and I want you in my bed every night. I want you as the mother of any children we may be blessed with." He pulled her into his arms and kissed her with all the passion he felt for her. "Very compatible indeed."

A little dazed by the desire his kiss had stirred within her, Alethea stared up at him. "Passion can fade, Hartley."

"I know, but companionship does not, nor does trust and liking."

She warmed at his words, knowing he meant every one, but her heart also ached. She wanted him to tell her that he loved her, that she was the sun and the moon and the stars and other such fulsome declarations. Alethea had to bite the inside of her cheek to keep herself from immediately saying yes. Then, like a snake in the garden, a sudden reason for this abrupt proposal slithered into her mind.

"Do you seek a mother for the children who will soon be living with you?"

"No. They do not need a mother, especially one who is only a few years older than Germaine. Howbeit, I will not lie and say that I am not hoping you will help me with them."

"And what about all your women?"

"There are not that many that I have known, nowhere near the numbers rumor claims, and many of them were women I seduced because they had secrets and knowledge the government sought. But—there will be no more of that. I believe in vows taken before God, Alethea. I will not break them."

It took Alethea less than a minute to say yes. He was not offering the love she needed, but she could not walk away from him. There was a chance he could come to love her, but she would not pine for it, she swore to herself. At least this time there would be passion and, God willing, children of her own. The moment she said yes, however, she found herself being rushed to the altar. There was no time for second thoughts. As she spoke her vows in a tiny chapel with a somewhat disheveled minister, she prayed that she had not just made the biggest mistake of her life.

Alethea looked around the massive bedchamber Hartley had escorted her to and tried not to feel too intimidated by the signs of wealth and prestige surrounding her. She smoothed her hands down the thin linen and lace nightdress she wore and wondered where Hartley was. They had had a rushed marriage and a fine dinner with Iago, Aldus, and Gifford. Kate had been thrilled for her and busied herself packing all of Alethea's things to be brought to Hartley's townhouse. And here she now stood, ready for her wedding night, and no husband. It brought back some painful memories of her first wedding.

Hartley stepped into the room, and his body immediately hardened with need at the sight of his new wife wearing a very thin, lacy nightdress. She stirred his blood as no woman ever had before. He could already feel his body crying out with the need to be inside her.

He stepped up behind her and wrapped his arms around her waist, grinning at the way she leapt like a scalded cat. The more nervous she became, the more at ease he grew. From the moment he had put his mother's ring on Alethea's finger, he had become calm, almost peaceful in his heart and soul. He nuzzled the curve between her neck and her shoulder, and she shivered in his arms.

"You smell good," he murmured as he nipped at her earlobe.

"Lilac soap."

She turned in his arms and looked up at him. Her husband. That she had a claim to such a man awed her far more than the fact that she was now a marchioness. She slid her arms around his neck and touched her lips to his. Passion would still her groundless worries and fears for a while. She did not want such things to interfere with her wedding night.

Within moments she found herself naked and

sprawled beneath an equally naked Hartley. A little more of her fear was chipped away at this sign of his desire for her. There was the seed for the love she needed from him. Alethea made herself a promise that she would learn all there was to learn about what pleased him in the bedchamber, and learn it so well that he forgot every other woman he had ever known.

Hartley was so hungry for her that he had to fight for enough control just to stop himself from ravishing her like some untried boy. The only thing that soothed his unease about the strength of his need for her was the certainty that she felt the same for him. He kissed and caressed her, his desire stirred to new heights by the way she tried to return each touch, each kiss, in equal measure. The soft noises she made as her passion soared were sweet music to his ears.

"I do not have the patience to do all I wanted to do on our wedding night," he muttered even as he began to join their bodies.

"We will have many more nights," she whispered against his ear, and then ran her tongue along the length of the life-giving vein in his throat.

Hartley lost the last of his control. He gripped her hips and buried himself deep inside her. The way her body held him so tightly within her heat drove all sense from his mind. He could hear the bed thumping against the wall as he pounded into her but could not stop himself. As his release swept over him, he heard her cry out with her own, felt her body clench around his, and gave himself over completely to the waves of desire that crashed over him.

Hartley came to his senses to find that he had maintained enough of his usual finesse to roll a little to the side when he collapsed on her. He looked down at her smooth white belly and wondered if his seed had already taken root. The mere thought of her rounding with his child made his heart leap in his chest.

Lifting his head from her breasts, he looked at Alethea and breathed an inner sigh of relief when she smiled at him, her eyes still glinting silver with the remnants of the passion they had shared. Perhaps he had not made as bad a showing as he had feared.

"Did I hurt you?" he felt compelled to ask, recalled to the fact that she was only newly initiated into the secrets of desire and lovemaking.

"Oh, no." Alethea sighed, knowing she was about to fall asleep, and stroked his badly mussed hair. "It was wonderful."

Hartley was tempted to sit up and thump his chest in pride as he looked down at his well-satisfied bride. "Welcome to my home, Wife," he said and kissed her.

Chapter 11

This was not what she had expected, Alethea thought as she stared at the two children standing before her. Hartley's men had been a little too eager to toss this responsibility in her lap and rush off in search of the marquis. It made one wonder just how much trouble the siblings had caused on the trip home to England. Both children watched her as warily as she suspected she watched them. Germaine and Bayard de Laceaux had lost more than their childish innocence in the last three years. They had also lost their ability to trust, their hope, and their faith. Alethea feared that the reunion between Hartley and his niece and nephew was not going to be as smooth or as joyous as everyone had hoped.

And they were not really children any more, she reminded herself. Germaine was eighteen, an age where young ladies in England were indulging in their first season, thinking of catching a husband and having children. Bayard was fourteen, nearing fifteen, tall and coltish like many young boys were but already holding a hint of the man he would soon be. It would have been easier if they had been children, scars and all, but she

was going to be dealing with small adults who had
spent three long years struggling to survive.

"Not the best way for you to come home, I suspect,"
Alethea said. "I believe your uncle will be home soon.
He was not expecting you to arrive so quickly. Shall we
go into the parlor and have some food and drink?"

When they both nodded, she had Alfred take their
pitifully meager belongings up to the bedchambers that
had been readied for them. She then ordered Hartley's
butler, Cobb, to bring them food and drink. In silence,
she led the pair into the parlor. The way Germaine and
Bayard studied the room made Alethea think they were
making a careful survey of all possible escape routes.

The silence continued until the heavily laden tea tray
was brought in. Alethea noticed how both children
stared at the food in a way that told her they had often
gone hungry. Once the food and drink was arranged on
the table between her and the siblings, Alethea waved
the servants away. Since neither Germaine nor Bayard
made any move to help themselves to the food, Alethea
put an assortment of small sandwiches and cakes on
two plates. She noticed that Bayard's hand shook faintly
as he accepted his. Germaine took her plate with a
grace that belied her ragged boy's clothing and then
fixed Alethea with a cool, unblinking stare.

"When did my uncle marry you?" Germaine asked.

"Right after we received the news that you had been
found," Alethea replied, trying not to be unsettled by
the hard look in the girl's beautiful sky blue eyes. "A
short courtship and a special license." Courtship was
not the way to describe what had passed between her
and Hartley before they were married, but she decided
it would serve for now.

"Are you with child, then?"

Alethea nearly choked on the tea she had been sipping. She carefully set her cup down and looked at Germaine. There was no doubt in Alethea's mind that the girl knew she had just been appallingly rude. Germaine had to have been well-trained in etiquette by the time she had been forced into running and hiding, and such training was not lost in a mere three years. It might need a little polishing, but the basics would have remained in the girl's mind. Alethea put aside her sympathy for all the girl had been through for the moment. Instinct told her she needed to be strong and firm now or the girl would trample her.

"Not that I know of," she replied calmly and reached for a small lemon cake. "That was not the reason for our marriage."

"Did he think we needed another mother?"

There was so much anger revealed in those words that Alethea was surprised Germaine could even sit still, did not tremble from the force of it. "No. I am but two, three years your senior, Germaine. A poor choice for a mother to a grown woman and a young man. What Hartley needed was a wife, an heir, and someone to tend his home. Is that not why most men marry?"

"And what did you need?"

"Hartley."

Germaine said nothing for a few moments as she ate two little ham and cucumber sandwiches and a lemon cake. Alethea waited patiently for the next strike. The blunt truth she had just told Germaine had been the right choice. Germaine would respect the truth. Alethea just hoped she could continue to hold her own.

"Leo told us that you helped them find us," Germaine said after delicately wiping her mouth with a napkin.

"Hartley had men looking for you and Bayard for three years, Germaine. I but helped to point them in the right direction at a time when they were almost resigned to your loss."

"With visions? Dreams? Where did this great insight come from? Cards? Tea leaves?"

For a girl with such a beautiful, soft, full mouth, Germaine sneered impressively, Alethea mused. "I will say this just once. Yes, I have visions. And dreams. And simple knowings which are a certainty that something will happen. I do not expect or demand that you believe in them, or in me, but I will not tolerate scorn. Especially since many of my family have such gifts, and I will not have them insulted. I suggest you be patient and gather a little knowledge before you speak so disparagingly of something you are completely ignorant of." She picked up her sketchbook that she always kept close at hand and gave it to Germaine. "I draw what my visions show me. Perhaps this will help you to understand."

Germaine and Bayard kept eating as they looked at Alethea's drawings. Germaine gave her a narrow-eyed glance a few times, but said nothing. Then Alethea realized they were about to turn to the page that was filled with drawings of that day on the beach, a page now preceded only by the one depicting the dark visions she had gained from holding Claudette's handkerchief. Alethea reached out to snatch the sketchbook away, only to have her wrist grabbed by Germaine.

Despite how thin the girl appeared, she was strong and easily held Alethea's hand aside. Alethea waited tensely as the siblings studied what she had drawn concerning the day that had shattered their young lives. It was hard to subdue a flinch when Germaine finally looked at her and slowly eased her tight grip on Alethea's wrist. There was such fury and grief in the girl's beautiful eyes, Alethea wanted to weep.

"You have not drawn the face of that murderous bitch," Germaine said, her voice cold and hard.

"I have," Alethea said and pointed to the black rose.

"Ah, so you can smell as well as see when you have these visions." She looked at the page holding the drawings of the vision Alethea had had when she had picked up the handkerchief. "Who are these men?"

"Ones she had killed because they were trying to stop her crimes. See? There is the black rose again."

"There is the farm," said Bayard when Germaine turned the page. "That is how you found us, *oui?* You saw the farm?"

Alethea nodded and sat back as Germaine closed the sketchbook and set it aside. The girl no longer looked scornful, but it was difficult to read what she did feel in her smooth, emotionless expression. Bayard, on the other hand, looked fascinated. There was no hint of fear in either of them, however, and Alethea decided that was enough for now.

"This"—Germaine waved her small, delicate hand toward the sketchbook—"will not hang her, will it?"

"No," replied Alethea. "No judge would accept such things as proof of her crimes."

"I saw her that day on the beach. You know that. There is your proof."

"It could be. Your uncle will know better about such things. Then again, you saw her, but you did not see her kill anyone. She and her allies could use that to steal away the strength of anything you might have to say. And that woman has gathered some very powerful allies. I have discovered that Madame Claudette has gathered power and coin since she slithered into England. She chose her lovers with an eye to how they might help her in evading punishment and in gaining useful information. She will not be easy to bring down."

"She will run, far and fast, once she hears Bayard and I survived. She will go to ground."

"Yes, I believe she will, but she will also wish to avenge herself upon the ones she feels have destroyed the life she has built for herself. That is her weakness. Vanity and anger. That is what will ensnare her." Alethea could not believe she was discussing strategy with this girl and her brother, but they listened closely as she told them all that had been done and was being done to bring Claudette and her sister to justice. "She has already revealed, by her attacks upon me, that her vanity and greed, her overweening sense of invulnerability, can make her act recklessly."

"She is very good at fooling people. She fooled my father and Theresa. They thought Claudette was no more than a shy maid, one as afraid of the ill wind in France as they were. They trusted her. The day my father died, he finally saw how he had been deceived. Claudette *was* the ill wind blowing our way. I suspect she is still very good at fooling people."

"Very good. She has made a very nice life for herself with the skill, but, believe me, Germaine, she *will* fall, and soon."

"And have you seen this?'

Just the way Germaine asked the question told Alethea that the girl accepted her gift, and she nearly smiled. "It is one of those things I call a *knowing*. There is no doubt in my mind that she is rapidly tumbling down a hill to her own destruction. What I cannot know is when it will happen and how many innocents she may kill before it happens."

"She can never truly pay enough for all the lives she has taken," said Bayard, the angry man within the lanky boy turning his dark eyes hard. "Never."

"No, she cannot, so one must think of how destroying her will save others," Alethea said quietly and breathed an inner sigh of relief when he nodded and turned his attention back to his food.

A glance at the food revealed that it was sadly depleted, and Alethea was standing up to ring for more when the parlor door burst open. She watched Hartley as he stood there, his gaze fixed upon his sister's children. He looked an odd mix of elated and nervous. Then his niece and nephew stood up and walked over to him.

"Hello, Uncle," said Germaine. "It was good of you to find us."

"Good of me?" Hartley shook his head. "Good of me? You are my blood, my only sister's babes. What else could I possibly have done? Of course, I bloody looked for you. I would have torn that cursed country apart if I could have."

Alethea was about to go to him and try to soothe him when Germaine suddenly grinned. The smile changed her solemn beauty into something breathtaking. Alethea could see how stunned Hartley was and had to cough to hide an errant laugh. She could foresee a great deal of trouble ahead for him once Germaine was dressed properly and presented to society.

"I would like a gown," Germaine said quietly and reached out to touch one of his tightly clenched fists. "Pink with a lot of lace."

Hartley choked and wrapped his arms around the too-slender shoulders of his niece and nephew. He pulled them close for a hug, pressing his face against their hair where their heads met against his chest. Alethea had to swallow hard to hold back the tears that choked her. When he glanced at her over their heads, she could see the gleam of tears in his eyes and ached to hold him. Instead, she smiled and, puckering her lips, sent him a kiss. To her relief, his tears retreated and he eyed her with the hungry look she had begun to recognize.

"I was just about to get some more food," she said and moved to the bell pull. "Would you like tea or coffee, Hartley?"

The grateful look he and Bayard sent her as they eased away from each other nearly made her smile. The show of emotion, although completely understandable, had made them uncomfortable once the strength of that emotion had eased a little. Men, she thought, would be better served if they did not try so hard to be what they believed men should be.

"Coffee, if you would be so kind," he replied.

"Bayard and I would like a cup as well," said Germaine.

Alethea was thinking about protesting serving such a strong beverage to the siblings, but a subtle shake of Hartley's head made her swallow the words. She gave her orders to Alfred and then returned to her seat. Germaine and Bayard sat across from her and Hartley, and Alethea waited to see who would speak first. Despite the emotional welcome just shared, they were still strangers in many ways.

"Do you truly want a pink gown with lace?" Hartley suddenly asked Germaine.

Germaine grinned. "No, Uncle, but a few gowns would be most welcome. I am so very weary of wearing a lad's clothing. And I wish to let my hair grow again."

The knot of tension eased inside Alethea as Hartley and the children talked of what they needed regarding clothing. It would not be easy, but the first steps to making a family with these children was now taken. They had accepted their uncle and did not blame him for the fact that they were lost in France for so long. Alfred came in, set out the new food and drink, and left with the old tray and dishes before they were done speaking of dressmakers and bootmakers. Alethea began to serve out the food and coffee.

"How did you end up at the farm?" asked Hartley.

Germaine took a sip of her coffee and then replied, "At first, we just ran. As far and as fast as we could. Then we hid and tried to think of a way to get back to the beach, to any port. We passed through large villages and towns and became very good at begging but could find no one we trusted to help us or a way to get on a ship that we could only pray was headed to England. After almost a year, we turned around and headed back."

"The Moynes needed farmhands, and we foolishly thought that would be a good job," said Bayard. "Instead, we saw no coin and little food. They charged us to sleep in the barn, for the clothes on our backs, and the food in our bellies. And they were very slow to replace our rags or feed us. We were told there would be others to help with the work, but those others never arrived. By the time we realized how they were playing a game with us, they owned us. We tried to walk away, and they nearly had us put in prison for trying to run from an indenture."

"That fat fool Moyne told everyone that our parents had owed him a large debt and sold our time to them," said Germaine even as she eyed a tiny cake, obviously fighting the temptation to eat just a little more. "He planned to keep us for ten years, although I suspect he intended to keep us far longer than that if he could. Everyone in the village kept a close watch on us, and we were locked up tight at night. I did get away once, but it did no good. There was nowhere to go, no one to find, so I went back to discover that they had beaten Bayard. I made no more attempts to get away."

"Damn, and Leo paid them," said Hartley.

"I told him he should just shoot the pair, but Leo said that would be too much trouble and too much noise."

Alethea grinned. "Sounds like Cousin Leo. The note said you tried to run from the men."

Germaine nodded. "I did not know who they were, did I? They grabbed Bayard quickly, but I thought I could slip back later and set him free. Leo told me that was a foolish idea when he found me. His man Bened had tracked me down like a hound running down a bleeding rabbit. I do not know how he did that. I have become very good at leaving no trail."

"Yes, I suspect you have, but Bened is an exceptionally good tracker."

It was nearly time for dinner before they left the parlor. Alethea was not sure how the siblings could even think to eat any more, but they had hurried up to their bedchambers to clean up for the meal. Hartley had rushed to his office to write a few letters concerning the return of his sister's children and whatever other plots he had going. Left by herself at long last, Alethea wandered out into the gardens. She needed time away from all the heightened emotions, time to consider how the presence of Germaine and Bayard might affect her marriage and her husband.

She was sitting on a stone bench watching a spider weave his web between two branches of a rosebush when Germaine strode up and sat down beside her. The girl was still dressed as a lad, but the clothes were of a nicer cut and style, and clean, as was she. Her fair hair gleamed and formed a riot of curls around her face. Alethea thought she looked very young and innocent until she looked into those incredibly blue eyes. In those eyes was far more knowledge of the ugliness of the world than any young girl should have.

"Germaine, did Moyne . . ." Alethea began.

"He tried to touch me once, but he drank too much. He could no longer do what most men seem to want to do." Germaine blushed. "Never gave me a dress, either, but soon even a lad's clothes could not hide what I was. I did fear for a time that he might try to make some money by selling my body to those who eyed me in that nasty way, but he did not do it. He never did. I am not sure why, but I doubt most sincerely that it was for any honorable reason."

Alethea sighed and patted the girl's clenched hands. "Men can be utter swine. But I pray that you do not now think that all men are that way."

"No. I never did. It did make me see how hard life is for a woman not of our class or with no man to protect her. 'Tis not right. Just because a woman has no money, no husband, or no title, she is not some bawd free for the taking."

"No, but you cannot change the whole world and its mind all by yourself. You can, however, change small pieces of it. Mayhap when you are settled in, you could look into the matter."

"I will. Did you truly marry Hartley because you want him?"

"Of course I did. I have land, a manor, and a portion that pays my bills. I had no need for a man. I am also a child of the countryside and have no real affection for the city and society."

"But you were not rich and you were not a marchioness."

"And thank God for that. Rich would have meant all the fortune hunters in England would have been after me, and a marchioness? Well, I mean no offense to your family, but who would wish more work to do and more nights spent trudging from event to event, listening to gossip, complaints, and bad music? No, I saw only one true benefit to marrying Hartley, and that was Hartley himself."

"So it was a love match."

Alethea could not completely stop her wince. "No, not truly. Hartley did not speak of love. Howbeit, he spoke of trust, fidelity, and companionship." She shrugged. "'Tis far more than many wives get, and I wanted him, none other. I also crave children, and one should have a husband for that, if only for the childrens' sake."

"Well, if I ever do something as foolish as marry a man, I will insist that he love me."

Alethea looked at the girl and then laughed at the impish look on her face. Germaine had not lost all of her love of life. The Moynes may have treated her and Bayard as no better than slaves, but there were so many worse things that could have happened to them. Alethea thought, for the first time since she had heard Hartley's sister's children were coming home, that there was some hope for a future for all of them, that they may have accepted her as they had accepted Hartley. After that first confrontation, all signs pointed to it. She doubted they would ever forget what had happened to them, but the scars of their travail did not appear to run too deep.

"I was sent out here to bring you in to dinner," Germaine said and stood up. "'Tis best if you eat and rest well tonight, for my uncle has already arranged for a dressmaker to come here on the morrow."

There was no holding back the groan rising in her throat at that prospect. Alethea stood up, brushed off her skirts, and then tensed. A tickle of alertness raced through her, and she recognized it as the warning of danger she sometimes got. She looked all around but saw nothing. That tense alertness that came from a sense of approaching danger did not ease, however. There was something close at hand that she was supposed to see as a threat, but the evening's shadows were hiding whatever that was.

"Germaine, get into the house now," she ordered.

"Why? What have you seen?" Germaine stepped up next to Alethea and looked around.

"I have not seen anything yet. I but feel that it is necessary for you to get into the house right now."

Then she saw the man. He stepped out of the shadows near the garden wall. It was the same man that had beaten her on Claudette's command. This time he held a pistol. His smile as he raised the pistol chilled her blood. To see that this man could kill a person while smiling made it all the more frightening.

For a brief moment she thought he was going to kill her. Claudette must have heard of her marriage to Hartley by now and wanted her dead. Alethea thought of all the things she had wanted to say to Hartley and wished she had not been such a coward. She would go to her grave never having let him know that he had been loved, and that grieved her.

Then, as she braced for the punch of the bullet, knowing that she could never get out of the way in time, not if she was going to protect Germaine, she saw that he was not aiming at her. He was aiming at Germaine, who stood by her side. The girl obviously thought to help her, protect her, when it was Germaine herself who was about to die. Alethea wondered how Claudette could have gotten the news of Germaine's survival so quickly. Had the cursed woman been down at the docks greeting each ship in case someone interesting arrived? she thought crossly as she ever so slowly moved her arm in front of Germaine. The girl's cold blue gaze was fixed on the man, his on hers, and Alethea prayed that would give her the time to push Germaine out of harm's way.

"You are one of Claudette's faithful dogs, *oui?*" said Germaine, the sneer in her voice so thick even Alethea winced at the sound of it.

Either the girl did not see the danger she was in or her rage rose so hot in her when anything to do with Claudette was near or spoken of, she was blind to everything around her. Her words made the man's finger tighten on the trigger of his gun, and he glared at the girl. He was a cold-blooded killer, but he obviously had his manly pride, and Germaine had just bruised it badly.

"'Tis a shame I must kill you quick," the man said, his eyes narrowing on Germaine. "I know many ways to make you regret those words, you little bitch."

A faint tensing of his arm and jaw warned Alethea. She shoved Germaine aside as the man fired his pistol. A heartbeat later something slammed into her shoulder so hard she stumbled back. Excruciating pain followed a moment later. Despite that, she flung herself on top of Germaine and pushed the girl onto the ground. On her hands and knees she urged the girl to crawl fast into the shelter of the many bushes and statues dotting the garden, even as she screamed as loud as she could, again and again.

"Move," she ordered Germaine.

"You are shot!"

"I believe I noticed that. We can deal with it later. I said move!"

Germaine tried to turn toward her, but Alethea just tugged her up into a crouch and pushed her toward the house. The sound of running footsteps and men shouting told Alethea that someone was coming, but she did not look for them or look back to see if the man who had shot her was still there. The only thought fixed clearly in her pain-fogged mind was that she needed to get the girl into the shelter of the house.

They stumbled through the open garden doors. It took Alethea a moment to realize the doors were open because all the men were out in the garden trying to find out what had happened. She prayed they found the man but sincerely doubted her prayers would be answered. The time that had passed between when the man had shot her, her screams, and the men racing out of the house had been long enough for a skilled assassin to escape. Since she was not sure any of the men had seen her or Germaine, she would need to find a way to tell them she and the girl were all right.

"M'lady! What has happened to you?"

Alethea looked at Alfred, and had to blink several times to steady her vision. "Man in the garden. Shot me." She stumbled and grabbed hold of Alfred's arm to steady herself. "Can you tell the men Germaine and I reached the house safely? I am not sure they saw us do so."

"I can hold her steady," said Germaine as she wrapped her arm around Alethea's waist and held her close to her body. "I think this is a particularly drastic way to get out of having to deal with my dressmaker," Germaine said as she started to inch Alethea toward a settee.

"It was all I could come up with on such short notice." Alethea smiled and then winced as Germaine jostled her wound when she tried to get a firmer grip on her.

Alfred barely reached the garden doors when the men and Bayard returned. Hartley looked at Germaine, obviously checking her for wounds. Alethea wondered what had happened to the man who had shot her. It was obvious that he had not been caught. She had heard no other shots, and the men had no prisoner with them. She dizzily wondered if it made her a bad person to hope that her assailant had been killed.

"I was not the one shot, Uncle," Germaine said and nodded at Alethea.

Hartley looked at Alethea, saw her blood-soaked gown, and swore, viciously and profanely. Aldus, Gifford, Bayard, and Iago all rushed to her side. Hartley ordered Alfred to send for a doctor even as he stepped up and ripped the shoulder of her gown away to look at her wound. The bullet had gone in but had not come out, which meant it would have to be dug out. The mere thought of the agony she would suffer made him ache to find the man who had shot her and make him suffer, too.

"Oh damn," said Iago. "We will soon have far more help then we may need or want."

Not sure what the man meant, Hartley ignored him as he pressed his handkerchief against the wound in a vain effort to stop the bleeding. "Did you see who did this?" he asked.

"Same man who beat me." Alethea was not surprised that her words came out as little gasps, for the way he pressed the cloth against her wound made the pain worse.

"Pierre Leon."

"Ah, so you have a name."

"Yes. Did he say why he shot you?"

"No. I thought Claudette had heard of our marriage. Thought this was her striking out at me."

"It was not that?" He started to turn to get some brandy to wash the wound.

"Hartley, catch me," Alethea whispered as blackness flowed over her.

He leapt forward as she slumped, and Germaine staggered, nearly dropping her. Everyone rushed to his side, but all of his attention was fixed upon Alethea. Blood soaked the front of her gown, her breathing was rapid and uneven, and she looked so pale, too pale. He wanted to bellow out his rage. If Alethea did not recover from this, Claudette and her allies would discover that he knew how to hunt and kill as well, if not better, than they did. He would make every one of them pay and pay dearly.

Chapter 12

Hartley paced his drawing room, ignoring the other three men who waited there with him. Germaine and Bayard sat close together on the settee, pale and silent. He had not even talked to Germaine about what had happened yet, although she had tried to catch his attention several times. He knew he should be over there trying to reassure them, but he was incapable of doing so. His every thought, every emotion, was fixed on what was happening to Alethea.

The doctor and Mrs. Huxley were taking too long, he decided, but fought the urge to race up to his bed-chamber where Alethea had been taken. He had been firmly ushered out once already. The scream that had escaped Alethea when the doctor had begun to dig the bullet out of her had maddened him, and he had tried to force the man to stop. Foolish but understandable, but the doctor had not seen it that way. His promise of better behavior had not been enough to get the doctor to allow him to stay, however. The man had refused to continue unless Hartley left. His only revenge for that had been to leave Kate there, watching the doctor's every move and making her opinions of his skill or lack thereof very well known. Afraid he might yet give in to the impulse to go back up there, he fixed his gaze upon a pale Iago and hoped the diversion of talking to the man would calm him. He suddenly recalled something Iago had said when he had looked down at the bloody form Germaine had been holding up.

"What did you mean when you said we would soon have help whether we wanted it or not?" Hartley asked.

Iago grimaced and combed his fingers through his hair, which had come loose of its tidy queue long ago. "When you consider who and what we are, Hartley, it should come as no surprise that the Vaughns, and to some extent the Wherlockes, are closely bonded. In many ways. Alethea is in pain, and she is in grave danger. That will draw at least some of our kinsmen here."

"There are others in your family who have visions?" asked Aldus.

"Some, but mostly it is a bonding we share." Iago shrugged, his face revealing his difficulty in trying to find the right words to explain himself. "The moment Alethea was shot, I promise you, several members of our family knew it. How many will come to London or come here from their homes in the city will depend upon who is close at hand when those who do sense something is wrong make their way here. Modred, the Duke of Elderwood, will definitely know, but I do not believe he will come. He will send someone in his place. He finds such crowded places a torment."

"He is *that* uncomfortable around other people?" asked Hartley.

"It can be a sheer hell for him to be amongst so many people, with all their emotions tearing at him and thoughts like discordant, unconnected shouts in his head," replied Iago. "There were times when we feared he would go mad. He has learned how to shut himself away from the cacophony, that constant barrage of others' emotions and thoughts, but it is difficult. It requires constant control, constant concentration. We have others in the family who are very empathic, but not in the way Modred is."

"He can actually *hear* what people think?" Hartley noticed that his niece and nephew looked intrigued and wondered what Alethea had told them.

"Some. Mostly he just catches pieces of a thought, but at times there is much more. He can be at ease around most of our family. We think that is because we are all so tightly bound together, by blood and our varied gifts. It could even be that our gifts are the reason we have these, well, shields against such an intrusion. There are also some people who are naturally shielded. Modred has several servants who are. In such cases he can sense their feelings only when the emotion is fierce, strong enough to break through those inner shields."

"And he is close to Alethea?"

"He was, but they saw little of each other after she married. Her husband found Modred unsettling, he said, although I never saw that. I do not think Modred was fond of the man, either. Probably knew that the man was lacking in emotion, but I do not think he ever told Alethea so. Alethea and Modred have kept up a regular correspondence, however. Forced into seclusion as he is, Modred is very fond of letters." He grimaced. "The two of them have always shared a special bond. You see, his mother was as terrified of him as

Alethea's mother was of her. She fled, just as Alethea's mother did. Our aunt Dob has had most of the raising of Modred, and the pair of them often visited with Alethea and her brothers."

"What is your aunt's gift?"

"Knowledge." Iago smiled faintly at the brief looks of confusion Hartley and the others gave him. "Aunt Dob has a true understanding of it all, some natural insight. She knows ways to help one control the gift, to harness it in some ways. Her empathy is boundless, as is her patience. I truly believe she is the reason poor Modred has not gone the way his father did. The man came home from a local gentlemen's gathering one night, walked into his library, and shot himself. He left a note saying he could no longer abide the noise."

"It does not sound like much of a gift, does it?" said Germaine.

"No," Iago replied. "The whole family holds its breath each time a child is born, fearing the babe will have the gift poor Modred is cursed with. As I said, there are a number of us who are empathic, but it is not the crippling gift that it can be for Modred." He grimaced at the sound of voices arguing in the hall, the sound drawing ever closer to the drawing room. "I believe at least one of the family was in the city and very close to hand."

Hartley frowned when a small, dark-haired woman marched into the room. On her heels were a tall, dark-haired man he faintly recognized and a young, fair-haired boy. Neither the males with her or his softly protesting butler, Cobb, did anything to halt or slow the intrusion. Hartley wondered if that was because the woman was very, very pregnant as his friends, nephew, and Iago scrambled to their feet.

"Ah, so 'tis not you who was hurt," said the woman as she stopped in front of Iago.

"No, Chloe, not me," replied Iago and kissed her cheek. "Before I explain, allow me to introduce you, Argus, and Anthony."

The moment Hartley heard the name Kenwood, he knew whom he was politely welcoming into his home. The scandal of the Marquis of Colinsmoor's wife and uncle trying to kill him and his son had rocked the ton three years ago. Even in his fear and worry over his niece and nephew, he had heard all the sordid details. He had occasionally wondered if that was why one rarely saw the marquis and his new wife. Looking into Chloe Wherlocke Kenwood's inky blue eyes, he changed his mind. The marquis obviously had all he needed in his wife and growing family.

Sir Argus Wherlocke's name was also familiar. Hartley was not quite sure what the man did for the government, but his name was often whispered through the ranks of one of the groups Hartley had been briefly connected with. Those whispers had held a note of awe. Hartley was beginning to think that the Wherlockes and Vaughns were already proving their worth to the government. He was surprised that Aldus had not known of the man and then realized it could be just a matter of Aldus not mentioning what he knew. Aldus did not freely share all of his knowledge.

"Julian will not be pleased about your rushing over here," said Iago as they all sat down again and Alfred and Cobb hastily brought in trays of food and drink.

"I will deal with my husband," Chloe said. "He will

understand. Eventually. Tell me what has happened, Iago."

Iago succinctly explained, and Chloe looked at Germaine and Bayard. Germaine and Bayard met her unwavering gaze with a calm that surprised Hartley. There was a lot he had to learn about his niece and nephew. He was distracted from that thought when every hair on his body suddenly began to stand on end. He looked at Iago, only to find him and Chloe glaring at Argus.

"Calm yourself, Argus," said Chloe. "Alethea will be fine."

"Are you certain?" asked Argus.

Chloe closed her eyes for a moment and then looked at Argus and nodded. "Very certain."

When the hair on his body went flat again, Hartley fought against the urge to ask Sir Argus exactly what his gift was. He saw Germaine look from Sir Argus, to her arm, and then back at Sir Argus again. When she opened her mouth, he made a quick slashing gesture with his hand that caught her attention, and then he shook his head. She closed her mouth and, for just a moment, looked like a disgruntled young girl. His heart ached for her when the hard, seasoned-warrior expression returned to her delicate features.

"What are you doing to catch the woman who ordered this done?" Chloe asked, looking from Iago to Hartley and back again.

Hartley took over the explanations and answered her. As he did so, he found himself wishing there was more—more direct action, more proof, more chance of an immediate retribution. He was startled when Chloe stepped over to him and patted one of his tightly clenched fists. She looked at the small boy while continuing to pat his arm, and cocked her head toward Germaine and Bayard. Kenwood's young heir hurried over to the siblings and began to talk about how he had once had pretty hair but his father had cut it. Hartley briefly wondered if there was a touch of madness in the Wherlocke-Vaughn bloodline, and then recalled that Kenwood's heir had none of that magical blood in his veins. He met the laughing gaze of Chloe.

"Anthony is still sulking over losing the last of his baby curls," she said and grinned, but she quickly turned serious again. "That woman will fall soon, but you must be especially vigilant in the days to come."

"Why?"

Chloe shrugged. "She is coiled to strike." She looked at Iago. "Modred comes."

"To London?" Iago asked, shock roughening his voice.

"Yes," Chloe replied. "He and Olympia. She was visiting him, so he knew immediately when Alethea was hurt, although I suspect he would have anyway. Someone would have immediately dispatched a message if naught else. He is the great gatherer of news concerning the many members of our clan. Use him."

"Use Modred? No. He could be harmed. These are very dangerous and vicious people, Chloe. I have seen what swirls around them, seen the fury of the ones whose blood is on their hands. God alone knows what poor Modred would sense in them, would see in their black hearts. These sisters thought nothing of killing babes to further their need for the trappings of money and vanity. It would be too much for him."

"Use him, Iago. One of the sisters is weaker than the other. Use Modred to get the truth from her. Argus could also help. But this is a chance for Modred to see that his gift is not just a curse, that it can be used to help people. He needs to see that."

"I am sure he understands how—"

"He *understands,* but he needs to *see* how that works. Use him. He is expecting it."

"Uncle," said Germaine as she stepped up next to Chloe. "You need to listen to me. It was not Alethea who was in danger in the garden. She was not the one the man was aiming at."

"Who else could it be? Claudette has had Alethea attacked once already and warned her there would be more trouble s-s-so . . ." He stuttered to a halt as he looked into Germaine's eyes. "No, it cannot be. How could the woman have known, so quickly, that I found you and brought you home?"

"I do not know, Uncle, but it was me that man was aiming at. He smiled at Alethea, you see, a cold, vicious sort of smile, and so I thought he was after her. I believe she did, too, but something warned her who the true target was, and she pushed me out of the way just as he fired so that she was shot instead. There is no question in my mind that he was aiming at me at that moment."

"Claudette must have men at the docks," said Aldus. "It would make sense, for she needs to be in touch with France to send out any information and collect her blood money. It would also allow her to arrange a swift escape. And you have been looking for Germaine and Bayard for three years. It is no secret. She would also want to try and keep a watch on that, too. After all, they were on the beach that day. Germaine saw her."

"She does not know that."

"She does not need to. The moment word spread that

you were looking for your sister's children, that there was even a hint that they did not die on that beach, she would take action. Claudette would want to know for certain that there was no one who could bear witness to that day. She probably even contacted the men she had with her that day and was told that only two children were there. That is, if she actually left them alive after the murder was done."

"Yes, she may have killed them, thinking she was leaving no witnesses."

"That and out of habit. She appears to hire ruffians to do work for her and then use a rich lover to rid her of the ruffians. I am astonished that word has not spread through the various rat holes she gets her men from and made it difficult for her to hire anyone." Aldus looked at Germaine. "Being trapped at that farm may well have saved your life, for I do not doubt for a moment that the very minute she heard a whisper you might have survived, Claudette would have begun searching for you as hard as Hartley was."

"I most certainly do not wish to be grateful to the Moynes for anything," said Germaine, her voice tight with anger. "Mayhap, if you are right and she wishes me dead, I could be used to—"

"No," said Hartley. "You will not be used as bait."

"Uncle, I am certain I would be well guarded."

"I suspect a lot of the people she has murdered considered themselves well guarded." He cursed when she paled and knew she was thinking of her family. "I am a clod," he said as he wrapped his arm around her shoulders. "I am also determined to keep you safe. Claudette has murdered men well trained in deceit and intrigue—neatly trapped them and sent them to their deaths. She has seduced God knows how many men of power and importance, and stolen secrets from them. I do not know how many people she has had killed and doubt we will ever know, but she is not a woman to be tricked by a tasty piece of bait left unprotected and apparently just waiting for her to collect it."

"No, of course not. It is just maddening that she continues to walk freely. She should be waiting for her hanging. Damnation, she should be naught but a rotting pile of bones and rags in a cage at some crossroads by now." She bit her lip when her uncle admonished her with one lift of a brow. "My pardon."

"Very understandable sentiment," murmured Iago.

Hartley scowled at Iago, but he just shrugged. "When Claudette gets the news that the attempt on Germaine's life was a failure, what do you think she will do?" Hartley asked Argus.

"Bolt," said Sir Argus as he helped himself to a blackberry tart. "She will know that there is only one person who could be looked at for such an act. Herself."

"How so? I think she believes us ignorant of all she has done. And what information we have about the blood on her hands comes from sources we cannot lay claim to—Iago seeing the ghosts and Alethea seeing the visions." A quick glance at Germaine and Bayard revealed no surprise on their faces at what they were hearing, and he knew Alethea must have told them something of her gift and made them believe her.

"She does not know that. There is none so suspicious as one who has committed a crime. She will see enemies everywhere and capture round every corner. It is what makes some criminals so difficult to catch. On the other side of the coin are the ones who are so foolishly arrogant they believe they can never be caught—right up until they hang. Which do you think she is?"

"The former, I should think," replied Aldus, "or we would have her by now."

"Alethea believes Claudette begins to be more like the latter," said Germaine and shrugged when the men all looked at her. "She has gone unpunished for so long, you see, that she thinks herself so much cleverer than we are, so much better."

Sir Argus nodded. "Very possible."

"She said that Claudette's weaknesses are vanity and greed. She also spoke of the woman's overwhelming sense of invulnerability. Said those things would make her act recklessly—those and a need for revenge when her well-constructed little life began to fall apart."

"Smart girl, our Alethea. That is exactly what will bring that murderous viper down." Sir Argus looked at Hartley. "Do you happen to know which men she entrapped? Who was seduced and may have inadvertently or knowingly betrayed his country?"

"We have made up a list," replied Iago.

"Then give it to me," said Sir Argus. "As soon as the doctor says how Alethea is doing, I will go and talk to some of the fools. Mayhap one of your friends will accompany me."

"Gladly," said Aldus.

"You think you can get them to confess something?" asked Hartley. "We have been trying, but they are very closemouthed."

"They cannot remain so with me," said Sir Argus. "I will get the truth from them. It is my gift. I can make them tell me what they know and what they have done.

There may be some that will find themselves facing charges of treason, however."

"You can make them put their own necks in a noose?"

Sir Argus smiled and looked at Hartley. A moment later, Hartley felt himself falling into the man's eyes. He tried to fight the pull, but a strange lassitude came over him.

"Stop it, Argus," snapped Iago, and he leapt up to put his hands over Hartley's eyes.

"It happened again," muttered Germaine, staring at the fine hairs on her arms, all of them standing up. "Just what do you do?"

"I make people feel compelled to tell me whatever I want to know," replied Argus and smiled when Hartley shook off the last of his bemusement and glared at him. "I can even make them forget they did it."

"Damn," muttered Aldus. "You looked dazed yet happy, Hartley. I have no doubt you would have done just that."

"Do not do it again, Argus," scolded Chloe. "He is family now."

"I was but answering his question," Argus said. "It is often easier to show what I can do than try to explain it." The man sounded so sincere and smiled so sweetly, Hartley knew he was lying through his teeth.

"As soon as we know how Alethea fares, we will begin to visit the men on the list," said Aldus. "I doubt we will be able to see to too many, but we can certainly make a good start. It might also be difficult to revisit the ones we have already tried to question, as they were obviously insulted by our queries."

"They will speak with us. Let us just hope that they were all fools seduced into idiocy by a pretty woman and not traitors," said Sir Argus. "I will not allow a traitor to forget that I just got him to confess all his sins."

Before Hartley could offer his opinion on a man who allowed a woman to make him betray not only his country but help lead good men to their deaths, the doctor was ushered into the room by Cobb. Hartley tensed, fear for Alethea a hard knot in his belly. There was nothing in the good doctor's dour expression to tell him if the news he was about to hear was good or bad. He stepped closer to the doctor even as Iago stood up to do the same.

"How fares my wife?" Hartley asked Dr. Hoskins.

The plump, balding man removed his spectacles and wiped them with a large handkerchief before putting them back on his somewhat bulbous nose and looking at Hartley. "The wound was high on her shoulder. I saw no damage to bone or muscle, but she did lose a lot of blood. If a fever does not take hold of her, she should heal well."

Relief swept through Hartley so swiftly and strongly he actually feared he might swoon. He felt Germaine grip him tightly by the arm, and that steadied him. The doctor stared at him as if he knew what had almost happened, and it took all of Hartley's willpower to subdue a blush. He supposed the man deserved a little revenge for Hartley's nearly strangling him.

"She must stay in bed for at least a week," the doctor continued. "No hearty food for several days, only broth. Introduce the sturdier fare gently after that. If she does take a fever, call me in. I have left some laudanum for the pain, although that aggravating maid of hers was not happy that I had given your wife some."

Hartley was not sure what he said, but the man

nodded and allowed himself to be escorted out by
Cobb. A glass was pushed into his hand, and Hartley
blinked in surprise when he saw that Sir Argus had
handed him a brandy. He wasted no time in drinking
it, however, and it helped to restore his calm. What he
needed to do was go and see Alethea for himself, to
make certain she was still breathing. He needed to push
the sight of her bloody and unconscious from his mind.

"I need . . ." he began and started a little when Chloe
kissed him on the cheek.

"Go," she said. "We can see ourselves out." She
grinned a little. "I may even get home before my husband discovers I left."

"Tell her we were here and will see her later, when
she begins to recover enough for visitors," added Sir
Argus. "In the meantime, your friends and I will see to
questioning Claudette's lovers."

"I should go with you," Hartley said, torn between
helping in bringing Claudette to justice and needing to
be with Alethea.

"Not tonight. We will still have a lot of men to speak
to once you have assured yourself that Alethea is healing as she should," said Aldus. "Remember, it was a
long list."

"And Alethea will heal," said Chloe.

Hartley nodded and left to go to sit with his wife. He
stepped into his bedchamber and looked to the bed.
Kate smiled at him as she silently rose from the chair
by the bed and slipped out of the room. He quickly
took her place in the seat and studied Alethea. She
looked as pale as the linen she slept on, but her breathing was steady. Tentatively, afraid of what he might
find, he touched her face and found it blessedly cool.

He knew that she could still come down with a fever, but she looked remarkably hale for someone who had just suffered as she had. When he took her hand in his and kissed it, her eyes fluttered open.

"Hartley," she whispered, her voice hoarse.

"Right here, Alethea," he said and bent forward to kiss her cheek. "Your family will be round to visit as soon as you have recovered enough to receive them." He was surprised to see her smile even as her eyelids slowly closed again.

"Poor Hartley," she murmured. "Best ready yourself. They can be a trial."

He opened his mouth to respond, only to see that she was asleep again. Still holding her hand, he settled in for a long wait. Despite how badly he wanted to go with the others to question Claudette's lovers, he would not leave Alethea's side until he was absolutely certain of her recovery. Then, and only then, would he put all of his time and strength into bringing Claudette and her allies to justice.

"He was torn," said Germaine as she watched the door close behind her uncle. "He wants to join the hunt, but he cannot leave Alethea."

"There will be a lot of hunting left to do even after she has healed enough for him to feel he can leave her side," said Sir Argus.

"I can go in his place."

"I think not, young lady, but I will give you points for trying. This is not something one drags a young miss into." He held up his hand to silence her when she opened her mouth to argue. "I know you and your brother have matured far beyond your years, but you are still too young for this. On the practical side of it all, someone wants you dead. I cannot be trying to gain information we need and keep a close watch on you at the same time."

"But it is not just you going," she began.

"The other men are needed to guard me and for intimidation."

Germaine scowled at him but did not argue. "I think you can be intimidating enough all on your own."

Chloe laughed. "She sees you clearly, Argus." She hooked her arm through his. "Take us home now. Then you may go ahunting." As she waved Anthony to her side, she smiled at Germaine. "Your uncle needs to see that you are safe right now, more than he needs anything else. His wife has been shot, and he has only just found you and your brother again after three years of fearing you were dead. There will be time enough for you to run free and put a few gray hairs on his head."

Germaine stood with Bayard and watched the guests leave, taking Aldus, Iago, and Gifford with them. "A very odd family our uncle has married into," she murmured as they moved to return to the drawing room.

"Fascinating, though," Bayard said.

"Very much so. And loyal to each other."

"You trust them. I can feel how much calmer you are. I was not sure you were going to trust Uncle's new wife."

"I was still wary about her right up until she was shot. Watching her purposely push me aside and take the bullet meant for me took away the last of my wariness. Now I am just trying to understand exactly what is going on between her and our uncle."

"What do you mean?"

"I mean she says she married him because she wanted him, and he married her for an heir, a companion, and to help run his house." She nodded when Bayard made a loud scoffing noise. "Exactly. I think our uncle is being just like a man." She ignored her brother's soft protest. "I shall be interested to see just how long it takes our thick-skulled uncle to see that he loves her."

"To see it or to tell her?"

"To tell her."

"A guinea says a fortnight."

"Eight days."

They both spit in their palms and shook hands, and Germaine said, "May the best man win."

Bayard grinned. "In the end, I believe the winner will be our uncle."

Chapter 13

Soft moonlight and candlelight illuminated the room as Hartley stared down at the woman on the bed. The bandages twined around her shoulder and chest were an obscenity to his eyes. She had been hurt while in his care, and that enraged him. Three days of battling with the emotions tearing through him had not dimmed that rage.

He was in deep, deep trouble. The emotions he struggled with were not those caused by a liking or mere physical attraction. Lust was certainly there, strong and hot as fire, more sweet and more fulfilling than any he had ever tasted. That alone should have warned him that he was stepping into far more than an affable, convenient marriage. As he thought over all he had felt and done since meeting Alethea, he had to marvel at his own blindness. All the signs were clear to see once one knew what to look for. He loved her.

Hartley almost laughed, and not just because it had taken him the three days since she had been shot to figure it out. He was filled—heart, soul, and mind—with an emotion he had scorned. He could hear himself arrogantly informing Iago that he did not believe in such an emotion as love, and all his fatuous reasons why. Now that he knew what it was, his dim memories of the times his parents had been together told him that they had loved. Their example was probably why, after long thinking himself a confirmed bachelor, he had so easily thought of marriage the moment he met the right woman—Alethea.

Sitting in the chair by the side of the bed, he took her hand in his. In his arrogance he had believed that when he married her, liking her, even enjoying her company, and the fierce passion they shared would be enough to hold the marriage together and make it a good one. Now he needed more. He wanted her to love him as he did her. How to accomplish that was the question. He was skilled at convincing a woman to give him her body for his, and her, pleasure, but he had never tried to win a woman's heart. Never wanted to. Hartley could do nothing but pray that Alethea had married him for more reasons than he had married her, deeper reasons, ones that flowed from her heart and not her head.

He tensed when she stirred, her hand clenching in his. She would live, but she was going to be in pain for a while yet. Even the three days she had spent drifting in and out of consciousness would not be enough to have eased that pain by much. There would also be two ugly scars marring the ivory perfection of her skin. They did not make him desire her less, but each time he saw them, he would be starkly reminded of how easily he could lose her. He brought her small, soft hand up to his mouth and kissed her palm. When he looked at her face again, her eyes were open and clear.

"Is there much pain?" he asked as he moved to help

her sit up enough to drink some of the cider Kate had left by the bed. "The doctor left you some laudanum."

"I loathe that foul medicine," she said, alarmed at how the simple act of being lifted slightly and having a drink had left her panting and trembling with weakness. "Kate has a potion of herbs that works as well. Is she here?"

"No. She was here all night, and I sent her away for a while, to have a rest from being in this room watching you sleep." Hartley sat down again. "She stayed with you while the doctor tended your wound. I was requested by the doctor to tie her up and gag her until he had finished with you, but I declined."

"Telling him what to do, was she?"

"In some very colorful language. When the doctor ordered me out of the room, I left her there as my revenge. Do you want some of Kate's potion now?" he asked, hoping to divert her attention before she asked why the doctor had banned him from the room.

"Not yet. I will be fine for a little while. Why were you banned from the room? Were you also trying to tell him what to do?"

"No." It struck him as just his luck that now was the first time she remained sensible enough to recall everything he said, and question him. "I was thrown out because I tried to strangle him." He shrugged when she stared at him in shock. "You screamed. I acted. He was not pleased."

Alethea laughed and then winced at the twinge of pain it caused. "Poor man." Recalling all that had happened in the garden the evening she had been shot, she whispered, "He was going to kill Germaine."

"I know. She told us. At first I did not believe her, but there was no arguing her conviction." Hartley shook his head. "She did try to gain my attention earlier, but I paid no heed. We were all so sure this had been another attempt on you, that it was because you had not left or because Claudette had heard that we were married."

"You must learn to pay heed to Germaine. And Bayard. They are now much older than their years. Nor are they the children you remember from three years ago."

She was right. In his mind's eye, he still saw Germaine and Bayard as the young children who had left with their father over three years ago. Time and tragedy had put an end to the bright-eyed innocence they had carried that day. Hartley knew he had to learn to respect the maturity his niece and nephew had gained during their travails in France.

"I doubt we shall know everything that happened to them," he said.

"Probably not, but that might be for the best. It is done, and to hear of their fear or pain now would only make us angry and feel helpless to change what cannot be changed. Did you catch the man who shot me? It was the same man who beat me."

"I know, and I fear we will not, not after three days of hunting him down and finding no sign of him."

Alethea stared at Hartley, trying to force her mind to make sense of his words. Her shoulder was on fire, her body ached all over, and her head felt as if it was stuffed with wool. It was difficult to follow the conversation they were having, even more difficult to participate in it, but she had thought she was doing well enough. Yet she could have sworn that he had just said they had been hunting her assailant for three days. That made no sense at all.

"Three days?" she asked.

Hartley kissed her on the cheek. "Three days. You did not fall ill with fever, but you did hate to wake up. The times that you did so you were lucid, ate a little, drank a little, and spoke clearly. Then you would go to sleep again. I worried over it for a while but then decided it was simply your way of healing. And, perhaps, due to the potions Kate kept pouring down your throat. We moved you in here yesterday."

"That makes sense, I suppose. I just wish I could recall doing all of that. I might have said something wondrously profound, and now I shall never know." She smiled when he laughed.

"Kate will be here soon to help you clean up a little and change the linens. I will have to leave then to rejoin the hunt for the man who shot you. Pierre Leon is proving very elusive, but I am getting quite a bit of help from your family."

"Oh dear." She frowned as a memory flickered in her mind. "You told me that once, did you not?"

"On the night you were shot, right after the doctor left. You showed great sympathy for me." He kissed her on the nose when she grinned. "Chloe came once but is only a step away from birthing and now sends demands to know how you are faring. Lady Radmoor, Penelope, has wandered round a few times, but the last time she sat here with you her husband arrived and dragged her home, as she is also very large with a coming child. She has a herd of boys and young men with her, plus one little girl, and they now come round in clumps."

"Clumps?" Alethea badly wanted to laugh but held it back, knowing it would hurt.

"That is what it seems like. They are young but bring some added measure of safety to Germaine and Bayard simply by adding to the numbers always around them. And they are good company as well. There is also a solicitor and a tutor, Andras Vaughn and a Septimus Vaughn."

"Good Lord, the Wherlocke Warren crowd. Penelope is a viscountess now, if I recall correctly."

"Yes. I recalled the scandal the moment she said her name and began to introduce all those boys and the little girl. For a family that tries to stay within the shadows of the world, you appear to have a true skill at falling into some very public brangles. And then there is your cousin Sir Argus."

"Oh. I think he came up here. I saw him briefly and thought I was dreaming."

"Not at all. He stopped here to see how you fared for himself, and you told him he needed to trim his hair, that he looked like some damned poet."

This time Alethea could not stop her laughter. "Ouch! That hurts. Do not make me laugh. Poor Argus."

"Nonsense. He laughed so hard I was surprised that you just went back to sleep. Slapped me on the back as he left the room and said that Chloe was right—you would be fine." He frowned at Alethea. "Just how old is Argus?"

The question was so sudden and so apart from all they had talked about, it took Alethea a moment to grasp the answer. "Oh, I believe he recently turned thirty. Why?"

"Good God! The man has two sons, and the eldest is fifteen."

"Argus likes to say he was an early bloomer." She grinned at his shock and patted his hand. "He had little direction as a child, but take note that there are no more natural children after Olwen, who is eleven, I believe. He also takes good care of his boys and sees them whenever he can. For being no more than a child himself when he became a father, I think he does well by them."

"He does. He is also a very frightening man when he wants to be. We have been questioning Claudette's lovers, and I fear there has been one who now faces a possible charge of treason. He was not a fool—he was an ally. Others were just idiots, and Argus wants to be sure they are not put in a position where they can hear or see anything too important again. But we are not finding out much about where to look for Claudette."

"She has disappeared?"

"Her lodgings are not completely closed or cleared out, but she is nowhere to be found."

Alethea really wanted to keep discussing the hunt for Claudette, but she was glad when Kate stepped into the room. She heard her stomach grumble with welcome at the scent of soup and bread. Despite the pain she still felt, a warmth spread through her when he stood up and brushed his mouth over hers.

"I will return later," he said, "and, if you are awake, I shall regale you with how the hunting goes."

Alethea watched him go and then grimaced when Kate approached her with a determined look. Although Alethea detested needing help for the simple chore of relieving herself, she did not complain. The embarrassment she suffered was greatly eased by a wash with scented soap, a clean nightdress, and clean linens on the bed. She settled herself very carefully against the bank of pillows Kate had placed at her back, not wishing to jar her wound in even the smallest of ways.

"That man has spent many an hour by your bedside," said Kate as she started to feed Alethea a thin but tasty broth.

"He is a man who takes his duty seriously," Alethea said, but her heart skipped with hope,

"Pishposh. He could serve that duty well enough by coming in, looking you over quicklike, and then leaving. He sat here, read to you a bit, talked when you woke, even though you made little sense at times, and always fretted that you were in pain or had taken a fever. I was that worried for you when you married him, but not now."

"You were not worried," Alethea grumbled. "You were too busy matchmaking to be worried. And do not deny it. So how could you be worried when the marriage was the fruit of all your devious schemes? I had thought it was just the once, you know, but later realized that you were never near when he was, that you did your best to leave us alone."

"Humph, and just why could I not worry, I ask? I could have been wrong. 'Tis pleased I am that I am right as always."

Alethea dearly wanted to argue with Kate, but she was feeling very sleepy again. That worried her, but Kate assured her that she was improving every day, staying awake longer each time she woke up. As she closed her eyes, Alethea wished that Hartley were by her side. She had only shared a bed with the man for a few nights, but she missed his heat, missed the way he wrapped her in his strong arms. The return of that pleasure was a good reason to recover as soon as possible.

* * *

Hartley followed Aldus, Gifford, and Argus out of Sir Harold Birdwell's small townhouse. Watching Argus question the plump, balding man had been fascinating, but hearing the man convict himself with each word had been heartbreaking. The sound of a shot made him wince even though he was not surprised. What choice had the old fool left himself? At least this way, they could use what he had told them to stop any damage he might have done and leave his family without the taint of treason destroying their lives. He stopped and looked at Argus when the shouts and screams began inside the house.

"Best we go back in," said Argus.

"How could he have been so stupid?" muttered Gifford.

"I have come to the conclusion that men of a certain age can lose their minds for a little while," said Argus. "They do things they would never have done before, everything from leaving for a long journey to India or some other hot place that does not have good whiskey or taking a mistress half their age or turning to wild nights of gambling and lechery. I think they face their mortality suddenly, and it unhinges them. Old Birdwell believed he had bewitched and won a beautiful young woman, and as long as he gave her all she wanted, she would stay with him and keep his flagging manhood from flagging any further."

"How would you know if it was flagging?" asked Hartley, as reluctant to step back into the house as Argus appeared to be.

"That is the usual reason a man like him starts trotting after a young beautiful woman, especially one who has been a faithful husband and loving father for—what?—five and thirty years? It usually ends with a ruined marriage and strain between the father and children, not in turning traitor and ending your life with a bullet in the brain. Let us go back in. If naught else, we can assure the widow that she will not be suffering for his mistakes."

"You think Lady Birdwell knows?"

"The wives usually know most of what their husbands are up to."

"That is rather frightening," muttered Aldus as he marched up to the door and let himself in, forcing the others to follow.

As his friends and Argus moved to deal with the hysterical servants, Hartley walked over to Lady Birdwell. She was, by his figuring, at least five and fifty, but she was still a good-looking woman, a bit plump, with more gray than brown in her hair, but stylishly dressed and not too careworn. She stood in the doorway to Sir Harold's office, staring at the man slumped over his desk surrounded by gore-stained papers. There was no sign that she was weeping, and he wondered if she was in shock. He touched her arm, and she turned to glare at him.

"See what you have done?" she snapped. "He was just a foolish old man. Why could you not have let it go, left him alone?"

"My lady, I think you know exactly why he did this," Hartley began, seeing the knowledge in her tear-filled eyes.

"I know. He did it because *she* bewitched the old fool. Stupid, stupid man," she muttered, her voice shaking with the grief she tried to hold in. "I thought if I just ignored it, it would pass, that it was just a need he had to feel young again. Do we not all feel that need from time to time? But then I began to realize it was more, far more, and something that could destroy us. I tried to tell him so, but he would not listen to me. And now see how it has ended. I will lose it all, not just my husband."

"And why should you lose everything just because your husband had an accident cleaning his gun?" Hartley asked very softly, not wishing the servants to overhear him.

Lady Birdwell stared at him. "No one will believe that."

"They rarely do, but it stands. He has paid for his crimes. There is no need for you and your children to do so."

Finally, she wept, and Hartley pulled her into his arms. He held her until she gathered her strength and pulled away, wiping the tears from her face. She glanced around her to see the other men watching her, and all her servants sent on errands. After studying their somber faces for a minute she looked back at Hartley.

"And what will happen to her, to the one who made him do this?" she asked. "My poor Harold did a stupid thing, but he was not alone. He was led to this by that woman."

"We know," Hartley replied. "We are working to bring her to justice. I am sorry the path to that has caused you grief."

"That did not. Harold did. Is there anything I can do to help?"

"Let us in there to go through his papers."

"Should you not wait until they have removed him?" Even as she voiced the question, two footmen arrived with several blankets and performed that duty. "I need to tend to the body. Do as you like."

"Lady Birdwell, I sent your husband's secretary to

make certain that whatever money your husband had here or at the bank or in funds is protected," said Argus.

"She would take that, too?"

"She has before. It needs to all be secured before she gets word that your husband is dead." Argus kissed her hand. "I am most sincerely sorry for your pain, my lady."

"No, you have naught to apologize for." She sighed and looked toward the desk where her husband had ended his life. "The pain I feel now is for that foolish man. He betrayed our marriage, but he did not deserve such a punishment for that. And mayhap I feel some sorrow for the fact that there is no more chance for my husband and I to regain what was lost." She looked at the four men watching her. "In truth, I am indebted to you all, for this could have cost me everything and left my children scorned and penniless. Good hunting, my lords, and be sure to invite me to her hanging."

Hartley watched her leave, walking away to see to the cleansing of the body of a man who had betrayed her. "I hope no one minds that I have, more or less, promised to keep this silent."

"Not at all," said Argus. "The man's wife and children do not deserve to suffer for crimes they did not commit. I never have believed in taking everything a traitor owned when it meant his entire family was destroyed. Wives and children have no control over what the lord of the house does. Now, shall we get this distasteful chore put behind us?"

For nearly an hour they searched through Sir Harold's papers. Hartley carefully set aside the few things he felt might be helpful yet did not incriminate the man. A glance through the ledgers Birdwell had been working on when he and the others had arrived to talk to him told Hartley that the man had been spending lavishly on his mistress, Claudette.

"Aha!" Sir Argus held up a sheaf of papers. "Our fair viper got herself a new house out of the poor old fool. This may show why we found nothing of interest in her lodgings."

"I would not be surprised if the woman has several bolt-holes," said Hartley.

"Let us go and search this one."

After bidding a somber farewell to Lady Birdwell, and gaining assurances that they could return to search more thoroughly if they needed to, Hartley and the others climbed into the carriage and headed for the late Sir Harold's love nest. Hartley knew Birdwell was no completely innocent victim; the man could have resisted temptation. He certainly could have refused to pay for his delights with his country's secrets. Yet it was sad that Claudette had brought a good man down, caused him to pull away from his family, hurt them, and stain his own honor.

He looked at his companions and saw that they, too, brooded in silence. "At least his family will not suffer. Once his treason was known, there truly was no other way for him."

"True," agreed Aldus. "And this way his widow does not have to suffer the scorn or the poverty. It is still a dreadful, sobering matter. On the other hand, if we had spies as cold-blooded and cunning as this bitch, we would rule the world."

"At least the male part of it," drawled Gifford. "I think, however, the female half of the world would soon have all those Claudettes dead and roasting in hell. Mayhap we move too carefully."

"We do," said Hartley, "but we have to. She can flee the country all too easily. Even if we got word of her flight, she could still be waving at us from the deck of whatever fast-moving ship she boarded. Between the smuggling and the spying going on between us and France, there must be a dozen ships slipping in and out of each country's borders every day and night."

"I know. I just feel as if we put the gun in the old fool's hand."

"Claudette did, and so did he. He broke his marriage vows, as many of our class do, but that does not excuse him for pleasing his lady love by handing over important shipping information."

"Many good men died because of that," said Argus, revealing by the tone of his voice that he had little sympathy for Sir Harold. "Alone and at sea, and with no wife to cleanse their bodies and give them a decent burial. And, now, there is the fine love nest he gifted Claudette with. I doubt we will find her there."

As the carriage stopped and they all climbed out, Hartley said, "Then we must hope that she had to flee so quickly she left something of importance and interest behind."

Argus just grunted and, without pausing to knock, let himself into the house. The hall was filled with servants who had obviously been busy stripping the house of anything valuable. It did not take long to get them all rounded up and secured. Leaving Argus to question them and Aldus to make sure that all the valuables were retrieved from the bags and trunks littering the foyer, Hartley and Gifford began to search the house.

It did not take much longer to realize that there were no incriminating papers left behind. A few half-burned letters added a few names to the list of people they needed to question, but there was little else. Hartley walked into the bedroom the lovers had obviously chosen for their own and grimaced. It looked and smelled like a bordello.

"My Ellen would cringe if she saw this," said Gifford.

"Your mistress has exquisite taste," said Hartley as he searched the clutter on the dressing table. "Except in her choice of protectors."

"So kind." Gifford sighed and began to search the bed. "Appalling as this is, it must have cost Birdwell a small fortune."

"She left in a hurry," Hartley said as he viewed the mess in her dressing room. "I doubt she has been gone very long."

"How could she know about Birdwell so quickly?"

"Had a servant in her pay, I suspect. Whoever it was probably ran here before the smoke from the gunshot had even cleared away. Mayhap ran to her when he heard we were questioning Birdwell." He sighed as he took a final look around the room. "I was hoping to find some jewelry. Some piece of what she stole from the compte and his wife would have been a very nice prize."

"Well, she missed one piece of her jewelry. Mayhap this will help."

Hartley looked at the ruby earring Gifford held up, and his heart skipped a beat. Grief pinched at him as he took the earring from Gifford. He could see his sister wearing the pair of ruby drops, smiling with pleasure over the gift her husband had given her on the birth of their son. He clutched it tightly in his hand, silently promising his sister that he would make the woman pay for what she had done.

"It was Margaret's," he said. "De Laceaux gave the pair to her when Bayard was born."

"With Germaine's testimony that she saw Claudette take the jewels, it should provide a nail in the bitch's coffin."

"It will help. We still have to catch her, though."

It was almost dawn by the time they sent the servants away and secured the house. Hartley was exhausted as he made his home and up to his bedchamber. He stood beside the bed, stared at the empty expanse, and then turned to go to Alethea. She woke even as he entered the room. Kate slept on a cot in the corner, and he made his way silently to the bedside.

He kissed her and savored both the passion and the peace the caress filled him with. Sitting by her side on the bed, he held up the ruby earring. She stared at it and then looked at him, the knowledge of what it was in her eyes.

"Do you want me to see if it tells me anything?" she asked.

"No. Mayhap later, if we continue to have trouble finding her. I recall all too well what touching something else the woman had held did to you and would prefer that you do not have to go through that again."

"It is proof that she was there that day on the beach, is it not?"

"It is, and it might be enough if we catch her. I want more, though. I want proof that she killed Rogers and Peterson, proof that she works for our enemies. I want every black deed she has committed to be known and have her condemned for all of them. I want all her allies to hang with her. However, if this is all we have when we find her, I will use it."

"Will you tell Germaine?"

"Not yet." He yawned and then stood up. "I would very much like to stay with you, to crawl beneath the covers with you and hold you, to let your sweetness wash away the ugliness we saw tonight." He told her about Birdwell.

"That poor woman. I am glad you let it end as it did. She does not deserve to pay so dearly for her husband's idiocy. If it was known what he had done, she would lose everything."

"Yes. I just hope that we stopped Claudette from being able to take what was left."

"Come to bed, Hartley."

"No. You are still too wounded to have a hulking great man in your bed." He kissed her again. "Soon, though. Sleep well, love."

She watched him leave and sighed. This was hard on him, and she was useless to help. That would end soon, however. Alethea was determined to get out of her sickbed as soon as possible. She needed to be there for him when he failed and when he finally won. Everything inside her told her that, although the chase was going to be a long one and danger was ever present, Hartley would win. As she snuggled down beneath the covers, she prayed that that was a true knowing and not just wishful thinking.

Chapter 14

"Oh! Foul, I say! Foul!"

Alethea laughed as she watched Germaine swing her racket at a laughing Bayard, who easily dodged it. Four of her cousins were also in the garden, and they hooted with laughter as Germaine chased Bayard around. Two were Penelope's half brothers—Artemis, who was eighteen, and Stefan, who was sixteen, both much closer to being men than boys. The other two were Argus's natural sons, the fifteen-year-old Darius, and Olwen, who was just eleven. She knew they gathered here to help in protecting Germaine and Bayard, to ensure that there were plenty of eyes searching for a threat as well as many voices to cry out for help if it was needed. Armed men stood guard elsewhere. She also knew that many of her relatives helped in the hunt for the man who shot her, as well as for Claudette and her sister. Yet the presence of the boys also helped Bayard and Germaine reclaim a little of their lost childhood.

It all should have comforted her, and it did, but it also made her feel like a prisoner in her new home. Alethea also missed Hartley. He was always gone,

trying to hunt down their enemies or find more proof
to send Claudette and her allies to the gallows. For
eighteen long nights she had slept alone. The doctor had
removed the stitches from her wound only yesterday,
the wound an ugly scar but firmly closed. Yet she slept
alone last night—again.

No matter how often she scolded herself for need-
lessly worrying, Alethea couldn't stop herself from
wondering if Hartley would ever return to her bed. He
might even be waiting to see if she was already carrying his child, that he had only come to her bed to breed
one. With each new reason she conjured up for why her
new husband was not sharing a bed with her, Alethea's
spirits sank lower.

"Stop it."

That deep, sharp voice startled her out of her increasingly melancholy thoughts, and Alethea looked
up to find Artemis glaring down at her. He stood like a
challenging warrior, with his feet apart and his arms
crossed over his chest. She started to ask him what he
wanted her to stop and then recalled that he was extremely empathic.

"I beg your pardon," she said, fighting to subdue a
blush. "I was just thinking."

"Very loudly. I do not usually sense one of our blood,
so you had let your shields down." He sat down next
to her. "What were you thinking about? Why your
husband is not here?"

Alethea frowned at him. "You do not have Modred's
gift, do you?"

"God save me, no. 'Tis not difficult, however, to discern one type of happiness from another. Having lived
through Penelope's romance with Radmoor, her bouts

of thinking herself unworthy, cast aside, unlovable, and so on"—he waved one long-fingered, elegant hand in the air to imply that the *so on* was infinite—"I recognized your increasing sadness as similar to hers."

"Oh." This time there was no controlling her blush. "It matters not. Foolishness, that is all."

"It certainly is foolishness—unless, of course, you think he is setting up a mistress, or three."

"Three?" Artemis just cocked an eyebrow at her, and Alethea decided not to question that any further. "No, Hartley swore that he would be faithful, that he believed in holding to vows spoken. Said that was why he had never sought out a wife before now despite needing an heir."

"Good man. Could be exactly why he did not marry years ago as so many others would have. Last of his line and all. Can make a man take whatever he can just to breed that all-important heir. Had to be very certain in his choice. At least most reasonable people would see that clearly enough."

Alethea crossed her arms and scowled at him. "You are a wretch. I am astonished that Penelope has not been driven to beat you daily." He laughed, and it was such a contagious sound, she joined him.

"Be at ease, Cousin," Artemis said. "Do not borrow trouble. The man swears fealty and has chosen you above all others after having enjoyed so many rakish years. That is no idle thing."

"I know. 'Tis just that I am but a newlywed, and my honeymoon ended after only two nights."

"And you want him to love you as you love him." He grinned and kissed her on the cheek when she growled at him. "Do not chew over that bone for too long.

Consider what he does, Cousin, not what he does or does not say. Men can be idiots at times, not even realizing that words are needed."

She watched him rejoin the others and sighed. It was no great surprise that such a young man would know all about emotions and how they could twist a person's heart and mind. He was an empath and, apparently, a very strong and precise one if he could differentiate between one sort of sadness and another. Artemis was also surprisingly wise for such a young man. She should heed all he had said, but feared she would not. Emotions could wreak havoc on wisdom.

No, it was not wise words she needed to soothe her fears. She needed Hartley back in her bed, in her arms, in her body. She was healed. Despite all her stuttering and blushing, the doctor had understood her query after her stitches were removed and had declared her ready to take up her marital duties again. Alethea just had to think of a way to make Hartley understand that.

Hartley wanted to hit something or someone. He was not particular. He wanted to hurl himself into a street brawl, fists flying. Eighteen days had passed since Alethea had been shot and since someone had tried to kill his niece. Yet he had nothing. No proof save for one small ruby earring. A name and a picture but still no criminal. It was frustrating beyond words. They had Alethea's sketches, and they had the name of her assailant, but no one would admit to knowing the man.

He stood outside yet another low tavern with Aldus, waiting for Argus to arrive. They needed his strange skill at making people talk. Whoever the man was who had attacked Alethea, he was deeply feared by the denizens of London's criminal warrens. That much Hartley had discerned. There was a chance that no one in this tavern really knew the man, but the chance that no one in any of the many taverns they had entered had ever heard of or seen him was very slim.

Even worse, they had lost two more of the men on the list of Claudette's lovers. One young Sir John Talbot had been stabbed in a brothel, and another had apparently fled the country. Hartley wondered about the murder, wondered if Claudette had discovered how they were questioning all her lovers and had decided to get rid of them. It might be time to warn the men as well as question them.

He also wanted to go home. It was getting dark, and Hartley did not wish to spend another night hunting their quarry. He wanted to spend it making love to his new wife. His whole body ached for her. He would wake in the night and spend far too long fighting the urge to go to her bed or drag her into his. She was healed now, and he would not sleep alone for another night. Nor, he thought as he watched two men swagger into a brothel on the other side of the street, would he spend another whole night roaming the rat-infested areas of the city.

"I think we need to sit back and look at what we already have," said Aldus as Argus's carriage pulled up. "We have been working at this night and day and may need to just step back, take a breath, and study what we do have."

"That would suit me," said Hartley. "We will have Argus talk to these fools in here and then go home. I would like to spend a night with my new wife."

"Ah, newlyweds," drawled Argus as he walked by

and headed into the tavern. "Such heat, such neediness, such constant pining for each other. Love is in the air. I do believe I feel a little nauseous."

Hartley shook his head and followed the man inside, a chuckling Aldus at his heels. Once they had found a table and ordered some ale, he watched Argus work his magic. It took two long hours to garner anything of importance, and it was not much. Even Argus looked disgruntled.

"Perhaps we are looking in the wrong places," Hartley said as they left the tavern.

"For a hired killer?" Argus frowned. "This is where they usually linger, waiting for someone too cowardly to do their own dirty work to hire them. And this is the time those who want to be hired begin to gather. Sun starts to go down, and the sewer rats start to creep out."

"This man dressed better and spoke better than anyone here. Alethea said he had a hint of an accent one might associate with men such as this, and he needed a bath." He exchanged a brief grin with the other two men. "Yet why could he not be low gentry, or someone she has blackmailed into doing this work for her?"

"Or someone who just enjoys doing such work," murmured Argus. "Someone who is just a little higher than these dregs. Killing can be a profitable business. He may be trying to rise up in the ranks, so to speak."

"Well, 'tis evident that no one here knows him. You got a hint, a nibble, but no more. So, at best he has wandered through here, but he is no longer a part of this lot."

Climbing into the carriage after telling the driver to take them to Iago's, Argus sat on the seat opposite Hartley and Aldus and rubbed his chin. "I believe I need to more carefully study the list of her lovers."

"You think she may have found one among them who is willing to do her killing for her. I saw no Pierre Leon on the list."

"The person we got the name from might not have the right one. As for one of her lovers? Quite possible. Especially if the price was right. And we must consider the chance that Leon has already paid the ultimate price for his failure that night in the garden, so she will need another killer."

Hartley swore. "Quite possibly, thus sending us on yet another wild-goose chase. I also wondered if Sir John Talbot's death was what everyone thinks it was."

"You think it might have been murder ordered and not done in the heat of the moment?"

"Why not? The woman prefers all witnesses or potential ones to be silenced permanently."

"A good point. I think we need to step back and look at all we have discovered so far."

"Aldus just spoke of the same thing."

"If Aldus is willing, he and I will carefully examine the list of her lovers and see if there might be something there. I also have obtained a dossier on her family. We can study that as well."

"Family," Aldus muttered. "Was not Pierre her family? It might be that we need to cross him off that list. What of Margarite?"

"I doubt she is the killer," said Hartley. "Alethea was positive it was a man, and the name of the man she drew was Pierre."

Aldus waved Hartley's words aside with a sharp slash of his hand. "I did not mean that she was the killer, but where is she? Mayhap she is the one who hired the man or saw to it that Sir John Talbot was silenced.

She has to be an intricate part of it all or she would not have disappeared, too."

Argus rubbed his hands over his face. "Hartley, go home before your wife forgets what you look like. Let us all get a good meal and a good night's rest and then study what little information we have. We are running in circles right now, and it clutters up our minds."

Hartley had no objection to that plan and felt his heart lighten as Argus told his driver to stop at Hartley's home first. Despite his eagerness to find Claudette and the man who shot Alethea, he needed to step back. He needed to think of something aside from where to look next or whom to question. He needed Alethea.

Alethea heard the library door open and panicked. She shoved the book she had been reading behind her and looked toward the door. Germaine and Bayard walked in, and Alethea had to fight hard not to blush. The very last thing she wanted these two to know was that she had been reading a very salacious tome she had found in Hartley's library and to explain why she had been doing so.

"Here you are," said Germaine, grinning as she sat next to Alethea on the plush settee.

"Why, yes, here I am," Alethea replied and hoped her voice did not hold any hint of how guilty, embarrassed, and nervous she felt. "Is there something you want?"

"My dressmaker is arriving to do some final fittings in a short while, and I wondered if you could abide being there, to offer advice and all. I do not want her to make my gowns too risqué. So—will you join us?"

"Is it not a little late in the day for that?"

"She is stopping here after closing her shop so that she can take the final fittings and get straight to work. It troubles her greatly that I have no gowns."

"Of course. I will come up as soon as she arrives."

"That will be in a few minutes," said Bayard as he studied his uncle's collection of books. "Germaine has a strange idea of what a short while really is. Quite often, she means immediately."

There was no way she could stand up without revealing what she had been reading. Alethea sat and stared at Germaine, trying and failing to think of a reason why she was not getting right up to go and do as she had just promised. She should have locked the door, she thought despairingly.

Just as she was going to make an excuse as to why she could not go immediately, hoping that it would not sound too inane, Germaine jumped up, grabbed her by the hand, and pulled her to her feet. The book fell to the seat of the settee with a soft thud. To Alethea it sounded like a clap of thunder. She yanked her hand free of Germaine's to grab for the book before either she or Bayard could see it, but Germaine was quicker. A blush spread over Alethea's face as Germaine looked at the book and her eyes slowly widened.

"Well, what have we here?" Germaine said and started to grin.

"Wretched girl, give me that."

Alethea tried to snatch the book out of Germaine's hands, but the girl danced out of her reach and over to her brother's side. Her blush grew even hotter when Bayard looked at it and grinned. She wished a hole would open in the floor and swallow her up. There was no way to explain this without sounding like a fool—or, worse, a lovesick fool who was desperate enough to try and use the sins of the flesh to make her husband love her.

"Oh, Alethea, you do not need this," said Germaine as she returned to Alethea's side and kissed her on the cheek.

"No?" she snatched the book out of Germaine's hands. "Do you not recall your uncle's reputation? A rake, lots of beautiful, experienced women." She sighed. "I just thought I might learn something, but this book is full of things I do not believe the human body is capable of." She had to smile when Bayard started laughing so hard he collapsed into a chair.

"These books are written solely to amuse men. They are not instruction manuals," said Germaine.

"What are not instruction manuals?"

Alethea shoved the book behind her and stared at Hartley in horror. A quick glance showed her that Germaine and Bayard were not as disconcerted as she was. In truth, they looked like they wanted to start laughing again. Although she loved to hear that sound of happiness, it was not so enjoyable when it was at her expense.

"Just a book we were discussing." Germaine grabbed a grinning Bayard by the hand and started to drag him out of the room. "If you have a moment, Alethea, I would not mind having your opinion."

Escape, she thought, and started toward the door. "Of course, I am coming."

"What? No hello for your husband?"

Hartley caught her by the arm and pulled her close, then kicked the library door shut behind his niece and nephew with his foot. Alethea stared up at his handsome face and heard the siblings' laughter fade as they skipped away free. He was staring at the door, a pleased look on his face, and she knew she had only one chance. If she could get the book to the floor without making too much noise, she could kick it under a chair. Her brilliant plan failed immediately. The book landed with a soft thud, but her husband had good hearing.

"You dropped your book, Al—" Hartley stared at the book he held. "Where did this come from?"

"Top shelf, left side, third book in."

He idly looked through the book, and realized it had been his brother's. It was filled with colorful drawings of sexual positions, exaggerated male organs, and supine women who seemed to smile no matter what was done to them. He then looked at his blushing wife and slowly grinned.

"Catching up on your reading?"

She blushed even more and grabbed for the book, but he easily kept it out of her reach. He stopped at one page, and despite how ludicrous he found the drawing to be, the position shown had his mind filling with ideas. In fact, the longer he looked at it, the more he could see himself and Alethea in the picture. His body now clamoring for her, he tossed the book onto the settee, and caught her by the hand.

"Hartley?" she asked softly as he led her to the big desk in the corner, pausing only to lock the door as he passed it.

"I am now intrigued." He picked her up and sat her on top of the desk.

"Oh, no, there is no need, I was just curious," she began.

"So am I."

His mouth stopped any further protest. Alethea wrapped her arms around his neck as his kiss roused the desire that had been unsatisfied for far too long. She was so drugged by his kiss that she made no protest at all when he pulled off the fine French drawers she wore. The way he stroked her legs had her trembling with need for him.

He tugged down the top of her gown and feasted on her breast, sending her passion soaring. Alethea twitched only briefly when his fingers touched the aching spot between her legs. Those same clever fingers soon had her arching into his touch.

Hartley savored her wet heat, the proof of her readiness. He pulled her to her feet, turned her around, and gently bent her over the desk. Pushing up her skirts, her looked at her taut, well-rounded bottom, and nearly tore the front flap of his breeches in his haste to open them. It had been a long time since he had taken a woman this way.

Alethea came out of her daze enough to wonder what Hartley was doing. Cool air on her backside roused her a little more. Before she could ask what he planned to do, he did it. She gasped in both pleasure and surprise when he entered from behind. She had the brief thought that this was how animals did it, and then his fingers reached around to stroke the front of her mons as he thrust in and out from behind. Alethea gripped the edges of the desk to steady herself and lost all interest in whether or not it was proper for a wife to let her husband make love to her like this.

It was rough, and fast. Hartley felt her body tighten around him, felt the ripples of her climax stroke him, and had to bite his lip to keep from roaring as his release tore through him. It was not until he was flopped onto his wife's back, panting, that he had the thought that she might not like being treated in such a way. Women had some of their own ideas about what was acceptable behavior between a man and his wife. Taking her from behind as she was sprawled on the desk in his library was probably not one of those ways.

He carefully eased out of her and tugged her skirts down. Bracing himself for a show of feminine horror and disgust, he turned her around and looked at her. She pushed her hair off her face and smiled at him. Hartley breathed a sigh of relief.

"Was that a good enough hello?" she said.

Hartley laughed and picked up her fine lace pantalets. Just as he was about to offer to help her put them back on, there was a rap at the door. He grinned even more when Alethea turned bright red and hid her pantalets behind her back.

"M'lord?" called Cobb. "Lord Covington asks to see you immediately."

Muttering a curse, Hartley started to ward the door. A soft rustling behind him told him that his wife was donning what little clothing he had managed to take off her. He slowly unlocked the door to give her time to right herself, and then opened it to scowl at Cobb.

"Did he say what he wanted?" he asked.

"His lordship said they had some word of Pierre Leon."

"Tell him I will be there in a few minutes."

Hartley turned to look at his wife. She was attempting to tidy her hair and blushing. He wanted to stay with her. Wanted to take her to bed and try a few more of those positions in that book, at least the ones that looked as if they could be done without hurting himself.

"I had intended to stay in tonight," he said.

Alethea walked over and kissed him lightly on the mouth. "This will end soon."

He hugged her close and rested his chin on the top of her head. "Have you seen that?"

"No, I am just certain. It will end soon. Go and see what he wants. I will go and make sure the dressmaker remembers that Germaine is a young maid who has not even had a season yet."

He laughed softly, kissed her, and hurried off to see what Aldus wanted. Alethea sighed and went to put the book away. When he had arrived she had hoped for an evening and a full night together. Instead she had had barely any time at all with Hartley. Glancing at the desk, she almost smiled. It may have been a short time together, but he had certainly put it to good use. He still desired her, and that would have to be enough for now.

The next time he was home, however, she was going to seduce him. He had done little more than chase after Claudette and seek proof of her crimes. It was time he took a night off from that. She intended to make it a very long and pleasurable night as well. And if she had to talk to all his compatriots to see that he got that night off, she would, no matter how embarrassing it might be.

She hurried up to the room where the dressmaker was making some final alterations to Germaine's wardrobe. There was still time to offer her opinions. Alethea took one step into the room, looked at Germaine, who was standing still while the dressmaker adjusted a soft green gown, and nearly gasped. She was definitely needed here, she thought as she marched over and demanded to know what had happened to the bodice of the gown.

Hartley grimaced as he looked at what was left of Pierre Leon. It took a long, hard look simply to see that he had died from having his throat cut. The mudlarks that roamed the edges of the river for a living had found the body, but not before the fish had.

"I cannot believe I gave up a night with Alethea for this," he muttered.

Argus grunted as he stood up from searching the corpse. "His pockets were cleaned out." He looked at the burly man who had claimed to have discovered the body. "Were the pockets empty when you found the body?"

Hartley started to say that such a man would have naturally cleaned out Pierre's pockets and, as soon as they left, would take all the man's clothing as well, but then he saw how the man's eyes had glazed over. Argus would get the truth.

"Had some coin and a few papers," the man answered.

"Where are the papers?"

"Here." The man pulled an oilskin packet out of his patched coat and handed it to Argus. "I thought they might be worth something since they were all wrapped up safe like."

"Yes, they are worth something, but not to you."

The moment Argus released the man's gaze, he blinked and then stared at what Argus held. "Here now, where'd you get that?"

"You gave it to me." Argus handed the man some money. "Do with the body as you want. It is of no interest to us."

"Do you think Claudette had him killed?" asked Hartley as they walked back to their carriage.

"If she did, she may have made a serious error. That fool was right to say that a man does not wrap up papers this carefully unless they are important. We are going to have to study these."

Hartley looked at the thick packet and sighed. There would be no spending a long, passionate night with Alethea tonight. He would be lucky to get home before dawn.

Chapter 15

"Margarite has similar tastes to her sister," Gifford said as they entered the woman's townhouse and looked around.

Hartley had to agree. They had held back in searching Margarite's home, for she had still been easy to follow. Alarming her with a search, stirring up her small cadre of powerful lovers, would have gained them nothing. From all they had observed while watching the sisters, Margarite was the follower, the ally. He had no doubt that she was the sister Chloe had referred to when she talked of one of the sisters being weaker. Unfortunately all they had thus far was a dead guard that had been watching the house for them and no Margarite. And one could not even prove that Margarite had anything to do with the dead guard.

Argus frowned. "They know how to get money but not how to spend it wisely. A few more bedrooms and this could be a proper whorehouse."

Hartley had to agree. For two women who had made a place for themselves in the rarified echelons of society, their taste in furnishings was appalling. What he did notice, however, was that the place had not been stripped bare by the servants.

"Either Margarite paid her servants well," he said, "or she let them all go before she fled this house."

"I would say they were gone before she fled," said Aldus as he started opening doors. "An owner flees in the night because of debt or legal difficulties, and the servants will always help themselves to things before they also leave. Mostly because they have been badly treated or not paid. Something tells me this woman would not treat her servants kindly."

"Then she is thinking she will be able to return."

"Possibly." Argus wiped his finger over a table just inside the door to a parlour done all in various shades of blue and stared at the dust on his fingertip. "She let the servants go before she felt the need to run and hide. Nothing has been done here in days, and I do not see the woman you have all described to me as one to allow her servants to be anything else but extremely diligent."

"And I suspect she took the time then to be rid of anything that might incriminate her." Hartley kicked the garish settee before sitting down. "They have not yet fled the country. At the moment, Margarite does not have to, even though it would be wise if she put as much distance between herself and her sister as possible. Those papers we found may be helpful, but they are in code, and decoding them will take time. Two more of Claudette's lovers have been attacked. Both will survive, but one may never walk right again. They are cleaning up behind them."

"And very well, too. Do we have a list of Margarite's

lovers?" asked Argus as he searched through a little desk set in the corner of the room.

"Yes, and one of them is Iago." He nodded when Argus looked at him in shock and a touch of alarm. "He had an extremely brief affair with the woman. As he puts it, once his blind lust eased he could not abide to touch her. Something about sensing that she was cold or dark. Had the soul of a cold-blooded killer. You will have to talk to him. You will probably understand what he means better than I."

"That could prove awkward if we ever catch the woman and she is tried and convicted."

"No, I do not think so. He was but a small fish in a very big pond. He also has no connection to any branch of government or access to any information. I believe he was just a handsome young man she decided she wanted. Or, she was searching for a new husband."

"God help us."

"How shall we divide up the search, then?" Hartley asked as he stood up.

"There is no need for you to stay this time. The three of us can search. I believe we will come up empty-handed again."

Hartley opened his mouth to insist on doing his part and then thought of Alethea. He had not gotten home until dawn and been too tired to do more than kiss her and fall asleep at her side. By the time he had woken up, she had been gone, and Argus and the others had been waiting for him. He was a newlywed, and he wanted to act like one if only for one day.

"Are you sure?" he asked.

"Very sure. Iago will no doubt join us soon." Argus looked around. "The thought of him and that woman in this house doing . . ." He gave an exaggerated shudder and then looked back at Hartley. "Why are you still here? Go spend some time with your wife and those children."

Hartley did not hesitate any longer. "Do not come after me unless you find one of them," he said as he grabbed his coat and left.

Hartley handed his horse's reins to his stable boy and nearly ran into his house. He knew he ought to feel guilty about leaving the others to do the tedious work of searching Margarite's house, but he did not. His marriage was nearly three weeks old, and he had spent only three of those nights sleeping with his wife. He did not count last night, as it was a brief one and he had only slept. Tonight he intended to spend a long, luxurious night making love to his wife. He almost considered starting now, but decided the middle of the afternoon was not a good time and he needed to spend some time with Germaine and Bayard.

His spirits high, he went in search of his wife. He found her in the drawing room, but his first sight of her did not cheer him at all. She was in the arms of another man. Hartley saw red, and, his fists clenched tight, he took a step toward the couple only to be brought up short by a firm grasp on his arm. He looked at the woman stopping him from pounding the interloper into the ground.

"I would appreciate it if you did not kill the duke," the woman said.

"The duke?" Hartley frowned. "Which duke?"

"The Duke of Elderwood."

It took a moment for the rage clouding his mind to clear enough for him to recognize the name. "Modred. Her cousin. And you are?"

"Olympia Wherlocke—another cousin."

Hartley took a deep breath to restore his calm and bowed to the woman. She was tall, voluptuous, and quite beautiful. Lady Wherlocke was the sort of woman he would have been trying to seduce in the days when he played the rake. With her raven black hair and bright blue eyes, she was a woman any man would lust after. Instead, all his thoughts were on his wife, who had not even noticed he was home yet.

"Modred," Olympia called. "Come and meet Alethea's husband."

Alethea looked over Modred's shoulder, saw Hartley, and smiled. She kissed her cousin on the cheek and then rushed over to greet Hartley. He stood a little stiffly as she slipped her arm around his waist, and she wondered what was troubling him. But then Modred stepped up to introduce himself. She watched closely as Modred and Hartley exchanged names and bows. There was no sign on her cousin's face that he felt anything at all as he stood but a foot away from her husband, and Alethea breathed a sigh of relief. She had feared that Modred would be able to see into Hartley too easily, and then they would never have been able to be the haven for the duke that she had hoped they could be.

"Good shields?" she asked her cousin.

"Excellent ones," Modred replied and smiled.

Hartley looked at the young man smiling at him. The young duke was extraordinarily handsome, with thick black hair and sea green eyes. When he had been told about how close this man was to Alethea, he had not considered the possibility that the reclusive duke would be the type of man who could have any women he wanted with just a smile. Hartley looked down at his smiling wife and tried not to be jealous. This man was part of her family.

"What do you mean by good shields?" he asked.

"You have some very sturdy walls, m'lord," Modred replied. "I feel nothing from you except for a hint of irritation. It is so faint, however, that I might well be reading that on your face. Have we come at an inconvenient time? We could go and stay at the Warren if you cannot house us at this time."

"No, of course not. You and Lady Wherlocke are welcome to stay here, Your Grace."

"Please, call me Modred. We are family, after all."

"Of course, and you must call me Hartley." He glanced at the woman.

"And you must call me Lady Wherlocke," she said haughtily and then laughed when both Alethea and Modred scowled at her. "Call me Olympia, please, Hartley."

As soon as Hartley had seen the guests shown to their rooms, he dragged his wife into his small office and shut the door. "You did not tell me your cousin the duke was a young, handsome man."

"What does that matter?" Alethea asked.

"It matters when I come home and see you hugging him."

She bit back a smile. He was jealous. She wanted to dance around the room at this sign that he might be coming to care for her more deeply than he had spoken of in his proposal.

"Hartley, Modred can touch very few people. He—well—just imagine if you had to be careful with everyone, always wear gloves, and never get too close. When he is with family, he can feed the need everyone has to touch someone, to hug someone he cares about."

He sighed and pulled her into his arms. "Perhaps he can be a little less effusive with my wife until I get used to him."

She laughed and kissed him. When he pulled her hard against him and returned the kiss with a hunger that rapidly stirred her own, Alethea moaned softly. He smoothed his hands down her back until he got a firm grip on her backside. She shifted against his hard length, and he pressed it against her, aching to have him inside her.

"Uncle? Are you in there?" Germaine called, rapping at the door.

Hartley groaned and pressed his forehead against Alethea's as he struggled to tamp down the need clawing at his insides. "Yes, I will be with you in a moment."

"We will be in the parlor with Modred and Olympia."

He looked at Alethea and sighed as the haze of desire faded from her eyes. "When this is all over, we are going away, just the two of us, and have a damned honeymoon."

"That would be lovely," she said and stepped back from him to brush smooth her gown. "But for now, I can see that life intrudes, and we best get back to it."

Humming softly to herself, Alethea arranged the flowers she had placed on the table near the fireplace.

She had slipped away from the others so that she could
prepare the bedchamber. The evening had been wonderful, with so many of her family stopping in to see
Modred, but the visits had finally ended, and it would
soon be time for her and Hartley to be alone. She
wanted the bedchamber to be perfect for a night of love
with her husband.

"Well, it certainly sounds as if you are happy."

Alethea glanced over her shoulder and smiled at
Olympia, who stood in the doorway. She had sensed
Olympia weighing and judging Hartley all evening
long, but was not worried. Hartley had all that was
needed to win the cynical Olympia's acceptance, although she knew her cousin would be slow to fully
admit that.

"Yes, I am very happy. Were you concerned?" she
asked as she placed a few candles on the little chest
next to the bed.

"Well, your first husband was a disaster."

"He was that, but Hartley is nothing like Channing.
Hartley has all the emotion Channing lacked—he just
does not always realize it."

"You love him."

"Yes, I do. Very much. Is it not a good thing for a
wife to love her husband?"

"Yes, if he loves her back."

Alethea sighed and sat down on the edge of the bed.
"He likes me, wants me, and trusts me. That may not
sound like much, but I believe it is a lot. He also accepts
who I am, what I can do, and my family."

Olympia sat down next to her. "Which are all very
good things, no arguing that. He seems to like Modred.
That is no small thing, either. Nor is the fact that

Modred says Hartley, his niece, and his nephew all have very strong walls. He is down there now thoroughly enjoying himself, and it lightens my heart. Of course, he almost found himself tossed out a window when your husband first came home."

"I know. Hartley was jealous." Alethea smiled. "I see that as progress."

"Toward winning his heart?"

"Yes. That is the prize I seek—a return for the love I have for him. Do you think I ask too much?"

"Not at all, and I am sure you will soon gain what you want."

"Have you seen it?" Alethea could not keep all of her hope out of her voice.

"A little. I do not fully trust what I see when it concerns family, especially ones I am close to, however."

"Because it could be wishful thinking."

"Exactly. Yet, I do see no clouds upon your horizon. Not concerning Hartley, anyway."

"Good. That well satisfies me for now."

Olympia kissed her on the cheek. "I best continue on my way to bed so that you can finish setting the stage for seduction. Tomorrow we can discuss your troubles."

Alethea hugged her cousin, and, as soon as the woman left, she hurried off to her bath. She wanted to be clean and sweet-smelling when Hartley finally joined her.

Hartley collected up the cards and smiled at Modred. They were the only ones still up, and Hartley had every intention of making his way to bed soon. His jealousy had faded with every hour spent in the duke's company.

Modred Wherlocke was a good man, with a heavy burden, and not just that of the gift that was more of a curse. He was head of a large, gifted, and somewhat eccentric family, many of whom had stopped in to welcome him to London.

"I have enjoyed our game, Modred, but I intend to go to my wife now." He hid his surprise when the younger man blushed faintly.

"You will be good to her, will you not?" Modred asked.

"Always."

Modred smiled. "I had hoped to be able to, well, read you a little to reassure myself, but you, Germaine, and Bayard have very strong walls. 'Tis just that Alethea needs someone who cares for her. Her brothers do, but they are rarely home, and Alethea needs a home, a real home, not just a roof over her head."

"She has one. She also has someone who cares for her now. Do not fear for her heart, as I have no intention of breaking it. As soon as these troubles plaguing us are gone, I mean to give my marriage my full attention."

"Fair enough. As for these troubles that were spoken of tonight, you must let me help."

"These are particularly evil women, Modred. If they do not have strong walls, you could find yourself seeing a lot of ugliness."

"It does not matter. I must help. Not only is it my duty as head of the family, but as Alethea's friend."

"As you wish, but do not feel you must continue if it becomes too much. Duty does not require you to torture yourself. Now, good night. You are good company, my friend, but I want my wife."

He left, Modred's soft laughter following him.

Hartley could almost pity the young duke were it not for the huge, supportive, and sometimes loving family the man had. And yet, for all he was head of a huge family, a duke, young, rich, and unsettlingly handsome, Hartley did not need any special gift to know that the man was alone and, worse, lonely.

He was still puzzling over Modred as he entered his dressing room, set between the two bedchambers he and Alethea had been using as she had recovered from her wound, and dismissed his valet, Dennison. They would soon have only one, he decided as he shed his clothes and washed up. Donning his robe, he made his way into the room Alethea was currently using.

All thought of Modred fled Hartley's mind as he entered the bedchamber where his wife waited for him. The scent of wildflowers and expensive spices filled the air. He looked around at the flowers and candles crowding the room and then looked at Alethea. She sat cross-legged on their bed, wearing what he supposed was a robe although it certainly provided no warmth or modesty. He could see her nipples through the lacy bodice, and his body immediately hardened in response. The sight of her glorious hair hanging down to her waist, its thick waves struggling to hide all that the robe displayed, only added to his hunger for her.

"This took planning," he said as he walked to the side of the bed after firmly latching the door behind him.

"Some," she replied. "Not very much, though."

"You asked Argus to send me home." His guess was confirmed by the way she blushed, and he sighed dramatically. "Am I doomed to be under the cat's paw, then?"

Her fear that he was angry about her interference

fled, washed away by his jesting manner, and she laughed. "I just asked for one night, reminding Argus that we are newlyweds."

"It did not work for me when I tried it."

"Ah, but you are not the poor neglected wife who is also your cousin."

"Wretch." He reached out to stroke her hair. "And so you plotted a seduction, did you?"

"I tried."

"You did very well. Of course, it is unnecessary. You have but to smile at me, and I am thoroughly seduced."

"Oh." Alethea fought back the urge to clasp her hands and sigh over the fulsome compliment. "You are too kind." She inwardly winced over saying something so mealy-mouthed.

Hartley kissed her forehead as he continued to stroke her hair. His wife, he realized, was not certain of his desire for her. She was uncertain about her attraction for any man, and he suspected that was the fault of her late, unlamented husband. He had every intention of leaving her with no doubts about either by the time they collapsed in a sweaty heap of sated exhaustion. It was his duty as her husband, he thought with a grin against her hair as he nuzzled his face in the thick, silken feel of it.

It was going to be difficult to go slowly. His hunger for her was still too new, too strong, and their times together still too few to have tamed it a little. Hartley was determined, however, to make love to her slowly, to show her with his hands, his lips, and his body, that there was more than passion between them.

He stepped back and undid his robe, letting it slide to the floor. The way she looked him over, her eyes wide with appreciation, could easily make him a very vain man. Then she slowly licked her lips, and his belly clenched with want.

In the hope of keeping himself from tossing her onto her back and leaping on her like some untried youth, Hartley began to slowly untie the ribbons holding her delightful excuse for a robe together. He watched as her breathing increased with each patch of her lovely skin he exposed to his eager eyes. The way their hunger matched was an aphrodisiac. He had bedded some very beautiful women but never before had the simple act of getting naked stirred him so deeply. It had mostly been a means to an end.

"Beautiful," he whispered as he bent forward to kiss the hard tip of one breast.

Alethea shivered and closed her eyes as pleasure swept over her. When Hartley picked her up and laid her on the bed, she opened her arms to welcome him. The moment he took to completely remove her robe was too long, and she sighed with satisfaction when his body finally settled on top of hers. She did not think there could be anything that felt as good as his skin touching hers.

He kissed her, and she wrapped her body around him as their tongues danced with each other. The sweet clouds of desire quickly swept over her mind, and she shifted against him in silent demand. Hartley's hand on her hip stopped her, and she murmured a protest.

"You will not hurry me tonight, love," he said. "I plan to savor you." He kissed his way to her breasts. "Every delicious inch of you."

He held true to his word, and by the time he had finished feasting upon her breasts, she was panting. Instead of answering her need, however, he began to kiss his way down her body, until he was warming her stomach with the soft heat of his mouth. When he slid his hand between her legs, Alethea did not even flinch. She opened to his caress and could not stop the soft cries and moans of pleasure that escaped her as he teased her desire to greater heights with his stroking fingers. It was not until she felt the heat of his mouth touch where his fingers had just been that she suffered any check in her rising need.

"Hartley?" She was not surprised that she squeaked out his name, for she was shocked by such an intimacy.

"Hush, love." He nipped her inner thighs when she tried to press her legs together and then soothed the pinch with slow strokes of his tongue. "Be still and enjoy."

Alethea was not certain how anyone could enjoy something so scandalously intimate. That thought had barely passed through her mind when her desire began to return in a heated rush. She quickly forgot her embarrassment and unease and reveled in the feelings his intimate kisses brought her. When her need for him was a tight knot low in her belly, she cried out for him, pulled at his hair to try and bring him back into her arms, but he ignored her, pushing her hands aside. With strokes of his tongue he took her over the edge of desire's precipice.

She had barely begun to return to her senses when he started to do it all over again. The next time she cried out for him to join her, he was there, uniting their bodies in one swift, strong thrust. Alethea clung to him as he drove them to their shared release with a fierce determination. She could hear her name upon his lips even as she sank into the deep well of bliss only he could bring her.

Hartley was climbing back into bed after washing them both clean before Alethea came back to her senses. Her cheeks stung with a deep blush as she recalled all he had done to her.

That color faded when he grinned at her as he pulled her into his arms.

"Do not fret over the right or wrong of what we share, Alethea," he said and kissed the top of her head.

"Easy for you to say," she muttered against his chest.

"And easy for you to do." He caught her chin in his hand and turned her face up to his. "You are beautiful all over, and I mean to savor that beauty as often as I can." He kissed her cheek, almost able to feel the heat of the renewed blush there. "Speak true—can you say you did not enjoy yourself?"

"I do not think you even need to ask that. I am surprised we do not have people knocking at the door, wondering what I was shouting about." She smiled when he laughed, and the last of her embarrassment faded away.

Alethea snuggled close to him, enjoying the way his warmth and strength flowed into her. They would soon be back to his hunting down Claudette until dawn and her sleeping alone. She did not want to waste a moment of this time they had together. She did not even want to think of Claudette, spies, murders, and intrigue but did have one question no one had yet answered to her satisfaction.

"Why did Margarite wait so long to flee?" she asked. "Do you think she was hoping all blame and punishment would fall on her sister?"

"No, I think she thought she could ride out the storm and even be a shelter for Claudette. In truth, nothing happened to make her flee. We were watching her. She was beginning to suffer the same cold shoulder Claudette was, but it was Claudette we were chasing. Margarite did not invite as many important men to her bed, and the ones we talked to did not believe she had any aspirations to be a spy for her sister. Argus just thinks she was very poor at it, that the riches a lover could give her were of more interest than what he may or may not know." He gently massaged her shoulders. "We will get them. Claudette might be the worst of the pair, but Margarite is far from innocent."

Alethea nodded, her cheek rubbing against the warm, taut skin of his chest. She suddenly thought about that scandalous thing he had done to her. If he truly believed there was nothing to be shamed of for enjoying that, then why would he not enjoy the same thing? She glanced down at his manhood, which rested peacefully in its nest of curls between his strong thighs. Just seeing it erect and boldly signaling Hartley's desire for her always made her blood heat. It would not be so difficult to pay it homage. But could she be so bold? After a moment of thought on the matter, she decided she certainly could be, and she pushed aside her fear of disgusting him with that boldness.

She kissed his chest, inhaling the crisp, warm scent of his skin. *This is going to be fun,* she thought as she reached down to caress his strong, lightly haired thighs. She gave him an opened-mouth kiss on his taut stomach, and out of the corner of her eye watched his manhood twitch and then begin to grow. A sense of feminine power crept over her, and she slowly curled one hand around that rapidly growing manhood, enjoying the hard, silken feel of it. He groaned, and she grinned against the light line of hair low on his stomach. Suddenly being bold no longer worried her. Alethea slid just a little bit lower and ever so slowly ran her tongue up his length.

Hartley was enjoying just lying in bed with his naked wife in his arms, recovering his strength for a second bout of lovemaking. Then he felt her open mouth on his chest and her soft hands lightly stroking his ribs. He opened one eye and watched her dark head inch down toward his stomach. His heart beat fast with the hope that she was about to do what he so wanted her to do. He could feel himself grow hard. When she curled her fingers around his erection, he could not fully repress a groan.

He buried his fingers in her hair and wondered if he should attempt to nudge her along, silently direct her in giving him what he now craved. Just as he was about to try and hoping that would not scare her into stopping, she ran her hot little tongue up his length, and he shuddered from the pleasure of it. He opened his other eye, not wanting to miss anything. When, at the silent urging he made with a move of his hips, she took him into her mouth, he knew he was going to need a lot of strength to gain the control to enjoy such a pleasure for a long time.

The moment he felt his release tightening his body, he grabbed her under the arms and pulled her up his body. Hartley sat her on him, and, to his relief, since he did not think he could form a coherent word, she joined their bodies with only a slight awkwardness. Hands on her hips, he urged her on until they both cried out and shook from the force of the pleasure that tore through their bodies. He caught her as she collapsed in his arms and struggled to catch his breath.

"I think you had already read that book when we all discovered you with it," he said, not surprised to hear a breathlessness still lingering in his voice, and then he grinned, for he could feel the heat of her blush warming his chest.

"I may have peeked at a few pages," she admitted. "Mostly I followed the rule that says what is sauce for the gander is sauce for the goose."

"Is that not t'other way round?"

"Not this time."

"I think we are going to have to bring that book up here and study it together."

"Later." She yawned. "You have worn me out."

He laughed and kissed the top of her head. That book was definitely going to be brought into their bedchamber. Now that he knew he had a passionate and adventurous wife, he intended to take full advantage of it.

Chapter 16

Hartley looked at the note Cobb had just given him and then looked back at his bed. Alethea was curled up facing him, her luxurious hair a wild tangle around her face and blanket-shrouded body. One small hand rested on the spot he had lain in just moments ago. He desperately wanted to be lying there again. *Duty calls,* he sternly reminded himself. Hartley did wonder why duty always seemed to call in the middle of the night or at the crack of dawn.

He strode into his dressing room, where Dennison was already setting out the bowl of hot water for him to wash in. In a very short time he was ready to answer Argus's summons. He paused and then went to the small desk in the far corner of his bedchamber. Idly thinking on how he was going to move his wife into his bed, he wrote Alethea a short note explaining his absence. Leaving that and the note from Argus with Dennison with strict instructions to give them to Alethea as soon as she rose, he headed out to his meeting.

A grimace twisted his mouth as he stepped out into the dim light of predawn, waving off a sleepy Cobb's offer to rouse someone to bring his horse around. This was not how he had planned to spend his morning. After an appropriate amount of rest following their last bout of lovemaking, he had intended to show his wife that the best way to greet the sun was with him buried deep inside her. His body began to harden at the thought of that pleasure.

An odd scraping noise broke into his thoughts of all the ways he could convince Alethea that morning was one of the best times to make love. Hartley began to spin around, but, even as he shifted on his feet, he knew he was too late. Something slammed into his head, and the pain brought him to his knees. A second blow robbed him of all ability to halt the darkness washing over him. His last clear thought was to pray that Alethea was safe.

"Hartley!"

Alethea bolted upright in her bed, her heart pounding and her body trembling. The cool morning air rapidly dried the sweat of fear on her body and made her tremble even more. The echo of her scream was still ringing in her ears. She was just looking around for something to put on so that she could go find Hartley, when Olympia burst into her bedchamber. Alethea hoped she did not look as wild-eyed as her cousin, who had obviously just leapt out of bed, thrown on a robe, and then rushed to her side. She suspected she did, and then heartily wished she could find a robe as easily as Olympia had.

"Hartley is in danger," Alethea said before Olympia could speak. Yanking the blanket loose of the bed so that she could keep it wrapped around her, Alethea got out of bed. "I need to find him."

"Not wrapped in a blanket," said Olympia, her voice uneven and still a little hoarse from being yanked out of a sound sleep. "Get dressed, or at least find a modest robe, and I will go have a look for him."

Alethea washed hastily and threw on a simple gown. She detested the time it took but knew that Hartley would not appreciate her racing through the house wearing nothing but a blanket. Just as she started out of the room, a now-dressed Olympia ran back in, Modred, Dennison, and Cobb right behind her. The looks on all their faces froze Alethea in midstep, her blood turning to ice as fear raced through her. She stared blindly at the two bits of paper Olympia held out to her.

"Put your fear away, Alethea," snapped Olympia. "It will help no one."

"And your walls are cracking," said Modred, giving her a faint smile.

It took a great deal of effort to continue—Olympia's sharp words and Modred's mere presence were highly unsettling—but Alethea regained her senses and took the notes. One was from Hartley explaining how duty called. She blushed a little at his not so subtle reference to what he would prefer to be doing as the sun rose. Then she looked at the note Hartley said was from Argus. Even before the vision swept over her, she knew her cousin had not written the note. Argus never stank of roses.

A dainty white hand weighted down with ornate rings. Anger. Hatred. A mindless need to get revenge. The shadowed walk from the house to the stables.

Menace. Alarm and then pain. Please let Alethea be safe.

Olympia was right there to steady her as Alethea was thrust back into the here and now. She leaned against her cousin, fighting the compulsion to find her sketchbook, and looked at the two servants. The urge to fall to her knees and weep was strong, but Alethea conquered it. She needed to do everything she could to get Hartley out of the hands of their enemies and back home safely. Only then would she allow her emotions to run free.

"Someone needs to get Argus, Iago, Aldus, and Gifford here immediately," she said, pleased by the firm tone of her voice. "Tell them it is an emergency. Claudette has Hartley. Someone snatched him away as he went to the stables this morning." She nodded in satisfaction as the butler and the valet rapidly left to follow her command.

"Are you certain?" asked Olympia. "I saw only an attack, danger." She looked at the note from Argus. "Touching an object gives me little, but if we take the walk to the stables, I can help to see what happened."

"Best we wait for that until Argus gets here. He will want to know, too, and there is no need to do it twice." Alethea swallowed hard. "She is going to hurt him. This is my vision, the one that brought me here. She is going to hurt him and then kill him."

"You must not think the worst. It will weaken you, and you need to be strong now. And, remember, you were not a part of *that* vision, were you? You have already changed fate by coming here, helping him, and marrying him."

Alethea was about to argue that opinion, when she

suddenly recalled a part of her vision that had already been changed. That knowledge offered only a thin strand of hope, but she grabbed it and held on tight. The vision had already changed once. It could do so again.

"Yes, you are right. That vision has changed, in more ways than you have listed. Hartley never went to Claudette's bed. In the vision, I saw him leaving her house, and it was very clear what he had been doing while he was in there. That never happened, either. He halted the seduction game before it could. Oh, and that was when he was taken. Just outside her house, and so that, too, has changed."

"You see now, do you not? What you saw in the beginning is not set in stone. And no one knew he was taken then, is that not correct?" Alethea nodded, and Olympia continued, "Yet another change in the vision. We know he was taken, and I do not believe he has been gone very long at all."

Alethea tried to recall the dream that had awakened her and then slowly nodded. "No, he has not. I felt the pain he suffered. He was struck down from behind. Two blows. And I immediately woke up."

"And Dennison judged it to be a half hour or less between when Hartley left and when I hunted him down. They can barely have gotten Hartley to where they were taking him."

"True, but where is that? Where have they taken him? This is a very big city. It could be impossible to find *where* he is in time to save him."

"Alethea, you need to recall that vision. There are clues in there." Olympia started to lead Alethea out of the bedchamber. "Mrs. Huxley was awake and will have some food ready for us."

"I cannot eat anything now."

"You can and you will. You will need the strength it will give you. And while you eat, you can think about that first vision, the one that brought you here, and find the clues that we need. There may even be something in your sketches that will help."

By the time the men arrived, Alethea had managed to choke down some food and think about that first vision until her head ached. She had stared at her sketches until her eyes burned. Despite all that, she had come up with very few clues as to *where* the place was that she had seen, where she had felt Hartley in so much pain. She touched her throat, recalling in vivid detail how she had shared the pain he had suffered as his throat was cut. It was that dark memory that caused her fear for him to writhe like a living thing trapped inside her, one she kept caged with great difficulty.

Argus came over and kissed her on the forehead. "We will find him, dearest. Remember who we are and what we can do. Within the hour we will start to fill the streets with family, all of them using their many talents to find him."

"They will be hurting him, Argus," she whispered as she briefly pressed her face against his broad chest.

"We cannot stop that, and you know it, but we can do our best to make his time in their hands as short as possible. Trust us."

"Oh, I do." She looked at the others gathered around the table. "All of you."

"Then let us follow Olympia outside and see what she can see."

Olympia did her best. She could sense where the men had come upon Hartley, how they had caught him unaware and knocked him out. The ghostly trail Olympia sensed allowed her to follow the assailants' path as they had carried Hartley away, right to the point where they had put him in a carriage. They all silently followed her as she walked the path the carriage had taken, but Alethea could see the frustration growing in her cousin's intent expressions. Even at such an early hour there were too many carriages, carts, and horses moving over the street, all leaving their own ghostly trail of passing. She was not surprised when Olympia finally stopped and spit out a curse that had both Aldus and Gifford gaping at her.

"Tsk, Pia," Argus said, "such language. I am to assume that there is too much here now to discern the exact path the carriage took?"

"Yes." Olympia sighed. "If I had knowledge of the carriage, had ridden in it or touched it, it might be easier, but there is too much here now. All I know is they headed east, but they could turn in any direction after here." She gave Alethea a sad smile. "I am sorry."

"No, nothing to be sorry for. The city itself works against us," Alethea said. "Too many people, too much noise, and too many hiding places."

"Exactly what were you following?" asked Gifford as they all started to walk back to the house.

"Everything leaves a faint trail behind it," Olympia said. "The more dramatic or violent the action, the stronger its mark and the longer that mark lingers. I can see that mark, see the remnants of what happened. It is as if the event itself left its ghost behind."

Alethea could tell by the look of concentration on Gifford's face that he was trying hard to understand how that was possible. Her interest in that was abruptly ended as they all walked into the breakfast room. Germaine and Bayard stood there looking both worried and accusatory.

"Where is my uncle?" Germaine demanded, her voice sharp and unsteady with fear.

Modred walked over to her and touched her cheek. "Your wall is cracking, Germaine," he said quietly. "Breathe, slow and deep. All that anger you have tried to bury needs to be resolved, for it is eating away at your heart. Now is not the time to do that, however."

Germaine did breathe as Modred told her, and he slowly smiled at her. The girl looked at Alethea then and asked much more politely, "Where is my uncle?"

"Sit and eat," said Alethea as she moved to the table. "Both of you. We will tell you what has happened and what we need to do."

The moment Bayard and Germaine were seated and eating, Argus told them all that had happened. Alethea quickly sat down beside Germaine and took hold of her hand when the girl paled. She noticed that Bayard was not looking much better. They may not have decided exactly how they felt about the uncle they had not seen for so long, but he was the last of their family.

"We will find him," she told the siblings. "It is just a matter of time."

"That is not a knowing, is it?" Germaine asked.

"No, it is full confidence in the people who will work to make it so."

"Child, do not forget who we are," Argus said quietly. "This will not be an easy thing to accomplish, but the skills our family will bring to the hunt are the best one can get. I will send out word to every Vaughn and

Wherlocke in the city and within a short ride of here. They will quickly put their skills to work to help us."

"I cannot lose any more of my family," Germaine whispered, and Bayard reached out to clasp her free hand in his. "I cannot."

"And you will not. I refuse to allow that woman to beat us."

"That woman needs to be killed."

Alethea opened her mouth to tell the girl she needed to ease the anger and need for revenge behind her hissed words, and then shut her mouth. It would be hypocritical to tell her not to say what Alethea herself had been thinking. Claudette also fully deserved those dark emotions directed at her. The woman had been the cause of far too many deaths.

"She will be," said Alethea. "If not now, then when she is hanged for all the evil she has done. Our job now is to find where she has taken your uncle."

"We need to go to Margarite's house."

Everyone stared at Olympia to ask what she meant by that, but Olympia was staring blindly at the wall. A moment later she shuddered slightly and then looked around as if surprised to find everyone looking at her. Olympia did not often have visions as Alethea did, but she did get many strong knowings, and Alethea felt her hopes rise just a little.

"What did I say?" Olympia asked.

"That we need to go to Margarite's house," replied Argus. "Do you think they have taken Hartley there?" His doubt about that was clear to hear in his voice.

Olympia frowned for a moment and then shook her head. "No, but there is where we will find information we need."

"We have already searched her house and found nothing," said Aldus.

"Except that Hartley told me she had left it as if she thought she would be returning to it some day," said Alethea.

"Then that is why we must go there," said Olympia. "She will be returning. Late today. The sun will be going down. And we will need a few more men."

Germaine looked at Alethea. "Have you seen that, too?"

"No," Alethea reluctantly replied. "I am too close to Hartley. I see nothing. The only reason I woke up and knew he was in trouble was because it happened so close to home, and he suffered pain. That is the greatest weakness of the gift I have. The closer I am to people, the less I can see about what may happen to them. However, I am not the only one with such a gift in the family. I am sure I will hear from any one of the others if they have a vision that can help. For now, we shall follow what Olympia's knowing told her."

"And I will still contact as many of the family as I can." Argus looked at Aldus and Gifford. "You two can find what men you can and get them searching."

The men quickly dispersed—Argus, Modred, and Iago to notify what kinsmen they could, and Aldus and Gifford to go and gather some men to help in the search for Hartley. That left Olympia and Alethea with the siblings. Alethea could see that Germaine and Bayard desperately wanted to believe what Argus had said, but sad experience had robbed them of the ability to hope easily.

"We *will* find him," Alethea told them.

"Is that what you know or what you want to believe?" asked Germaine.

"It is what I have to believe."

"Why would they take him if they did not plan to kill him?" Germaine studied Alethea and Olympia and then sighed, the soft sound unsteady as she held back her tears. "They want him to tell them something. They will try to make him tell them anything he might know, and to do that they will have to hurt him, will they not?"

"I fear they will, and there is nothing we can do about that. We can only pray that we get to him before he has to suffer too much pain."

"Then find him fast, please. Use all your gifts, all your family, all the men those departments they work for can spare, and find him. I have lost too many. I will not lose him, too."

"That is exactly what we plan to do." Alethea leaned over and kissed Germaine's pale cheek. "I cannot lose him, either. And we will make them all pay dearly for every moment of pain they have caused him."

Hartley groaned as consciousness returned. His head throbbed, and it took him a moment to recall why it should. He started to raise a hand to check what wound there might be and tensed. His hand was secured to something. Cautiously, he opened his eyes and nearly cursed aloud. He was tied to a chair.

Taking several deep breaths to calm the urge to thrash about and strain against the bonds holding him firmly to the chair, Hartley fought to clear his vision. He needed to study where he was and assess any chance of escape. A small voice in his aching head taunted him for thinking he could escape when he was bound to a chair, but he ignored it. If he allowed it to win, he would lose all hope, and he knew he needed it to survive.

A few lanterns dimly lighted his surroundings, and there was nothing he saw that immediately told him where he was. All he was sure of was that he was not in a cellar or a house. Some place of business, he mused, although it could be an unused office in one of the many warehouses that dotted the city, especially along the river. He took a deep breath and tried to sort out the various smells that assaulted his nose.

Hartley was certain he was somewhere near the docks. Faint though it was, there was the rank odor in the air that was peculiar to the Thames. That could cause a problem for the people who were looking for him, and he knew there were some. If nothing else, one of the Vaughns or Wherlockes running freely in his house would have a vision or a seeing or some such thing that would tell them he had been taken. There were some advantages to finding oneself wedded into a family many people would run screaming from, he thought.

The thought of the family he now belonged to through marriage made him think of Alethea. He could still see her curled up in their bed, sleeping the sleep of the sated, a hint of passion's blush still on her cheeks. That image gave him strength, and he used it to push back his fear of never seeing her again. Fate could not be so cruel as to give him what he needed to complete his life and then allow some murderous viper of a woman take it all away just so she could fatten her purse.

He shook his head, and a wave of nausea poured over him. Closing his eyes tightly and breathing in slowly and deeply, he fought the churning sickness in his belly. The last thing he wanted to do was vomit on himself. At least give him one of his enemies to aim it at, he thought. It would be a pathetic defense, but there would be some satisfaction in it.

It took several minutes to push aside the urge to empty his belly, but he knew he had succeeded when the cool, damp air in his prison began to dry the sweat on his face. Then the door opened and Claudette walked in, followed by five big men, and Hartley silently cursed. His luck had obviously not begun to improve yet. His sickness had passed, and here came the very targets he had hoped for.

"So, you are awake," said Claudette and smiled as she stood before him.

"Why, I do believe I am," he drawled. "How perspicacious of you."

"Do not try my patience, Redgrave. I believe I hold the upper hand right now."

She did, he silently agreed, but he had no intention of letting her see that he acknowledged that. Claudette looked so pleased with herself his palm actually itched with the need to slap her, and he had never raised his hand to a woman in his life or wanted to. He knew what she had planned for him. Alethea's vision had warned him, and he was as prepared as anyone could be for what was to come. What disturbed him and made his skin crawl was the knowledge that this woman would enjoy it.

"For now," he said and smiled when she frowned.

"No one knows where you are, Redgrave. You cannot be so foolish as to think they are all going to come riding to your rescue."

He shrugged. "Not so foolish. I have married a Vaughn, after all, and with Alethea comes all of that family, including the Wherlockes."

To his surprise, he saw the hint of fear briefly flash in her eyes. Claudette was one of those who believed in demons and witches, he realized. Her threat to Alethea had held some truth about her own feelings. Hartley would freely admit that a few of the gifts that family had made him uneasy, but he had yet to meet one he could dislike or actually fear. It also astounded him that, in this enlightened age of reason, anyone could still believe in such things as demons in human form and witches who cast spells or consorted with Satan. It was a shame that he only saw the fear Claudette held now, when it was too late to put it to good use. That did not mean, however, that he could not taunt her with it.

"A foolish lot of eccentrics and recluses who think they have some power," she scoffed and flicked her hand in a dismissive gesture.

"But they do have power. A great deal, in fact."

"Am I to believe then that the great rake Hartley was seduced by such a little country wench because she cast a spell on him?"

"In a way, she did. The spell of honesty and innocence. Two things I believe you have not been touched by in a very long time." He could see her anger in the narrowing of her eyes and the flush upon her cheeks and knew he would pay for his remarks, but he did not care.

"You were to be mine," she snapped. "I had chosen you."

"As your next victim? Like Peterson and Rogers?"

"What do you speak of? I know no Peterson or Rogers."

"Iago says different. He has seen their spirits around you. Them and the compte and his family. All angry and crying out for vengeance." She paled a little, and he knew he had struck at a deep fear. "Children, Claudette? You felt a threat from a boy so young he did not even talk yet and a tiny girl of five? Did you think they would grow and take back the jewels you were so hungry for? I am surprised you can wear them, that the stink of that sin does not burn your skin each time you put them on."

The slap she gave him caused enough movement of his head to bring on the nausea again. He actually considered letting it flow, but she was already out of reach, pacing in front of him with her hands clenched tight at her sides. Hartley fought to push the sickness aside again and fixed his gaze on one of the men who stood a little distance away from the others. He had the look of a man who found himself involved in something he no longer wanted a part of.

It was because of the talk of murdering children, Hartley decided. It was when he had spoken of the compte's children that the man had taken a step back. Obviously the man was willing enough to take coin for beating, torturing, and killing a grown man, but the murder of children stirred what little conscience he had.

Hartley was just wondering what use he might make of that when Claudette whirled around to face him again. He watched as she nervously rubbed her hands over her arms as if trying to brush away something and nearly smiled. Claudette's mind had accepted the talk of the ghosts of her victims clinging to her. A miasma of hate and fury, Iago had called it, and Hartley could almost swear he saw a faint glimmer of it.

"You talk nonsense," she said. "The dead stay buried.

It is good that Iago did not continue the affair with my sister, I am thinking. He is not right in the head."

"He did not continue the affair with your sister because he felt her cold emptiness. A spirit like a soulless killer, he said. He felt she probably did not do the killing but did not care who died, mayhap even chose a few. No, once his lust cleared away, he could not abide to touch her. I do wonder why she wanted him, however. The two of you tended to pick lovers with ties to the government or the military. He had neither. I suspect your sister disappointed you a little there as she chose a man simply because he was handsome."

"There is nothing wrong with Margarite. I will not listen to any more of this nonsense. You try to upset me and make me fear, but I am stronger than that. Stronger and far more clever that the lot of you."

"Why? Because as a poor farm girl you have managed to get yourself accepted in society? Your face and body did that, and you know it. Foolish men who wished something beautiful on their arm brought you out of the gutter, naught else. But you will soon be back there. Even if you do as you intend to me, even if, by some miracle, my allies do not prove what a murderous bitch and traitor you really are, you will still never be accepted back in society."

"You made a mistake when you turned away from me. You may have saved yourself all of this by making me your marchioness."

"I would rather endure this than have you in my bed. And do not think me such a fool as to believe having anything to do with you would have saved me. This has been planned for me from the beginning. In fact, it was foretold by my wife. It is yourself you can blame for the fact that I found the woman I wished to marry. She came here to save me from you."

"Then she has failed," Claudette hissed. "I now have you, and you will tell me what I need to know. I may have lost my place in the pathetic group of idiots you call society, but I mean to leave this country with my purse full. You will give me the information I need to make that happen."

"No, I think not. I doubt you got much off of Rogers or Peterson, either."

"They were fools."

"Why? Because they chose not to betray their country before they died?"

"Yes. Of what good is honor to a dead man?"

"Only a person who has none could ask that question."

"Fool. I will ask you a lot more questions, and you will answer me. Mayhap I will even allow you to live." She smiled. "Although you may not wish to when I am done with you. Still, you may consider the fact that if you die, you leave your little wife alone."

Fear shot through Hartley, but he quickly conquered it. Alethea would not be alone, for her family would see to her safety and care. "No, she will never be alone. And you will not be able to enjoy whatever money you flee with. My niece and nephew will see to it that you are hunted wherever you go, hunted down and made to pay for killing their family on the beach that day. And they will have all the help my wife and her family can give her."

"You but try to make me cower and run, but it will not work." She stood up and brushed off the sleeves of her gown again. "First my men will soften you up a bit, *oui?* And then I shall start to ask you questions. You think you are such a brave, big man that you can stand firm beneath what I do? I think you are in for a very big surprise. Men, begin please, and do try to remember that I want him alive and able to speak afterward."

Hartley watched one of her men roll up his sleeves. His arms were thick with muscle. When he clenched his hand into a fist, Hartley had to admit it was an impressive one. *This is going to hurt,* he thought as that big fist swung toward him.

Chapter 17

An itch on her ankle was driving Alethea mad, but she remained still. She did not know how long they had been watching Margarite's house, but she thought it had been long enough to begin to consider that this may have been a mistake. Olympia's vision was undoubtedly correct, but they all knew that visions were rarely specific as to when the foreseen event would occur. Olympia would readily admit that her visions were more of a knowing, a certainty about something, and nowhere near as exact as Alethea's could be. Her cousin was certain that Margarite would return to her home, but that did not have to happen today or even this week. The time of late in the day could be right, but which day? It could be next year, and all that would be left of Hartley was his bones.

A hand began to rub her back, and Alethea pulled herself free of the trap her fear for Hartley kept ready for her. She glanced over her shoulder at Modred. He was such a beautiful man, he looked odd hiding in a shadowed alley with her and the others, she mused, and then mouthed the word *sorry*. Modred did not need to be pummeled by her wayward emotions now, not when he was determined upon using his gift to get information out of women like Margarite and Claudette.

Alethea understood why Modred was so insistent upon helping. He needed to see that what he saw as a curse could actually be used to help someone, that there could be some good in it. She just wished he had not chosen women like these to do so. Nothing they had told him about Claudette and Margarite had changed his mind, however. She felt guilty that a large part of her was glad of that, for no one had a better chance of getting the information they needed to save Hartley than Modred did.

"There she is," Argus whispered from where he stood in front of her.

In the dim light of a cloudy late afternoon, Alethea did not know how Argus could tell Margarite from any other heavily cloaked woman, but she did not ask. Although, she mused, not many women walked around with six big men. If Argus said this was Margarite, then it was. He was rarely wrong about such things. The fact that the woman went to the door of Margarite's house and, with a quick, sharp movement of her hand, quickly dispersed the six men around the house, confirmed Argus's opinion.

Alethea was almost able to smile. Those men were in for a nasty surprise. In the shadowy areas around Margarite's home were an equal number of men, both Hartley's and, to her surprise, Argus's. She supposed she should have guessed by Argus's highly efficient hunt for proof of Claudette's crimes—and then for Claudette herself—that her cousin was doing the same sort of government work as her husband. She just could not recall anyone having said so explicitly.

When the signal came from one of Argus's men that told him Margarite's men were no longer a threat, Argus casually brushed himself off and strode out of the alley they had all been hiding in. Alethea, Modred, Olympia, Aldus, and Gifford had to scramble to catch up with him. The way Gifford and Aldus heeded Argus's commands despite their higher stations told Alethea that whatever position her cousin held in the secretive branches of government, it was a high one. When this was all over she was determined to find out just how many of her family were lurking in the shadowy corridors of the government and the military.

"Are we just going to rap on the door and wait for her to invite us in?" she asked Argus when she caught up with him.

"Oh, my dearest cousin, I had not intended to rap first," he replied. "Why announce ourselves after suffering all this discomfort to remain a secret?"

He took her hand as if he sensed that her fear for Hartley was beginning to get the best of her again. Her husband had left the house when the sun had just begun to rise. Now it was almost full set, and they still had not found him, did not even know where he was being held. She kept thinking of how much pain he must have endured by now and was not sure how much longer she could bear it.

They walked into Margarite's house without making a sound. The woman had dismissed all of her servants, so there was no one to warn her of their secretive invasion. Alethea blinked in astonishment as she looked around at the somewhat garish décor. She looked toward Olympia, who just rolled her eyes. Having money, cunning, beauty, and power obviously did not prevent one from having extremely bad taste, Alethea decided.

Margarite did not see them at first. She was on her knees prying up a board in the floor of the parlor as, one by one, they slipped into the room. They had nearly encircled her before she sensed something was amiss. Whirling around, she stared at them in horror and then glanced behind them. A heartbeat later, she looked at each window. Alethea realized the woman was looking for her guards to rush to her rescue. By the time Margarite met their gazes again, she had begun to get control of her expression and just looked a little shocked, with a hint of confusion. Alethea hated to admit it, but she had to admire the skill that kept the woman from looking as afraid as she must feel now that she knew her guards were not coming to her aid.

"I am afraid your burly ruffians cannot help you now," said Argus as he stepped over to Margarite.

The way Argus yanked the woman to her feet, dragged her to a chair, and shoved her into it shocked Alethea. Argus was a lot angrier about what Margarite and her sister had done than he had revealed before now. The look of grim satisfaction on Olympia's face confirmed Alethea's opinion that barely repressed fury was at work here. If Argus had some dark part of him that caused him to be rough with women, Olympia would have known about it. She would also have gelded the man by now, brother or not.

"You cannot come in here like this," Margarite protested, her expression now one of righteous outrage. "You certainly have no right to treat me so roughly."

She rubbed the arm he had grabbed. "I am sure to have bruises."

"If all goes as I wish it, madam, you shall have yet another bruise, a brilliant one around your neck caused by the noose you so richly deserve to wear. Now, where is your sister and, most importantly, where is Lord Redgrave?"

"I have no idea where my sister is, and, as for Lord Redgrave, I suggest you ask his little wife."

Before Alethea could say a word, Argus bent toward the woman. He put his hands on the arms of the chair, and Margarite pressed into the back of it in a vain attempt to escape the furious man drawing so close to her. Alethea was glad she could not see her cousin's face, for whatever was there leeched all the color from Margarite's face.

"You will tell me what I wish to know, madam," Argus said in a voice so cold it made Alethea shiver.

"I just told you that I have no idea where Claudette or Redgrave are. Why should I? Perhaps they have slipped away for a tryst. He has the wife to give him an heir, *oui?* So now he can play."

Argus stepped back, put his hands on his hips, and stared up at the ceiling for a moment. "Aldus, see what she is hiding beneath the floor." As Aldus moved to do so, Argus looked at Margarite again. "I am curious to see what would have a woman on her knees trying her hand at ripping up a floor."

Alethea was truly astonished by the woman's control. Not by a flicker of an eyelash did Margarite reveal that she was in any way overset by the chance of Aldus revealing her secrets. It was very possible that the woman had not hidden anything that could get her or her sister hanged.

"I have nothing hidden there," Margarite said. "I was but trying to fix a loose board."

"By yourself? With six burly men roaming about outside? I become gravely insulted, madam, that you should think such weak explanations and excuses would be enough to turn me aside from what I seek."

"You said you seek Claudette and Redgrave. I certainly have not hidden them beneath my floors."

"Sweet heavens, but she makes me ache to slap her blind," muttered Olympia in a quiet but very hard voice.

"I feel the same," said Alethea in an equally soft voice so as not to disturb Argus. "You can almost smell the arrogance and conceit of the woman in the very air around her. I would like to believe that Aldus will find something of importance beneath the floor, but I cannot. Margarite is far too calm, cocky even, for someone about to be revealed as a traitor."

"My guess is that there is money and jewels under there, enough to make for a very comfortable life somewhere safer for her than London is now."

"If that is so, then why stay here once it did grow dangerous if she had the funds to leave?"

"Because for someone like her, enough is *never* enough. More, always more, is wanted."

"Olympia, if you will work your magic on this hovel, I would appreciate it," said Argus.

"Of course. Madam, if there is anything you wish to confess to, do it now, for it might be to your benefit to do so before I uncover the crime."

"What *are* you talking about?" asked Margarite.

"Your secrets, your sins, leave their mark, madam,"

Olympia said as she began to walk toward the fireplace. "The greater the crime, the heavier the sin, the longer that mark remains." She shrugged when Margarite just stared at her as if she were mad. "Have it your way."

The way Olympia strode directly to the fireplace told Alethea that her cousin had already been closely surveying the room for signs. Olympia's gift was one she did not completely understand. Alethea understood Iago seeing the spirits of people, but how could Olympia see the spirits of events? However the woman did it, she did it well, and Alethea had no doubt that Olympia had already uncovered something Margarite would rather not have discovered.

"If I recall the drawings I was shown," said Olympia as she ran her hand over the ornate marble mantelpiece, "that man Pierre Leon was recently here. That is who I see standing here."

"That is no great secret," said Margarite. "Of course he was here. He is my cousin. And most people stand by a fireplace when they first enter a room. He was probably cold or damp."

"A very close cousin, too. You were lovers."

Margarite began to look a little nervous, but she shrugged. "That is no crime, either. Pierre is a very handsome man."

"And foolish enough to think he could trust you." Olympia idly rubbed her hand up and down the side of the mantelpiece. "He thought you had accepted his failures, understood that he had done his best to kill Germaine and make Alethea run home. But you had not. Neither had Claudette. Oh, my. That is interesting. You were both with him."

"How is that interesting? As I just told you, he was our cousin."

Alethea saw the faint smile on Olympia's face and knew why it was there. Margarite had slipped. She had said *was,* not *is.* No one showed that they had noticed that slip, however, and so Alethea struggled to keep her knowledge of it out of her expression. She knew that cracking a nut as hard as Margarite would not be quick and easy.

"And so very, very close to both of you." Olympia shook her head. "Poor, poor fool. If he had not tried to kill young Germaine and beat my cousin, I might actually feel sorry for him. He did not realize that the moment he failed to do as you and Claudette wanted, he was already a dead man. Blood ties mean nothing to you or her."

"Of course they do. We honor our family and are all very close."

"Well, you and Claudette were certainly very close to him that night. He thought he was in for a very special delight. The fact that he felt no surprise at what was offered tells me that he had indulged before." Olympia gave a dramatic shudder. "That is something I would rather not think about, and I am pleased the act was never finished here. No. As you, madam, kept him dazed with passion, your sister slipped her knife out of her sleeve and cut the poor fool's throat. I believe if we look hard enough, we will find his blood around here somewhere. No one can clean up such a mess completely."

"How dare you accuse me of such things!"

The protest was spoken with an admirable amount of outrage, but Alethea could see the glint of fear in

Margarite's eyes. The guilty might not understand how their secret had been discovered, but the very fact that it had been laid out in front of them, in detail, was often enough to unsettle them. Alethea had never seen it done to someone guilty of so many heinous crimes before, however. It was interesting to see that the control needed when faced with one's sins was as hard to grasp in the most evil of criminals as it was in the petty ones.

"My dear, do not try to argue with our Olympia," said Argus. "She just tells you what she sees."

"By touching things? Do not think me a simpleton, sir. No one can see things by touching something." Margarite spoke in a voice heavy with scorn, yet she never took her gaze off Olympia.

"Oh, but they can. Our Alethea is very good at that. You and Claudette left a handkerchief at Iago's house, and it was very talkative." Argus met Margarite's startled look with a smile. "Farm girls. You are naught but lowly farm girls who reach far and above their station."

That stung, Alethea thought as Margarite glared at her cousin. "Chickens," she murmured, knowing she was adding to the insult. "You slaughtered chickens for nothing, and very little of it."

Margarite was starting to become afraid. Aldus sat on the floor looking through several small chests he had pulled out of a hollow beneath the board Margarite had been pulling up. The rest of her unwanted company stood around telling her things they had no way of knowing. Alethea was just surprised that it had taken the woman so long to lose her bravado.

Modred stepped forward, and Alethea tensed, wanting to know what he might discover and wanting to protect him from such evil. She clenched her hands at her side, fighting the urge to pull him back, away from what she saw as a danger to his heart and soul. He was a grown man, head of their large family, and he had the right to prove himself.

"She is as Iago said," murmured Modred as he stared at Margarite, his head cocked slightly to the side. "Cold, empty."

Margarite glared at Iago. "If I was cold, it was because you were such a poor lover."

"No, you wanted him back," said Modred. "You wanted him to be your next husband." Modred glanced at Iago. "You would not have survived the marriage for long."

"I am not surprised." Iago shook his head. "I had not realized what a narrow escape I had until Alethea arrived to tell me of her dream. Although, marriage had never been on my mind. One wishes one's wife a little less experienced than she."

"She killed her first husband and the man she married when she came to England," Modred said and watched Margarite calmly as he set the accusations before her. "The first she turned in to the authorities as a traitor. The second, she poisoned. He liked a drink of brandy before bed. That is where she put the poison. I believe he is the only one she killed by her own hand."

Modred idly adjusted his gloves. "You were right to say she has the soul of a stone-cold killer. She sent both men to their deaths for petty reasons. The first she killed because he tried to be the man of the house, and the second because he irritated her. The worst irritation was how he ate his soup."

Alethea could see that Margarite was stunned and

growing more terrified of Modred with every word he said. Modred looked a little pale, the pulling of secrets from the woman costing him in strength and peace of mind. More than any of them, Modred led a sheltered life. He would have had little to do with the kind of evil Margarite and Claudette had inside them.

"The only thing she felt when Pierre was killed right in her arms was irritation over the ruination of her gown. And she does know exactly where her sister is holding Hartley," Modred finished and smiled at her. "She thinks she does not need to tell us, that she only needs to remain silent for a little while longer and we will give up and go away, returning to blindly running about London looking for him."

"Ah, a sound plan, madam," said Argus. "But you must see that it will not work. We shall just have Modred here pluck it out of your mind. And, if Modred is feeling a bit wearied of peering into that sewer, I will make you tell me what we need to know."

"What is he?" Margarite whispered, ignoring Argus. "He was in my head. I could feel him there."

"Could you? How intriguing. Tell me where Redgrave is."

"Why should I?" she suddenly snapped, glaring at Argus. "It will gain me nothing. You are all of a mind to hang me anyway."

"Yes, but you might at least meet your maker with one less stain upon your soul. I might even feel kindly enough, seeing as you never actually killed anyone, aside from your English husband, of course, with your own dainty little hand, to get the court to transport you instead of hanging you."

"Transportation? To go to some stinking land and

work as someone's slave? Return to working someone
else's lands until my body is broken and bent and my
skin as tough as old leather? I think not. I would rather
hang."

"And so you will." Argus looked at Modred. "Do
you want me to finish this?"

"If you would be so kind," Modred replied. "Chloe
said one sister was weaker, and I believe this is the one
she referred to. Still, it was not easy to dig out the
truth. Not in the beginning. Once started, what walls
she had tumbled down very quickly. However, if her
sister is the strong one, I shall need all my strength to
deal with her."

Alethea grasped Modred's hand as he stepped away
from Margarite. She could feel the slightest of tremors
in his hand and knew he was not as calm as he appeared. Iago stepped over and, pulling a fine silver flask
from his coat pocket, handed it to Modred. Alethea
released Modred's hand and watched him shudder as
he took a drink, but the color slowly returned to his
face. If a woman who had done little of the killing herself troubled him, what would looking inside Claudette
do to him?

"Modred, mayhap this is not good for you," she
whispered.

"It certainly is no fun, but I will survive," he said.
"I just wish I could do as Argus does. He can make
them tell him what he wants to know with just the
power of his will and does not have to see all the other
filth that is inside them." He took a deep breath and let
it out slowly as he handed the flask back to Iago. "It is
done, and we will soon know where they have taken
Hartley. For that, it was worth it."

"Thank you."

Argus soon had Margarite staring at him in that dazed manner he could inflict upon people and answering all of his questions. The moment the woman said where Hartley had been taken, Alethea wanted to race there immediately, but she fought for patience. In a way, her vision had warned her against such a rash move. It was the sudden arrival of someone that had gotten Hartley's throat cut. She was going to have to wait as a plan was made. And, perhaps, if she kept telling herself that, she would not go insane with worry.

"What have you done?" Margarite said as she came out of the daze Argus had put her into to find her hands tied behind her back.

"Just asked you a few questions, which you answered." Argus smiled at her, and Alethea thanked God he never looked at her that way. "You know you told me everything, as I saw no need to make you forget it. And now, my man here will take you to prison." He looked at the man who grabbed Margarite by her bound hands and started to drag her to the door. "I am sure the rest of the men have gathered up her hirelings and tossed them into the wagon. She can join them. Gag her if you must," he added as Margarite began to loudly protest.

Argus then turned to Aldus. "Find anything interesting?"

"I believe she was indulging in a little blackmail. Other than that, just some jewels and money. A great deal of money."

"We can look at the papers later. Now that we know where Hartley is, we have to make a plan. First we need to send a few men there to reconnoiter. I know that warehouse, and it is empty, but I am sure Claudette will have guards around it, and we need to know how many and how they are placed. They have to be disposed of before we go in."

Alethea walked to the window to watch the wagon with Margarite and her men leave. She listened to Argus issue orders and the men he chose hurry away. It was going to be a long, hard wait, but she would not make a nuisance of herself. And neither would she allow the men to deny her when she joined them. She would stay out of their way, obey all their commands, but she would be there when they found Hartley.

"Alethea," Argus said as he stepped up beside her and put his arm around her, "we are almost done. Soon you will have him back home."

"But in what state?" she asked, voicing her fear in a shaky whisper.

"Alive. And that is what is important. She wants something from him and will not want him to die before she gets it."

"But she has had him for a whole day."

"He is a big, strong man, love. And she will not have him for much longer. I suppose I cannot ask you to wait at home until we bring him to you."

"No. I need to be there. I swear I will do whatever you tell me to, but I need to be there when he is found."

"Fair enough. Now, shall we step outside? This place smells like them, and I would like to breathe some fresh air."

Alethea followed him outside. They stood near the carriage as Aldus, Gifford, and Iago brought out the chests they had found in the floor and secured them in the back. Modred paced the walk in front of the house slowly, Olympia at his side.

"Is Modred all right?" she asked Argus.

"He is doing just fine," replied Argus. "He needs to do this, for you, and to prove to himself that he is worthy of being the head of our family. I think it is good for him in another way, too. This is the worst he will face, and he is facing it. It will help him ease away from Chantiloup, from hiding behind those great walls. He is a man now, no longer a boy, and he needs to stop hiding so much. This is also showing him that there are places, such as the home you share with Hartley, where he can go and find peace even as he finds friends and company."

"Of course. I was very glad to see that he could be with Hartley and the children with ease. You are right. He needs to slowly come out of his cave. I just wish it was not such an ugly introduction to the world."

"Sad to say, there is a lot of ugliness out there. If he is to ever have anything approaching a real life, a full life, he has to learn how to deal with it. He also has to see that there are people in this family more than ready to help him do so."

Alethea nodded and looked in the direction his men had gone. "Do you think it will take them very long to do this reconnoitering?"

"Not too long. Then we will plan how to deal with the guards and get into the place without being seen. And this, sweetheart, is the hard side of intrigue. Waiting. Planning. Thinking out every step one takes. But it is the only way to do it. Rushing in may seem heroic and daring, but it gets people killed." He kissed her cheek. "Be patient. All this is to ensure your husband's safety, as well as our own."

She held his words close to her heart. They would need to be kept there, and kept to the forefront of her mind, for every single moment until Hartley was safe, for she knew her fear could easily make her do something foolish. That could cost Hartley his life and put the lives of her friends and family in danger as well.

It seemed like hours before the men returned and even longer before all the plans were made. Alethea soon understood what was meant when someone said they wanted to tear their hair out. The tension grew in her until she thought she would snap like a dry twig.

When the order was given to finally leave, she nearly threw herself into the carriage. She listened patiently as Argus told her that she faced even more waiting. She would not be allowed near the warehouse until the guards were secured, and then she would have to wait outside until Hartley was freed. Alethea hated it but swore she would follow the orders given her. All she asked was that, the moment Hartley was freed and all his captors dead or secured, she be allowed to go to him.

Olympia clasped her hand as the carriage started rolling. All the men save the one driving and a guard had already disappeared into the night, their horses all as dark as the men's clothing. Alethea softly prayed that they would be in time.

"We will save him," Olympia said.

"Have you seen it?"

"No, but Argus is certain, and he is rarely wrong, arrogant, annoying man that he is." Olympia sighed. "I also just *feel* it. Deep inside, I just *feel* it. And remember, I saw you happy."

Alethea did remember that. Unfortunately, a voice in her mind softly reminded her that Olympia had not said for how long she had been happy.

Chapter 18

A fiery sore throat greeted Hartley as he dragged himself out of the blackness of unconsciousness. Obviously he had finally screamed, although he could not recall doing so. His pride was pinched by that knowledge, but he told himself not to be an idiot. What fool did not suffer from the pain inflicted when being tortured? His honor had been preserved. He had told them nothing.

Alethea. His heart clenched as her name caressed his mind, sending longing throughout his battered body. If he was not found soon, he knew he would never see her again, never hold her again, and that was enough to make his eyes sting with tears. He would never make love to her again or see her smooth white belly grow round with their child. Nor would he ever hear the laughter of that child. Hartley was almost glad that he was firmly strapped to a chair, for he feared that, otherwise, he would fall to his knees and loudly bemoan his fate. His captors would undoubtedly see that as a weakness instead of the honest grief for all he was losing that it was.

Pain was making him morbid, he decided, and
fought against the fatalistic turn his thoughts had
taken. They would make him weaken, perhaps even
weak enough to say things he should not and inadvertently betray his country. Hartley sought for thoughts
that would make him strong, would bring him comfort
and hope. He thought on how Alethea's family would
protect her. Secretive, reclusive, gifted with skills he
did not always understand, and apparently very, very
numerous, they would shield her and help her.

If he had already gotten her with child, they would
assist in the raising of him or her, and he doubted he
could have chosen better himself. He might fervently
wish he could be there, but he did find comfort in the
fact that he would not be leaving her alone and unprotected. Nor would Germaine or Bayard be left alone.
Alethea would see to that. And, he thought grimly,
Alethea's family would never rest until they found the
hell-born sisters who had murdered him. He could
almost smile at that thought, but his battered mouth
would undoubtedly make it a painful exercise.

The tap, tap, tap of Claudette's expensive shoes
echoing through the room pried him from his thoughts.
Hartley was a little surprised at how badly he wanted
to stay alive so that he could watch the woman hang.
He had seen a hanging once and had vowed that he
would never watch another. But to see Claudette dance
the Tyburn jig, he would break that vow without hesitation. Not just because she would be his executioner,
either. No one was safe as long as she remained alive,
no woman, no man, no child. She was an abomination,
one of those who took great pleasure in the inflicting
of pain and who killed on a whim.

"You sadly disappoint me, Redgrave," she said. "I had thought you an intelligent man, yet you do nothing to save yourself from this agony."

Hartley opened his eyes as much as the swelling would allow. Her men had *softened* him up for her torture with great skill. They had inflicted a great deal of pain and damage yet broken no bones or made it impossible for him to speak. The bone breaking had come later. He glanced down at his hands, his arms now strapped to the arms of the chair, and winced at how badly swollen they were. Most of his fingers were broken now, and blood trickled from more shallow, stinging wounds on his body than he cared to count. He thought of the others she had killed in this way and knew, broken fingers or not, that if he could get free of his bonds, he would strangle her and welcome the way she would die beneath his hands. She might not be killing his spirit, but she was stripping away all of his civilized ways.

He looked at her and used a curt two-word phrase with a harsh four-letter word he had not used since he was a youth testing his boundaries. It did not really surprise him when she revealed no shock at his words, only anger. Hartley suspected a lot of the poor bastards she had sent to their deaths had spat the same coarse words at her.

"You do not have much skin left to slice, Redgrave, or bones left to break," she said. "I think your little wife and her family, all those witches and demon-possessed souls you so counted upon, have left you to rot."

"The only one who is demon-possessed is you, you sick and twisted bitch." The rage that contorted her face robbed her of all beauty. "They will find you, you know. They have so many wondrous gifts to help them hunt you down, and they will not stop until you are captured and hanged. Three long years I searched for Germaine and Bayard, the children who escaped the callous slaughter of their family that you ordered, and found nothing. Once Alethea and her family joined the search, those children were home with me within weeks. No matter how much money you hoard and no matter how many powerful fools you trap between your thighs, you will not keep them from finding you and making you pay for all your crimes."

"You *will* tell me what I want to know!"

"No." He glanced at her men and realized there were now only three, although he was sure there were others guarding the outside of the building. "And if you continue to lose minions as you are, you will soon be doing this alone."

"Those deserters have paid for their disloyalty. I do not tolerate failure or betrayal."

"Or much of anything else, judging by the number of your past lovers who have been murdered or injured in the last few days. Damned dangerous rut you turned out to be."

"They knew too much, and their usefulness had ended. Take his boots off," she ordered her men. "I have now recalled that there are a few bones left unbroken."

Hartley bit back an instinctive protest. Considering how painful a stubbed toe was, he knew he was about to suffer an agony that could have him screaming like a girl. It could also leave him crippled. How could he return to his wife if he had been so badly broken he was no better than an invalid?

He stared up at the rafters as two of Claudette's men struggled to remove his boots, and then he blinked. Something moved up in the slender loft that ran down both sides of the room, something a lot bigger than a rat. He tried hard to discern what he was seeing, but the pounding in his head and the swelling around his eyes made it difficult to separate one shadow from another. Then, as Claudette sharply criticized her men for not moving fast enough, the shadowy figure stepped into a small shaft of moonlight coming through a crack in the ceiling. Only briefly, just long enough to be seen, before slipping back into the shadows he was so much a part of.

Aldus. Hartley prayed the sight of his friend was not some wild delusion brought on by the pain he was in. One of Claudette's men had a hammer, and the other was busily strapping Hartley's foot to a block of wood. If he had not imagined seeing Aldus, if rescue truly was at hand, Hartley prayed it came before that hammer started meeting his toes. Glancing at the way Claudette held her knife, he assumed that breaking his toes would be just the beginning. If his friends did not hurry, they would soon be able to discard any attempts at being silent. His screams would adequately conceal any noise they might make.

Alethea paced back and forth before the door to the building in which Hartley was being held prisoner. Argus had used the men with them to swiftly and silently dispose of Claudette's guards. Alethea was continuously astounded by her cousin's many skills, ones that had helped her keep her fears for Hartley controlled. At least controlled enough not to do something idiotic and dangerous. But, now, with Hartley so close, her fear for him, and for what he had undoubtedly suffered at that woman's hands, was a clawing, raging beast inside her. It was taking every scrap of willpower she had not to race into that building, screaming his name, and thoroughly destroy everyone's hard work.

"Enough, Alethea, or you will have dug a trench so deep in front of that door that we will be in need of a bridge to cross it," said Olympia as she grabbed Alethea by the hand and halted her pacing.

"I know, I know." She rubbed a hand over her forehead. "I just need to see him, to know that he is still alive. I wish I was a Valkyrie so that I could join in the rescue, screaming some pagan war cry and swinging a sword." She smiled faintly when Olympia laughed. "I want Hartley home." She took a deep breath and hurriedly confessed, "And may God forgive me, but I want to see that woman dead."

"Have no fear. I believe God will forgive you for that. Me? I would want her to suffer every pain, in body and in spirit, that she has inflicted upon others first."

"That would be true justice, but we can hope that what all the ministers tell us is the truth, that she is damned and will suffer greatly for her sins in the hereafter."

"Yes, and the devil is undoubtedly a lot more skilled at torture than that bitch is." Olympia sighed when Alethea flinched. "Sorry. I oftimes speak before I think. It will be over soon. There were only three guards left inside with Claudette, according to one of the ones left outside. Argus is also a master at sneaking up on people. That vile lot in there will be captured and bound up for the trip to the gaol ere they can even blink and wonder what that shadow was that they just saw out of the corner of their eyes."

"And there is just another thing on my mind. Just how and when did Argus become so good at all these things, this spying business. I have always thought that he was just, well, just Argus."

"He has been a part of that shadowy group of men for a long time. Many of our men are. Some are doing it as full members of that secretive society, others just lend a hand now and then. I worry about him, but he is doing what he feels he must do and what he loves to do. 'Tis the same with our cousin Leopold. In truth, I rather envy them for all I hate the danger they put themselves in. Then I recall, well, incidents like this one and decide that they are all a bit mad."

"It is going to be very difficult not to demand that Hartley stop doing this."

"Best you will swallow the urge to say so and bury it deep. However, I do not believe you have to worry too much. Once Hartley knows he is about to become a father, he will pull away from this dangerous game if he has not done so already for your sake alone."

Alethea blinked at her cousin, her mind scrambling to understand what she had just said. "I am not carrying Hartley's child. 'Tis too soon."

"All it takes is one time. Leopold is very fond of saying we are like rabbits."

"How flattering. How can you know I am carrying, be so certain of it, when I do not?"

"I just am. It came to me just now when I clasped your hand. I suspect your woman's time is late, but you have been too involved in all of this intrigue to have noticed it. Trust me in this—you are with child. Wait a while to tell him if you wish. I will say nothing."

She did wish. Alethea believed Olympia, could even sense the glow of wonder and delight over the thought of being a mother burst to life inside her. She would still wait, however, and not just to be certain. Hartley needed to heal, regain his strength, and give her some sign that he now sought more from her than the sort of comfortable marriage he had envisioned when he had proposed. She wanted a union of love, and now she had only a few months to build one.

"Have you studied this? Read books on the great inquisitors?" Hartley asked Claudette as he fought the urge to tense, to brace for the pain he was about to suffer. "Or does this sort of cruelty come naturally to you?"

"I do what I must to get what I need," snapped Claudette.

"You do this for money, greed, and some twisted sense of power. You think this makes you stronger than the poor sod you brutalize. Tying a man to a chair, then cutting him and breaking his bones while he is unable to defend himself, is the act of a coward. Enjoying it is the act of someone truly sick in mind and soul."

Out of the corner of his eye, Hartley saw the shadowy figures of what he prayed were his rescuers slip ever closer. Even if it cost him a toe or two, he would keep Claudette's attention full on him. Her three lackeys followed her lead, their attention firmly fixed on her. They obviously believed themselves secure within a well-guarded building. Hartley had only known Sir Argus for a short time, but he was already certain that

that man could get in anywhere he wished to, exactly when he wished to.

"I see how it is. Because I am a woman, you think I must be soft and submissive." Claudette laughed. "You are as big a fool as all men. A woman is as capable of doing what must be done, no matter how bloody or cruel, as any man. I suspect you would never call a man who tortured information out of another man sick in his mind."

"My dear, vicious lunatic, I most certainly would."

"As would I," said a deep voice as a hand grabbed the wrist of the hand Claudette held her knife in.

What happened next happened so quickly, Hartley doubted he would have seen it all even if his eyes had been clear and not swollen. Claudette struggled, but Argus had her hands tied behind her back in no time at all. Her three henchmen were swiftly subdued by Iago, Aldus, Gifford, and three men Hartley did not recognize. Argus's men, he supposed, and was light-headed with relief.

Aldus began to slice off the bindings holding Hartley to the chair. "Damn, old friend, they have made a fine mess of your good looks."

"Just as they did to Rogers and Peterson," Hartley said.

"Exactly, although not nearly as thoroughly, thank God."

"Thank God indeed." Hartley looked at Claudette, and, even though he knew it was a childish thing to say, it still felt good to say it. "Told you so."

"Get Alethea," Argus said to Gifford, "as well as something to carry Hartley out of here, as he cannot walk out. We will also need a little help with the prisoners." Argus handed Gifford a note he had obviously had prepared before coming to Hartley's rescue. "And have one of my men take this to the Wherlocke Warren. Everyone is staying there while Radmoor's townhouse is being enlarged. They will know what to do."

Modred stepped forward as Gifford left and looked at Claudette, the color slowly leeching from his face. "This one is the darkest soul I have ever looked into. Her sister's soul was cold and empty. This one is so eaten up with hate, jealousy, greed, envy, and anger it is as if she is diseased and rotting from the inside out."

Hartley hissed in pain as Aldus tried to wash some of the blood from his face. "Modred, do not soil your heart and mind by looking into hers. She confessed enough to me to hang her." He looked at his broken fingers and then at Claudette. "I would like my ring back. She took it."

"Yes. A souvenir," Modred said. "She has others. Many of them. She sees each one of them as a sign of her victory over a man or woman or someone she thought belittled or insulted her in some way." He frowned for a moment. "They are all in a chest, one she packed to flee the country once she had finished with you. Stowed in a cabin on the *Raven*. It is due to set sail on tomorrow night's tide. From here in the city."

"What are you saying?" demanded Claudette, staring wide-eyed at Modred. "'Tis lies! All lies!"

"No. The jewels she took that day on the beach are there as well. If you can match her souvenirs to the dead, you will have enough proof to hang her ten times over. Ah, and papers. She already has something to sell to our enemies, Hartley. She just hoped for more. And I see that she badly wished to make you suffer for marrying our Alethea. She had a lot of plans for hurting Alethea as well."

Hartley could tell from the terrified look on Claudette's face that everything Modred was saying was true. It was unsettling to watch him so easily pluck all of Claudette's secrets out of her mind, but Hartley was glad of that eerie skill. Now they had more than enough, more than just their word on her guilt and what she had been caught doing to him.

"Get him away from me!" she screamed, trying to back into Argus for protection even as he did his best to elude her touch.

Modred looked at her three men. "She meant to kill you, too, you know. No witnesses. Best not drink that wine she gave you unless you wish to escape the hangman by poisoning yourselves."

The three men looked at Modred in open-mouthed wonder, touched with a strong hint of fear. Then they turned as one to glare at Claudette. Chaos ensued as they fought with their captors in an attempt to get to her. Four of Hartley's men rushed in to help put an end to the struggle. And behind them came Alethea.

Hartley drank in the sight of her as she rushed to his side. The way she stumbled to a halt only a foot away and all the color left her face told him that he looked as bad as he felt. The arms she had held out to embrace him fell limply to her side, and he saw the glint of tears in her eyes.

"I will heal, Alethea," he said as Aldus knelt to undo the bonds at his ankles.

Alethea forced herself to nod. "Of course you will, and I know a number of people who can help you do so, and quickly."

"Already sent for, sweetheart," said Argus, stepping up to put an arm around her as one of Hartley's men took over holding Claudette. "They will undoubtedly begin to arrive at your home very soon." He winced as Claudette was dragged away, her screams on odd mix of denials, curses, and bloodcurdling threats. "Modred," he called to the young duke, who looked as if he was about to empty his belly. "You did us a great service today. I believe we had enough to hang her, alongside her sister, if only for what she did to a marquis, but what you pried out of her and Margarite will answer a lot of questions. Thank you. Now, do not get anywhere near that bitch again."

"I will be very glad to obey that command, Cousin," Modred said.

"Thank you, Modred," Alethea said.

"For you, Alethea." Modred bowed and then slowly walked away.

"He will be fine," Argus assured Alethea as she watched Modred carefully exit the building.

A cry from Hartley drew her attention back to him. She started to move toward him, but Argus held her back. All her fear and worry for him, and she had not yet been able to touch him.

Despite the care the men moving him to the litter took, she could see the agony it caused him and was not surprised at the damp rush of tears on her cheeks. His hands and face were swollen and deeply bruised. His chest and arms were covered with so many shallow cuts she doubted she could count them without being physically ill. As soon as he was settled on the litter the men had brought in for him, Argus released her, and she ran to Hartley's side. He was pale, panting, and covered in sweat. She doubted he would remain conscious for much longer and considered that a mercy. Careful not to bump the stretcher or touch his battered body, she knelt by his side, leaned forward, and kissed his forehead, the only part of him that remained unscathed.

"Love you," he said, his voice a hoarse, whispery remnant of what it should be. "Feared I would never get to say it."

Alethea was still frozen in shock by his words as she stumbled to her feet so that the men were able to lift the stretcher. With a groan that held all the pain he had to be suffering, Hartley gave up on consciousness. She was grateful when Argus returned to her side and wrapped his strong arm around her, for she was very close to collapsing.

"She hurt him so badly," she whispered. "I do not think there is a part of him that is not either broken or bleeding or bruised. How can he recover from that?"

"He is a strong and stubborn man," Argus said. "And, do not forget, nearly every healer in our family who can come, will come, and will be taking a turn at ensuring that he recovers fully. The cuts are shallow, and, from what little I could see, the bones were cleanly broken. He is alive, Alethea. Be grateful for that. Find your strength in that."

She did her best to heed his words. When Hartley was carried into the house, the immediate need to try and calm Germaine and Bayard helped her regain her strength. Alethea left them with Argus and the others as soon as she felt she could and rushed to Hartley's side. Although she had no healing gift, she was able to help with the bathing of his wounds and bandaging

the worst of his injuries while the healers in her family
each took a turn doing what they could for him. The
strongest of the lot were Penelope's half brother Stefan,
who paired up with the boy Delmar, her cousin Felix's
natural son.

By the time they had all left, Olympia hurrying after
them to make certain they got all the food and drink
they needed to restore the strength lost in healing,
Alethea's hope for Hartley's recovery was growing.
Hartley had not awakened, but he slept peacefully even
though they had been able to get only a small amount
of Kate's potion down his throat. She pulled a chair
up beside the bed and decided that, even if all the healers had done was to ease his pain, it was enough.

It was very late when Germaine and Bayard slipped
into the room. Alfred followed them and set a tray of
food and drink down on the small table in front of the
fireplace. After a stern look at her that said she had
better eat, he left. Alethea stood up, stretched, and then
moved to sit at the table. She realized that she was
hungry, her appetite returning as her fear for Hartley
began to fade.

"Does Alfred understand that you are now a marchioness?" asked Germaine as she took the seat opposite
Alethea, leaving Bayard to sit watch by Hartley's bed.

Alethea smiled. "Of course, but I am also the girl he
has known since she could barely walk. And the Pughs
have served the Vaughns for hundreds of years. They
are, in so many ways, as much family as servants."

Germaine nodded and looked toward Hartley. "Uncle
looks much better than he did when he was carried into
the house, even with all the splints, bruises, bandages,

and cuts. He sleeps as if he feels no pain. How can that be after what was done to him?"

"The healers did it, and I fear I cannot explain it. Since his fingers, left arm, and left leg are splinted, I cannot even be sure just how much of him they have actually healed. Yet he sleeps free of pain. That can only be good."

"Your family has so many different gifts. Is there anyone in your very large family who does not have one?"

"Some have one that is so very weak it is nearly useless, but only a few. We do not marry amongst ourselves, or very rarely do, and not because the church frowns on it. We all have the never-ending hope that we can breed it out of us, but that has yet to happen."

"I would cease trying. For most of you, the gift you have been given seems to be doing more good than harm. Even for poor Modred, whose bad luck appears to have started with whoever gave him that name." Germaine grinned when Alethea laughed, but quickly turned serious again. "He looked pale and shaken but also very pleased with himself. He helped, and I think that matters a great deal to him. It gave him some pride in himself."

"Yes. Yes, it did. Chloe said he needed to do it. I am just sorry that he had to prove himself on two such evil women. Is he resting now?" When Germaine nodded, Alethea sighed in relief. "I just pray that he suffers no nightmares due to what he saw in Claudette."

"I waver between wanting that woman dead and being appalled that I could wish for such a thing. All the time we were in France, the thought of making that woman suffer kept me strong. Now? Now I feel a little ashamed of that. Yet she should suffer for what she did to my uncle, to my family, and to so many others."

"Agreed," said Alethea, "and we must believe that she will."

"In hell?"

Alethea shrugged. "We can only hang her once." She studied Germaine. "Do you wish to go to her hanging?"

"Not so much wish it, but need to. She stole my family from me, save for Bayard and Uncle. I need to be there for my father, for Theresa, and for the babes. I also need to know that she is truly dead."

It was difficult not to argue that plan with the girl, but Alethea simply patted Germaine's hand and then turned to the chore of finishing her meal. They could sort it all out when the time came. At Bayard and Germaine's insistence, Alethea sought out her own bed. She wanted to stay by Hartley's side, her fear of losing him still running deep and strong, but she also knew she needed to sleep. As Hartley recovered, caring for him would require a great deal of strength and courage. All her instincts told her that he would not be an easy patient.

Once Alethea was tucked up in bed, she found sleep hard to come by even though she was more tired than she had ever been in her life. Hartley's words kept pounding in her mind, demanding she think about them. *Love you.* He had definitely said those words, but she was not sure how much faith she should put in them. He had been in pain, dazed with it, yet exuberant over his rescue. Emotions had been running high, and that could have prompted the words. He might also not have meant them as she so dearly wanted him to.

Alethea closed her eyes and worked even harder to clear her mind of all thoughts fighting to deprive her of sleep. She would wait to see what he did and said in the days to come. If he did not repeat the declaration, so be it. Alethea would accept that it had been spoken in the heat of the moment or a delirium born of the pain he had been in. Then she would do her best to make him say those words again while he was awake and clear of mind. Only then would she choose to believe him and gently place her heart in his hands.

Chapter 19

With a few final flourishes, Hartley signed his name to the last of the documents his secretary had brought to him from his solicitor. He had been a fool not to make out a new will the moment he had married Alethea. The troubles they had been wrapped up in were really no excuse for such a lapse. Now it was done, and, if anything ever happened to him, she would be financially secure, all her rights as his widow and the mother of whatever children they might have thoroughly protected. Before it had been uncomfortable to contemplate his mortality, but after having faced death, he was all too aware of how quickly and unexpectedly it could touch a man on the shoulder.

He held up his right hand and wriggled his fingers, and then he did the same with the left. Only three weeks had passed since he had been rescued from Claudette and her men, and he was nearly as good as new. In the last week it had only been weakness and a need to regain the strength lost that had held him back from a full recovery. Hartley might not understand what the healers had done, but he was grateful beyond words for it. His arm and leg had also healed rapidly and were growing stronger by the day. He could all too easily have ended up crippled in some way. It was a miracle he would thank God for every day. And, despite their refusals of any payment, he had seen to it that each Wherlocke and Vaughn who had helped him heal so well and so rapidly had been duly rewarded for their efforts on his behalf.

Now he could begin to turn his attention to his wife, he thought, and grinned. She had said nothing about his declaration of love just before he had become unconscious that day. Hartley decided she had convinced herself that it had been made due to the high emotion of the moment and was not heartfelt. He was determined to show her just how wrong she was. The wooing had already begun with small gifts and long talks alone in the garden as he had recuperated. Now that he was completely healed, he could begin to woo her in the bedchamber as well as outside it.

Germaine slipped into his office, and, quickly yanking his mind out of the bedchamber where his willing wife waited for him with nothing more than a smile on her face, he smiled at Germaine. The time he had spent healing had also served to bring him, his nephew, and his niece closer together. They had wept together when the jewels Claudette had stolen from the compte that day on the beach were returned. Bayard and Germaine had wept for their father, a woman they had grown to love, and their two young half siblings. Hartley had wept for the sister he had lost so long ago, the senseless death of the man his sister had loved, and the pain she would have felt if she had known how her children had suffered. In that shared moment of grief, they had finally become a true family.

"They are hanging Claudette and Margarite today," Germaine said as she stood before his desk and nervously played with a colorful stone he had collected as a child during a walk on the beach with his father.

Hartley inwardly cursed, for he had hoped that she would not discover that. He should have known better. In the three years she had hidden and worked in France, Germaine had picked up a few skills most young ladies did not have. One thing she was very good at was ferreting out any information.

"I am going so you do not have to," he said.

"I know, but I feel guilty about that. It is my place to stand there in lieu of Papa, Theresa, and the babies."

"That is what I will do, just as I mean to stand for the others those women killed."

"Is Alethea going with you?"

"No. She was prepared to go, but it was easy for even a cloddish man such as myself to see that she did not truly want to go to a hanging, and I understand that. It is an ugly way to die. I do not particularly wish to see it myself, but I will be with Iago, Argus, Gifford, and Aldus, as well as a large group of men who worked with or were friends with Rogers, Peterson, and the others she killed. And, I promise you, I will make very sure that she is dead."

Germaine slipped around the side of his desk and kissed him on the cheek. "Thank you, Uncle, and Bayard thanks you, too. He never wanted to go. We saw enough death in France." She started to leave, only to pause in the doorway. "Oh, and Bayard and I are going to spend tomorrow with the Radmoors at their country home. We are going to be leaving soon and will not return until late the day after tomorrow. Alfred and Kate are coming with us as our maid and valet. Is that still acceptable to you?"

"Of course. Radmoor has a very fine home and grounds. And, of course, all those young people. It will do you well to get some fresh country air. Have a good time."

"Oh, I am certain we will, Uncle. You have a good time, too," she sang as she hurried away.

Hartley intended to have a very good time indeed. Until recently he would have needed Alethea to take the upper hand in the lovemaking if they were to have any. That would have been agreeable to him, but she had been treating him like an invalid and lovemaking had clearly been the last thing on her mind. All her relatives had left, and now Germaine and Bayard were going away for a little while. Even Kate and Alfred would be gone. He would have Mrs. Huxley leave some food for him and Alethea and then give the servants a full day off, starting right after dinner and continuing until the morning of the day Germaine and Bayard were to return. He only had one last grim chore to see to, and then he would turn all of his attention to the seduction of his wife. Tonight he intended to show her that he was no longer an invalid.

"And that appalling show puts a firm end to it all," said Argus as he, Hartley, and the others walked away from the gallows grounds. "You can assure Germaine, Bayard, and your wife that the woman is most certainly dead. She and her sister. I think I would even tell them just how badly they died, too."

Hartley grimaced. The women had died badly. They had wailed and protested, even fought and dragged their feet every step of the way. The crowd had booed, jeered, and pelted them with rotten food and offal. He was very glad that Alethea and Germaine had not been there to see it all. The whole spectacle had been as appalling and as gruesome as he had remembered. The fact that Margarite had been nearly decapitated by the rope had only added to that. He had thought that knowing the condemned, knowing of all the crimes they had committed, including the ones against him and his family, would make it easier to watch the execution. It had not, except that now he could tell his family that Claudette and Margarite would never be able to trouble them again.

He left the other men to make his way home alone. Alethea met him in the foyer, an expectant look upon her face. He handed Cobb his coat and hat, and then gently drew Alethea into his office. As delicately as he could, he told her all about the hanging, not mentioning the near decapitation, for it was not necessary to the tale and he simply could not speak of that gruesome part to his wide-eyed wife. And then, pouring himself a brandy, he waited to hear what she had to say about it all.

"'Tis odd, is it not, that two people who killed so many other people would be so terrified of their own deaths." Alethea went to Hartley and wrapped her arms around him, resting her cheek against his broad chest. "I am sorry you had to witness that but very glad to know for certain that they are both gone."

"I went because their victims could not. Iago said that the spirits around Claudette are at rest now."

"Good. Then it is over and done, and we can get on with our lives now." She stepped away from him, even though she ached to linger in his arms. "A bath has been readied for you, and then there is dinner to be enjoyed. It will be strange to have just the two of us at the table again. That has not happened since only three days after we were married."

Hartley thought it would be a sweet pleasure to have her all to himself for a little while as he went to his bedchamber to wash away the stench of the gallows. Once dinner was over, even the servants would be gone. He could chase his wife through the house and make love to her in any room he wanted. He could also do his best to discover exactly how she felt about him.

He loved her, and he needed her to return that love in full measure. It was not going to be easy to bare his soul when he was still uncertain of the depth of her feeling for him, but he could do it. Catering to his pride now seemed foolish after what he had been through, after that moment when he had thought he would never see her again. His instincts told him that she loved him, but he needed to hear the words. Hartley knew he also needed her to believe him when he spoke the words to her.

Alethea looked around her bedchamber and sighed. It was a beautiful room, but she wanted to be sharing Hartley's bed. They had thus far spent very little of their marriage in the same bed. She was beginning to fear that Hartley liked that arrangement. He would just have to change his mind, she decided. They were husband

and wife, not some sinful couple sneaking a few trysts when time and the absence of other partners allowed.

She studied herself carefully in the mirror. Her hair was clean, thick, and shining with good health even though she did wish it was not as black as a raven's wing. The nightgown and robe she wore were dainty concoctions of blue linen and white lace meant to tease a man; at least, that was what the dressmaker had told her. Her breasts did seem to be more exposed than she liked, the neckline of the gown barely covering her nipples. Alethea had no idea what men liked to look at but, if it were breasts, Hartley would get an eyeful.

"Now or never, woman," she grumbled as she turned and marched toward the door that connected his bedchamber to hers. "Get a spine. This is for the rest of your life. Time to start as you mean to continue."

Alethea opened the door only to face a robed Hartley standing there in the act of reaching for the door latch. "Oh. I was just coming to speak with you."

"Good." He grabbed her by the hand and pulled her into his bedchamber. "I was intending to speak to you as well. I am no longer in need of gentle care and nights spent alone in my bed."

"Ah. Yes, I can see that."

Hartley had not tied his robe very tightly, and it was obvious that he was naked beneath it. She clasped her hands together in front of her to stop herself from slipping her hands inside that robe and running them all over that smooth, taut skin she loved to touch. He wanted to talk, and, since she did as well, it was best if she did not give in to her baser urges. There would be time for that later.

"Is this new?" Hartley could not seem to lift his gaze

above her breasts, and all his carefully planned words were fading away. "I do not recall seeing this before." He trailed his fingers over the plump swell of her breasts above the neckline of the nightgown and watched her tremble slightly.

Perhaps the best place to talk was in bed, he thought, his mouth watering to taste all that soft flesh she was showing. He might get the words he needed from her in the heat of passion. He would certainly find it easier to say them then. Hartley put his arms around her and tugged her close to his body.

"I thought you wanted to talk," she said as she slipped her hands inside his robe and lightly caressed his sides.

"We can talk in bed," he said as he slowly removed her robe and kissed the place where her neck met her shoulder.

The heat from that one soft kiss against her skin flowed through Alethea's body. She decided they could talk during or after. She no longer cared. It had been too long since she had been held by him, kissed by him, and touched by him. Her whole body ached for him to be inside her.

"I think this is going to be fast and furious," he said.

"Just do not rip the gown. You paid a lot for it."

He laughed as he tugged the gown over her head and then threw off his robe. When he pulled her back into his arms, he fell down onto the bed. The feel of her soft skin caressing his was a stark reminder of how long it had been since he had tasted her passion. He kissed her, showing her his hunger for her in each thrust and stroke of his tongue as he touched her everywhere.

Alethea tried to return every touch he gave her in

equal measure. She was starving for the heat of his skin and the taste of his kiss. Her passion was running so high and hot she could not keep quiet and briefly worried about being overheard. Then he took the hard tip of her breast deep in his mouth even as he thrust his fingers inside her, and she forgot all about a need to be quiet.

They wrestled each other in an effort to each touch the places that brought the most pleasure to their partner. Alethea finally grasped hold of his erection and stroked the hot, hard length of him. When he trembled in her arms, she knew a sense of sensual power that only added to her need for him.

"Now, Hartley," she demanded, her body shaking with the need to have him inside her.

"Ordering me about now, are you?"

He was not surprised at the hoarseness in his voice. Every inch of his body was taut and ready to possess her, and it had been a strain to hold back as long as he had. He sat back on his knees, grabbed her thighs, and spread her legs wide. A small part of his mind that was still sane grinned at the way her eyes widened, too. Pulling her forward until her legs rested on his hips, he pushed into her. The tight heat of her made him gasp, and he lost the last thread of what little control he had.

Alethea was shocked when he pulled her into such an indecorous position. Then he thrust inside her, and her greedy body revealed that it did not care how he did it, so long as he kept on doing it. Her release stormed over her, and she arched her body into his, straining to take him in as deep as possible. Hartley's hands tightened almost painfully on her hips, and then he pounded into her four more times, until he stilled and the heat of his seed bathed her insides. The way he cried out her name was pure music to her ears.

"That was certainly fast and furious," she said after they had washed off and then collapsed in each other's arms. "Noisy, too. I hope no one heard us. I will not be able to look anyone in the eye on the morrow."

"No one heard you." Hartley savored the sight of her naked and in his arms, trailing his fingers up and down her spine. "Everyone is gone."

"Well, yes, I know Germaine and Bayard, along with Alfred and Kate, have gone to the Radmoors', but—" She frowned at him when he placed a finger on her lips and silenced her.

"Everyone is gone. I sent the servants off right after dinner, and they will not return until the morning of the day after the morrow. We have the entire house to ourselves." He slapped her on her beautiful backside, gently rolled her body off his, and stood up. "And I believe I will now go to the kitchen and eat some of that food Mrs. Huxley left for us."

"Naked?" Alethea sat up, holding the blanket to her chest as she looked him over. It amazed her that after such a satisfying bout of lovemaking, that tickle of interest was yet again skipping through her body.

"My house. No servants. Yes. I am going to the kitchen to eat something, and I am doing it naked. Coming with me?"

She climbed out of bed and picked up her robe. "I will come, too, but not completely naked."

Hartley watched her march out of the room in front of him and grinned. He decided he would not tell her that the robe she was wearing hid very little. If it made her feel as if she was decently covered, he was not about to argue. He was enjoying the view far too much. Rubbing his hands together, he began to think of all the ways they could make love in the kitchen.

To Alethea's shock and then pleasure, Hartley made love to her on the kitchen table. She was barely recovered from that when he dragged her into his office and made love to her on his desk, saying that he would always remember this and it would warm him on the days he was buried in work.

In the parlor he stretched her out on the window seat and made love to her with his mouth. In the breakfast room she pushed him up against a wall and returned the gift. Alethea lost all sense of modesty by the time they made love on the stairs. She was not sure she could walk by the time they staggered back into bed. Her last clear thought was that they still had not talked.

Dawn was just lighting the sky when she woke to the heat of Hartley's mouth on her breasts. Alethea lifted her hand and threaded her fingers through his hair. "You are insatiable."

"Only for you." He gently bit the nipple he had nursed to a hard point.

"Hartley, you said you had something you wanted to talk to me about," she reminded him, fighting back the demands of her body to just give in to his seduction.

He slid up her body and kissed her. "I want you to sleep in here. Every night."

"Oh. Of course." She blushed. "I was actually going to talk to you about that, too. I do not like to sleep alone, and yet we have done little else since we got married."

Hartley kissed her again, relieved that she, too, was eager to sleep in the same bed. "Now, I said something to you when I was rescued, just before I passed out. You have never acknowledged what I said, and I know you heard me."

"It is all right, Hartley. I know you were in pain and yet so overjoyed that you had been freed and I-I—" She stuttered to a halt when he gently placed his hand over her mouth.

"I thought that might be the way of it. I meant it, Alethea. I meant each word and would have been more eloquent had I been able to speak." He was not sure the way her eyes widened so much it had to hurt was a good sign, but he continued, "I thought I was going to die."

She moved his hand. "I know, and that is why you felt the need to say—"

He put his hand back over her mouth. "I felt the need to say it because I was afraid that, in my cowardice, I had forever lost the chance. I sat in the damned chair waiting for that woman to break even more bones and started to think of all I was losing, because I did not see how I could get out of there alive. Oh, I told her you would come, boasted of your family's many gifts and how she could not run from them, but I did think I would die.

"And all I thought about was you. How I would not be able to hold you again, see you again, make love to you again. I even thought of how I would never see you round with our child or hear that child laugh. I did not think of my friends, or even Germaine and Bayard except to know that you would take good care of them. Not my title left without an heir or my lands. All I could think of was you and how I would die without ever telling you what you mean to me. I meant it,

Alethea. I love you." He frowned as a tear rolled down
her cheek. "Are you crying?" He slowly moved his
hand away.

"No," she replied and used her hands to wipe the
tears from her face. "Oh, Hartley, I am such a wretch.
All this time I never mentioned it because I thought
you did not really mean it as I hoped you did. I am so
sorry."

"Nothing to apologize for. I had guessed that. It was
not the best time to make a declaration, but it had been
one of the things I had thought I would never do, and
I felt compelled to say it right away, the moment I saw
you again." He frowned as he suddenly thought over
what she had just said. "Did you just say you hoped I
meant it?"

"Is that what I said?" she asked, staring at a lock of
her hair as she combed her fingers through and fighting not to smile.

Her heart was bursting with joy. He loved her. She
had heard those two hoarse words in her dreams ever
since he had said them and silently prayed every night
that he would say them again and mean them. Now that
he had she was giddy with joy and could not believe
she was teasing him before replying in kind. The words
had burned on the end of her tongue for so long she
was surprised they were not branded there.

She laughed softly when he cupped her face in his
big hands and made her face him. Alethea could see by
the mock anger in his expression that he knew she
loved him. If he had had a moment of doubt, he was far
past that now.

"Alethea, when a man makes a declaration to a
woman, I think she is supposed to respond," he said.

"Especially when she says something about hoping it is true and is lying naked beneath him."

"Ah, so that is why you were in such a rush to get me in bed. You hoped the nakedness would prompt me to spill all the secrets of my heart."

"Alethea," he growled.

She laughed and kissed him. "I love you. I have loved you almost from the beginning. I think the seed for it was planted with the first time I saw you in a vision."

"You have never said so."

"Have I not? I bedded you despite the fact that you made no mention of marriage, and I was a virgin. I also said yes to your poor proposal."

"What was wrong with my proposal?"

"Companionship, passion, and someone to help with Germaine and Bayard? Hartley, my own true love, only a woman madly in love with you would say yes to a proposal like that."

He laughed and nuzzled her neck. She was right. It had been an appalling proposal. If he had realized just how bad it was then, he would have known that she was in love with him the moment she said yes. For a rake, he knew very little about women aside from getting them in bed. Now he had two living in his house, a wife and a niece. It would be interesting to see just how different his life was going to be from now on.

Hartley murmured his pleasure when she stroked his stomach. "Are we done talking now?"

"Hartley, do you want children with me?" she asked in a small voice, her fears of her own heritage hard to shake off.

"Of course I do. Why would I not want children with the woman I love?"

"Because whatever children we have will have a very good chance of having some sort of gift. I know I mentioned this before, but you said you did not care. I wondered if you still felt that way after meeting my family."

"After meeting your family, I feel even stronger about it. Yes, they have skills I simply do not understand and may never do so. But the ones I have met are loyal, loving men and women. A child could not ask for a better family. If our child is born with a gift, they will all help in the raising to make sure the child understands the gift and uses it correctly. So, yes, I want a child with you. Do not worry about what I might say if there is a Vaughn or Wherlocke gift that comes with the baby. I will love any and all of the children we have, even if they can see ghosts."

Alethea was almost weak with relief. "I hope this child does not have too strange a gift. You will want to adjust to such things before a second one comes along."

Hartley propped himself up on his elbows and stared at her. "Alethea?"

She took his hand and placed it low on her belly. "Olympia told me there was a child the day we saved you, but I had no sign of it yet. Now I have. Yes, Hartley, you will become a father in seven or eight months."

He stared at her belly, nearly completely covered by his hand, and then looked at her. It took a moment for the news to really sink into his mind, and then Hartley felt a stinging in his eyes. He blinked quickly and gently kissed the place where his child grew. A heartbeat later he sat up and stared at her in horror.

"My God, woman, I just made love to you on the stairs!"

"And the kitchen table and the desk and—"

"But you were with child while I was doing that."

He looked so horrified, so afraid he had hurt her in some way, that Alethea was able to swallow her laughter. "It did not hurt the baby. You made love to me in odd places, Hartley—you did not bounce me down the stairs or the like. I am fine. The baby is fine. And we will both be fine no matter how often or where you make love to me."

With a sigh that was filled with both relief and disbelief, he pulled her into his arms. "I love you, and I already love the child. I do not suppose Olympia said which it was?"

"No, only that there is a child. I may be wrong, it may be just a wish to please you with an heir, but I think it is a boy."

"Do you have any names you dearly wish to use?"

"No. I think you do, though, do you not?"

"Yes, I would like to name the first girl after my sister and the first boy after my brother. They both died too young."

"Then that is what will happen. I always wanted a child, but, due to the sort of names our family has, I always imagined they would be called Mary or John. Something common. I am already impatient to meet him. It will be a long wait."

"And worth every month." He kissed her. "I love you."

"I love you, too."

"And I think we ought to celebrate."

"Really? How?"

He leapt out of bed, picked her up, and grabbed the blanket. "We have not made love in the wine cellar yet."

Alethea wrapped her arms around his neck and laughed all the way down the stairs.

Epilogue

"Alethea, where are you?"

"In the parlor, Germaine," Alethea yelled back. "I hear that tone in her voice, Justus," she said to her son, who stared up at her with his father's eyes. "She is just a little too happy."

A moment later Germaine swirled into the room. She curtsied to Alethea and then to her young cousin Justus, who was struggling to pull himself up on his feet. Only nine months old and already tired of being an infant, Alethea thought lovingly.

She then looked at Germaine and nearly groaned. By the look of it, Germaine thought she was in love— again. For a girl who was usually so mature and sensible, Germaine had revealed an alarming romantic streak that had her thinking she had met her true love every other month. She fell for a pretty face, elegant clothes, and fine manners much too easily. Neither she nor Hartley had the heart to deny her her fun, however, and they were also confident that she would never do anything foolish such as rush off to get married in the middle of the night or destroy her good name. However,

Alethea really wished she would get over this falling-
in-and-out-of-love stage she was stuck in.

"Who is the lucky man this time?" Alethea asked.

"Tristan Maccleby. Baron Maccleby." Germaine
placd her clasped hands on her heart and sighed
dramatically. "He is the most handsome, the most
dashing, the—"

"—most poverty-stricken, debt-ridden, whore-
mongering piece of pretty man flesh that has ever
donned a pair of breeches," Alethea said, having made
a close study of all the young men currently prancing
around the ballrooms and parlors of the ton for just this
reason.

Germaine stumbled to a halt and looked at Alethea
in horror. "Are you certain?"

And this, Alethea thought, was another reason she
and Hartley did not do anything about Germaine's
many romantic flights. The girl heeded them when they
told her what they knew about the chosen one of the
day. She trusted them to always tell her the truth, and
they treated that trust with all the respect it deserved.

"Afraid so. He is only welcomed everywhere because his father is a powerful duke."

Germaine sighed and flopped down on the settee next
to Alethea. Unfortunately, her action caused young
Justus to fall down. He landed on his well-padded
bottom and frowned at Germaine. Alethea laughed
softly, for he looked very much like his father when he
frowned, even though he had her black hair.

"Oh, I am so sorry, little man," Germaine said and
picked the boy up, kissing his cheek and apparently
oblivious to the drool dripping onto her fine gown.

Alethea saw something when Germaine stretched

out to get the boy and set her sewing aside. She inched up Germaine's sleeve and frowned at the long scratch there. "How did you get this?"

"Oh, a group of us were out in Lady Gideon's gardens, and I stumbled against a very large, very thorny rosebush. It was Lord Maccleby who helped me up, and he looked so much like a hero, with the sun glinting in his hair. You would never know to look at him that he is just a fortune-hunting, faithless, rutting swine. Oh, do not worry. It is just a scratch. It bled only a little."

"I think I will still wash it and put some salve on it."

Alethea stood up just as her son put his hand right on Germaine's scratch. "Ah, no, sweet boy, that has not been cleaned yet." She picked his hand off the scratch and gasped.

"What? Is it bleeding again?" Germaine looked at her scratch and frowned. "It is not nearly as red and ugly as it was a moment ago." Her words slowed to a halt as she looked at Justus, who was wriggling in his mother's arms in an attempt to get back on the floor. "But he is still just a baby! Should he not wait until he is older before he gets a gift?"

Alethea set her son down on the floor and then collapsed on the seat next to Germaine. "I know he is only a baby, but it sometimes happens that way. Our cousin Paul was only a toddling little boy when he began to get his warnings of danger. Maybe it is just that the air cooled off the cut, eased the irritation that made it red." She searched in her sewing basket for a needle as Justus struggled to stand up again.

"What are you going to do with that?"

"Try to see if it was real or just that your irritation

went away." Alethea poked her fingertip with the needle. "Ow!"

Holding her breath, she stretched her hand out toward Justus. He frowned that adorable frown and grabbed her finger. To her astonishment and amusement, he gave the tip a loud, smacking kiss. All amusement fled, however, as she felt a distinct warmth that had nothing to do with baby drool. She knew what that warmth meant. She had never had a healer touch her who did not have that warmth. Gently taking her hand back, she looked at her finger and saw nothing.

"Maybe it was such a small cut it just closed up, and his drool washed the blood away," said Germaine as she stared at Alethea's finger.

"That could be the way of it." Alethea had the sinking feeling it was not, however.

"Well, we cannot go around wounding ourselves and making him touch the wounds just to be certain. From what I recall of the healers that helped Uncle, healing anyone made them weak. We do not want to make poor little Justus weak."

"No." She looked at Justus, who had managed to get himself up on his feet and was bouncing up and down on his plump little legs. "He does not look as if he feels any weakness."

Germaine looked at her arm again. "If he has a gift at such a young age, at least it is the healing one. That should be no great problem, should it?"

"Not unless he grabs someone who does not understand or is superstitious and heals some wound or illness. When a child gets his gift at such a young age, secrecy becomes very difficult to maintain." She frowned. "Mayhap I should get Stefan and Darius over here."

"You think they can help tell us if Justus is a healer?"

"Well, Stefan is one, and sometimes healers can sense each other. And Darius sees auras, and he says he is learning how to tell the aura of a seer from the aura of a healer and so forth. He felt it might be a useful thing in our family."

"Then let us get them over here quickly."

Even as Alethea got up to go to the bell pull and summon Cobb, she asked, "Why in such a rush? Justus is not going anywhere."

"I would like an answer, and I think it would be very helpful if we have one for Hartley when he comes home."

Alethea thumped her head against the door. "Oh hellfire."

Although she knew they were doing their best, Alethea could not help pacing as she waited for Stefan and Darius to tell her what they did and did not know about Justus. Ever since Germaine had mentioned Hartley, she had been on pins and needles. He loved his son, and she had no doubt he would continue to love his son even if Justus proved to be gifted early. It would still be a shock, however.

"Well," said Stefan as he set Justus down on the floor and brushed baby drool off his shirt. "I think you have yourself a very powerful healer."

Darius nodded. "The aura is right." He held out his hand. "And look there."

She looked. "There is nothing there."

"Exactly. When I arrived, I had a cut there. It was starting to heal, and then Justus touched it. I felt that

warmth, Alethea. That warmth of a healer. And then I
looked, and it was all healed. He is going to be a very
powerful healer, Alethea. And look at him. He is not
even wobbling. For such a small boy to heal a cut and
not even get a little sleepy? Wonderful."

Alethea dragged her hands through her hair and ignored
the sound of hairpins dropping on the floor. "Oh, yes.
Wonderful. Just what am I going to tell my husband?"

"I do not know. What *are* you going to tell your
husband?"

That deep voice coming from behind her froze
Alethea on the spot. She noticed that Germaine, Stefan,
and Darius all blushed with guilt. Turning, saying
nothing was wrong, and smiling was obviously not
going to work now.

She turned to see Hartley frowning at Justus. He
walked over and picked up his son, who gave him a
big, loud, drooling kiss on his chin. After he looked the
boy all over, he turned to Stefan.

"Is something wrong with my son?" he asked. "Is
that why you are here, Stefan?"

Alethea rushed to Hartley's side. "Oh, no, no. Nothing is wrong. Truly. I asked Stefan and Darius to come
here because I think Justus is already showing signs
of having a gift."

"What? He is a baby."

"I know."

Alethea began to tell him all about Germaine's cut,
and how that had been healed and then poking her
finger. She knew she was babbling but could not stop.
She consoled herself with the fact that she was at least
telling him the whole story. There was a lot included in
the tale that did not need to be there, but she could not

think clearly enough to stick to the exact points that needed to be told.

Hartley listened to his wife go on about Germaine's latest infatuation, rose-briar scratches, pinpricks, drool, and calling on Stefan and Darius to discover the truth. When she finally stopped talking, he leaned forward and kissed her. Then he looked at Stefan.

"Justus is not sick," he said.

"No," Stefan answered.

"So you are here to find out something else about my son. About a gift?"

"Yes." Stefan sighed. "Seeing as the women have been struck speechless, I will tell you that we are fairly certain that your son is already showing the signs of being a very strong healer."

"I see." Hartley looked at Alethea and then back at the others. "Perhaps, Germaine, you could take the young men to the kitchen and see if Mrs. Huxley has anything good to eat. And I thank both of you young men for coming so quickly in response to my wife's call for assistance."

"No trouble," said Darius as he followed Germaine and Stefan out of the room. "It was wonderful to see the aura of a new, powerful healer. You should be very proud."

Alethea looked at Hartley, who was staring at Justus. "I am sorry."

He put his arm around her and pulled her close, then kissed the top of her head. "You have nothing to be sorry for. We both knew this could happen." He chuckled. "I just did not expect it to happen to a child who cannot speak or walk yet and who seems to be an unending source of drool."

"You are not upset?"

"Just answer me this—will there be more gifts?"

"No, I very much doubt it. Well, it is very rare for a healer to be anything more than a healer. There might be a tiny touch of something later, such as when he enters manhood, but nothing is as strong as the first gift that reveals itself."

"So, I have a son who can heal people but still has three months to go before he is even one year old."

"I am afraid so." She stroked her son's head. "He will be such a powerful one, too."

"I love you," Hartley said and kissed her.

"I love you, too."

"Do not look so worried, love. I am not upset. A little uneasy, as he is too young to know how to be discrete, but not upset at all." He grinned. "Hell, I have a very strong healer here. It could have been another Modred. Love the man though I do, I have dreaded the chance that our child could get his gift. No, Darius is right. I should be very proud, and I am. Now, since I know that Mrs. Huxley has baked gingerbread, I think we will wander down to the kitchens to celebrate."

Alethea slipped her arm through his, and they started down to the kitchen. Olympia was right in what she had seen in her future. Alethea was very happy.

Dear Readers:

Hope you have enjoyed the tale of Alethea and Hartley. I'm leaving the Wherlockes for the next book and returning to visit the Murrays, the Highlands, and the heather. Sir Simon Innes—who appeared in both HIGHLAND WOLF and HIGHLAND SINNER—has been whining for his own story and his own special heroine. And who better for him than a Murray lass? A lass raised to be strong, quick of wit, adventurous, and destined to find trouble if it doesn't find her first.

Ilsabeth Murray Armstrong is the daughter of Elspeth Murray and Cormac Armstrong from HIGHLAND VOW. Following in the footsteps of her illustrious ancestresses, she stumbles her way into a lot of trouble. She overhears her betrothed speaking with another man of a plot against the king. Before she can get home to speak to her parents she is warned that a man has been murdered, her dagger found in his heart, and that the king's men were already searching for her.

Knowing that she cannot drag her family into the midst of such treachery and suspicion, she seeks out a man who has already saved two Murrays from the hangman—the dark, sober Sir Simon Innes. Ilsabeth finds him to be a man very much to her liking despite the distrust he reveals as she pleads for his help. She is not one to back down from a challenge and sets her heart and mind on proving her innocence. But can she prove to him that she is the perfect woman for a man who is too much alone, his spirit burdened by the evils he has seen?

Sir Simon Innes is a man dedicated to finding the truth and he is not all that sure that the beautiful Ilsabeth is being completely honest with him. She may have Murray blood but she is also an Armstrong and they do not have a particularly sterling reputation. He finds himself tempted by her big blue eyes and her lively spirit, however, and is drawn deep into the danger and betrayal surrounding her. Passion soon rules them both and he risks his position as a king's man to try and save her.

Oh, yes, Simon and Ilsabeth have a hard row to plow, enemies to fight, and doubts to conquer. Will she win? Or will treachery defeat all her plans? And what of Simon? Can he give his well-protected heart to a woman he is not sure he can trust?

After the tale of Simon and Ilsabeth I do plan to return to the Wherlockes. There are so many stories about their vast and gifted family that need to be told. I am thinking it is time the cocky, randy, but oh-so-charming Sir Argus Wherlocke gets his tale. He is certainly demanding one. Nudging at my mind even as I turn my attention back to the Murrays.

But what sort of woman would deal well with a man who has two illegitimate sons? A man who has bedded far too many women, starting at a very young age? A man who can make anyone tell him their deepest, darkest secrets?

She would have to be a very strong woman. She would also have to have some defense against that strange gift of his. After all, what woman wants a man who knows all her secrets? Where would be the mystery in that? Matching that arrogant rogue will not be easy but I know there is a woman out there ready to take him on. And I think Argus should have to work very hard to deserve her, don't you?

Look for *Highland Protector*, coming in December 2010! Here's hoping you will enjoy a return to the Murrays!

Happy Reading!
Hannah Howell

More by Bestselling Author
Hannah Howell

Available Wherever Books Are Sold!

Check out our website at
http://www.kensingtonbooks.com

Romantic Suspense from
Lisa Jackson

See How She Dies	0-8217-7605-3	$6.99US/$9.99CAN
Final Scream	0-8217-7712-2	$7.99US/$10.99CAN
Wishes	0-8217-6309-1	$5.99US/$7.99CAN
Whispers	0-8217-7603-7	$6.99US/$9.99CAN
Twice Kissed	0-8217-6038-6	$5.99US/$7.99CAN
Unspoken	0-8217-6402-0	$6.50US/$8.50CAN
If She Only Knew	0-8217-6708-9	$6.50US/$8.50CAN
Hot Blooded	0-8217-6841-7	$6.99US/$9.99CAN
Cold Blooded	0-8217-6934-0	$6.99US/$9.99CAN
The Night Before	0-8217-6936-7	$6.99US/$9.99CAN
The Morning After	0-8217-7295-3	$6.99US/$9.99CAN
Deep Freeze	0-8217-7296-1	$7.99US/$10.99CAN
Fatal Burn	0-8217-7577-4	$7.99US/$10.99CAN
Shiver	0-8217-7578-2	$7.99US/$10.99CAN
Most Likely to Die	0-8217-7576-6	$7.99US/$10.99CAN
Absolute Fear	0-8217-7936-2	$7.99US/$9.49CAN
Almost Dead	0-8217-7579-0	$7.99US/$10.99CAN
Lost Souls	0-8217-7938-9	$7.99US/$10.99CAN
Left to Die	1-4201-0276-1	$7.99US/$10.99CAN
Wicked Game	1-4201-0338-5	$7.99US/$9.99CAN
Malice	0-8217-7940-0	$7.99US/$9.49CAN

Available Wherever Books Are Sold!
Visit our website at **www.kensingtonbooks.com**